Sunset Across the Waters

Sunset Across the Waters

Susan Evans McCloud

BOOKCRAFT
Salt Lake City, Utah

Library of Congress Catalog Card Number: 96-78766
ISBN 1-57008-285-5

First Printing, 1996

Printed in the United States of America

Since India and Lottie
are Pamela's,
this one is for
Amy and Sara,
with tender affection

Chapter One

LONDON IS A DIFFERENT PLACE TO ME NOW. But then, I am a different creature. It is said we carry with us all we have experienced and seen. Surely I am a conglomerate of many seasons and places; at times I feel as though I am an accumulation of various people as well, who all have something to do with one another but are not one and the same. Shakespeare wrote that experience is a jewel because it is purchased at such an infinite price, and Byron claims that adversity is the first path to truth. I agree with them both. The last thing my ayah, Vijaya, told me when I left India was a reminder, really: "You are only what you carry inside." I have loved much and suffered much, and it seems, in my twenty-one years, that I have known too much of humanity's greed, of the groveling weakness which motivates so many. I have been heartbroken, terrified, shamed, and betrayed. And yet now some benign power has deigned to bend over me in mercy—this truly miraculous intervention has once again altered my life. Perhaps *karma*—which seems to function only in the faraway, shadowed land of India—still plays its part in my life, and will, in justice, vindicate me. Perhaps. Meanwhile, Winston, Sita, and I live in this lavish and gracious mansion, soothed and healed by the kindness of an old woman who needs someone to love. I am grateful. At first I was stunned with gratitude, greedy for nothing more profound than the chance to rest, to stand back from the front-line fray of the battle that was raveling my spirit to bits. Now, that has passed. Now, with the pathetic forgetfulness of mortals, I go whole days, sometimes several altogether, without one grateful thought, one moment of quiet awareness. This is becoming simply my life, and as comfortable to me as that privileged existence I once enjoyed back in Barrackpore. I chafe at its little inconsistencies and annoyances, I expect certain things to happen! I who have stood on the edge of the abyss, with no escape before or behind. It saddens me. Am I becoming inured, even hardened? No one else seems to notice, except perhaps Seth, that unusual young man who is responsible for my being here. Perhaps only he is capable of gently prodding my sensitivities back to that high level where I wish them to be. But he would exact a price, for all that his help is so freely given. All things in life have their price. And I have learned the sharp truth that no one can quote that price accurately to you, for it is never quite known. Like everything else, it is layered, ongoing, subtly woven into the very warp and woof of one's life; for good or ill, exacting far more than one would ever have willingly agreed to pay at the start.

It was a stormy day, as cold as any that winter. Black crows scudded across the gray stretch of sky like tatters of cloth, or bits of coal. Their cries trembled through me, for they somehow held all the loneliness of the stark London streets I had known, as well as the pain and mystery of that "land of sorrows" which I had left behind.

"Someone here to see ye, miss." Tabby bobbed into the room and dropped me a quick curtsy. "Shall I put him in the east parlor?"

I nodded. Then, unable to help myself, I asked, "Is it someone I know?"

"Gen'leman, miss. Not one of your nice fellows, nor any of the guests the missus has here."

I felt a tightening around my chest. Why did strangers still have the power to frighten me, to set the ghosts of the past whispering around me? "Very well, show him in."

I took off my apron, straightened my collar, and nervously smoothed the knot of hair tucked into a net at the back of my head—thick auburn hair coiled like a smooth, shining rope and revealing the slender sweep of my throat. I wore one of the silk-trimmed frocks Geoffrey had insisted I have made during the first months after we came here; it was light cream in color and set off well the honey glow of my skin. I laughed at myself as I descended May Skinner's broad, curving staircase. No evil could touch me here. And what did it matter, the hue of my skin, or the shine of my hair? Mere months ago I had cared only for the few wilted, cast-off vegetables I could obtain to fill our bellies, and left-over bits of coal to heat our small rooms.

With such thoughts still teasing my composure I entered the parlor, which was fitted with a large mahogany mantelpiece and deep rosewood mouldings at ceiling and floor. The gentleman who rose to greet me had once been thin, as his tapered hands and still gangly legs attested. But the indulgences that attend opulence had unbalanced his appearance, so that now the rotund belly which threatened to burst the fastenings of his waistcoat appeared as his dominant feature; that and the narrow meanness about his eyes, which had survived the softening layers of fat which now cushioned his cheeks and chin.

"Mrs. Charlotte Hillard? Garrett Longhurst at your service, ma'am."

The name startled me—not his, but my own, so seldom spoken aloud these past six months and more. I nodded, which was an indication that he might resume his seat, but he remained standing. I did the same, folding my arms across my chest, and waited for him to speak.

"You are long acquainted, I understand, with a Dr. Alan Fielding, lately of Barrackpore, India?"

I could not have been more astounded. Of all the people in my past, save Karan only, Dr. Fielding was the dearest to me. Mr. Longhurst saw the response on my face and continued.

"I have here a letter from Dr. Fielding addressed to yourself . . ."

The weak flutterings of my heart froze. It had been too much to hope for, that he might be here, in England. The need which I had, for a moment, allowed to escape bit hard. I blinked and picked up the strand of the stranger's words.

"... and I shall await your answer."

He held the letter out to me, and I stared back, a bit stupidly.

"Would you mind reading it now, ma'am, while I wait?"

I closed my fingers over the paper and he sat down with some ceremony, indicating subtly that he was prepared to be patient. I tried to smile, and he tried to return the courtesy, but neither of us did a very good job of it.

"Make yourself comfortable," I said. "I shall have Tabitha bring you some tea."

Once outside the room, I hastened to my own private chambers, admonishing Tabby, after giving her instructions concerning the gentleman, that I should not be disturbed. I sat in the yellow chintz chair by the window where, just beyond me, the gray sky churned. I drew out the folded pages, pleased to see the close, crowded writing. My friend's face was achingly clear in my mind: gaunt cheeks, with the skin tightly drawn across them; lines of fatigue finely etched at his mouth and eyes; and those eyes, as soulful and tender as a woman's, seeing everything, yet judging nothing, as patient as the hands of the healer they served.

> *My dearest Lottie:*
>
> *I welcome with intense pleasure this opportunity to communicate with you after the painful silence of these last years. I feel a sense of failure, gray and bewildering, when I think of you. Yes—you need not jump to defend me, as I know you, in generosity, will. The truth is that I allowed you to marry Geoffrey Hillard, despite the doubts that plagued me. I allowed him to take you to Dacca, I allowed Ralph to bungle the business of your father's journal and your mother's life. I should have been courageous enough to break my silence and tell you what I knew of your mother before time and distance separated us irrevocably....*

I stifled a sob that was making my throat burn, and realized I was clenching the thin sheets so tightly that my trembling fingers ached. Ralph Reid had been like a father to me, and the pain of his cruelties, so unexpected, still hurt deeply.

> *But, alas, none of the past can be changed or undone. I have learned of the loss of the child you carried when you left Barrackpore. I have learned of the birth of your daughter and the death of your husband—most of this from Geoffrey's boy, Runjeet, upon his return. What you have suffered I cannot even imagine. But I am gratified to learn of your present situation in one of the great houses of London, where I hope you are being adequately nurtured, and where opportunities may be presented you in keeping with your rare virtues and gifts. . . .*

Oh, yes, by all means, I thought dully. *A marriage of advantage. Is that what he would wish for me? Does he not know that the British men here are but weaker, paler copies of their brothers in India, that I have yet seen nothing of substance or beauty they could offer me?*

> *Now, here am I, waxing bold enough to ask a favor once more at your hands. Dare I, Lottie? If the wound is too raw still, if the pain would be too much to bear . . . I would not, save I have no other to turn to. . . .*

I felt a violent shudder pass through me, and a sense of foreboding, so that I was both anxious and fearful of reading on. How did he know where I was? And what service could he possibly require?

> *I am given to understand that you have corresponded a time or two with Major Reid's sons, who were for several months in the south of France with their mother. They have now returned, to the address I have enclosed. The major is now also in England. I do not forget his coldness to you, indeed, his cruelty, Lottie. But he is dying—his doctors have assured us of that. He is but a wasted shadow of his former self, but his spirit is tormented yet more than his flesh. . . .*

Good, I thought. *Let him see what the torment of the heart tastes like.* The unworthy thought trembled between myself and the words as I continued to read.

> *Constance is more than unstable—she is unmanageable; he can do nothing with her. She fails to respond to his needs, to the needs of her children; she seems at times in danger of doing herself or others harm. He cannot bear the thought of dying and leaving his family thus. You can well imagine. . . .*

I would not let myself imagine.

> *Who is left to care for the fate of the boys, Lottie? No one I know of but their strict and narrow Aunt Alice. You, my dear, and you only know intimately the people involved. You alone care. . . .*

In agitation I rose and walked the length of my bedroom. The doctor was blackmailing me, and he knew it. He knew he could touch not my conscience, but my heartstrings; he knew how truly I had loved the major's dead daughter, Roselyn, he knew how sincere were my feelings for the major's two sons. But there was more than that. He was not asking me to succor only the two comfortless boys. I, alone, had any chance of reaching Constance. I laughed—a bitter, choked little laugh— as I read his next words.

> *There is no hope, save in you. For who else has a chance with her, Lottie? She is pathetic and to be pitied. Can you look past all the injustices and have mercy on two people who did not have mercy on you?*

Perhaps if you were here, I thought, *to help me, to steady me with your gentle and assuring gaze, as you did that time in hospital with Karan; as you did when you sent me, ill and mourning, to the terrors of Dacca.*

> *It is much to ask, and I would not ask it of any soul who was less than yourself.*

His words were not idle flattery—I knew that. But his good opinion of me had little power to strengthen me now. I shrank at the thought of the task set before me. Nor was it so much that I could not forgive. It was more the horror of spreading old memories before me, of reopening wounds, of re-living . . .

I sank down again, weak as a kitten, and read the remainder of the letter, my mind, all my senses somewhat frozen and stunned.

> *Do what you are able, Lottie—no more—and set your mind at peace concerning the rest. God forgive me for the torment I know I am causing you. But we are all such poor, ignorant creatures working our way through the snares of mortality. Surely the great Maker himself will bless you for having mercy on those who are so in need of it. I pray for you daily, my dear. May heaven and earth deal tenderly with you, may you walk in peace, may you never forget your devoted friend and servant,*
>
> *Dr. Alan Fielding*

I dashed the hot tears from my cheeks and rang for Tabby. Despite May Skinner's great wealth, she had far too few servants, nothing like the full complement that existed in an Indian house.

"Tell the gentleman downstairs that he must return tomorrow if he desires my answer, and see him out."

She nodded, masking poorly the curiosity that burned in her eyes. But she was well trained, and in a few seconds she had left me alone again—alone, but already crowded and haunted by images of the past, cruel ghosts that I had worked so hard to bury. I sat with my head in my hands, weighed down by despairs I could not put a name to, until Winston came into the room and rescued me, as he had so many times in the past. He tugged me gently to my feet and led me down to dinner, and to the return of sane, normal functions again.

The table was too long, the room too cavernous. Why did the English order their lives in such a stiff, ridiculous manner? I missed the intimacy of Indian meals served in small, cozy rooms; food both fragrant and tasty, accompanied by the soft, swishing administering of servants at elbow and hand. How unsavory were English manners and English meals!

My son Winston, now seven, left us to return to his place in the nursery with his sister, Sita, and I took my seat. For a moment we sipped our clear soup in silence. Then May's bright, birdlike voice tumbled into the void.

"You had a visitor today, my dear. Is he the cause of your pale cheeks and obvious distress?"

Dear, rare woman, with her sincere, direct ways. There was no dissembling, no pretense necessary with her, no holding to the niceties which were the under-structure of English society—those iron conformities which stifled the soul.

I explained briefly, and she listened with attention, raising one thin eyebrow and dabbing at her lips with her white linen napkin.

"You have not made up your mind yet." It was a statement, not a question. "I am certainly not one to advise you, heavens no!" She shuddered visibly. "I have always thought of myself as a compassionate woman, yet put to a test such as this—" She shrugged her narrow shoulders and smiled across at me. "No, I shall not advise." Yet she shook her head as she considered the weight of the matter. "Well, do eat heartily, dear."

As though food were an answer, a comfort, or even a diversion. I smiled in return and began on the wilted lettuce salad which had been placed before me, thinking fleetingly on curried rice and fresh mango drinks that soothed the throat as well as the belly. I did not think of the dilemma before me; every time I tried to, my mind seemed to freeze, to go numb and blank and useless.

We had not finished our desserts when I heard a knock at the door, but by then I had forgotten my obligation for the evening. So when Tabby bobbed in to announce that Mr. Taylor had arrived to take me to meeting, I felt an unaccountable irritation rise up within me. "I do not believe I feel like going this evening," I began. But then Seth Taylor strode into the room. People raised outside society, in a common manner, I have observed, possess no knowledge of what is proper or improper, nor any inner sense of such things to fall back upon. I glanced up at May, sure of her support. But she tisk-tisked at me lightly.

"I believe it would be good for you to get out among people," she announced. "Clear the cobwebs from your head and keep you from brooding on this unfortunate matter. The children will be cared for here during your absence."

I glared at Seth Taylor, who at least had sense enough not to ask questions. While he finished off the glazed fruit and cream, I made myself ready, and joined him with an ill grace which I knew must be evident.

"It never ceases to amaze me," I began, as he gave me his arm and helped me into May's fine, warm carriage.

"What never ceases to amaze you?" he asked, kindly picking up the thread of my conversation; I liked that about him.

"It amazes me that May Skinner is so open in her support of the Mormons, when all people of sense and breeding shun them in fear and loathing."

It was obvious that I was trying to goad him.

"She can afford to do so for the very fact that she is not selective; her liberated view embraces all eccentricities that fall under her eye, of which the strange sect of the Mormons is only one."

He spoke the words without smiling. Now his gaze searched my face slowly. "What is it, Lottie? What is the trouble?"

"I do not wish to tell you," I replied, a bit petulantly. But, in truth, I did. In truth, I longed for some outward comfort and counsel.

He sat quietly, with that patience which was one of the first things I had noticed about him. At length I sighed and began. He leaned forward a bit during the telling, keeping his eyes on my face. The sympathy I saw in those eyes acted like a salve on a throbbing wound.

"Your friend, the doctor, is a man of rare integrity," he muttered—I thought that a strange initial response. He caught up my gloved hand and held it lightly in his. "Obviously he knows you well, Lottie, and has great faith in you."

That is neither here nor there! I felt like shouting. "I cannot do this, Seth."

"You do not wish to do it—that is more than understandable. But you can do it—I know that as well as your Dr. Fielding does."

I pulled my hand away. "You know less of the matter than you suppose," I said through clenched teeth. I was thinking of Karan. I was seeing his face, not Seth's, as I stared into the frosty gloom of the closed carriage.

He lowered his head slightly in assent. "I know all I need to know."

"Which is?"

The carriage pulled up to the curb beside the hall where the Mormons held their meetings. Seth came around and handed me out, and the moist fog closed over me, stinging my throat and eyes. I disliked coming here; we were too close to the shabby rooms on Nine Elms Lane from which he had earlier rescued me. For all my finery, for all the comfort and security of my present condition, I shuddered inwardly still, and felt the old sense of desolation sweep over me, the sense of hopelessness that had eaten at the very core of my being.

"I know what death is," I said suddenly, looking up into Seth Taylor's calm, gentle eyes. "When all the terrors and trials of life have nibbled at the soul and taken their bits off here and there, when nothing is left but the hard, shriveled pit of the thing, nothing left to go on with—that is what we call death."

He almost smiled. "Trials eat at our marrow," he assented, "but, far from destroying it, they stimulate a growth, a strengthening of the sinews—"

I felt angry. "You know nothing of what you speak," I snarled back.

He took my arm and led me toward the protection of the building. "You are shivering, Lottie," he said. At the door he paused. "You're right. I know little of what you have passed through, save the ordeal of this last while. But there is such a seasoned strength in you, Lottie; I wish you could see it yourself."

I put my hand on his arm. "I am tired, I am so tired of being the strong one. And now . . ."

He leaned forward and pressed his lips to my forehead. I shuddered as the tenderness of his touch swept through me. I had been alone, and lonely, for so long.

The meeting had started. As we stepped inside they were singing a hymn, a new song written by Parley P. Pratt. The strains were so jubilant, so touched with hope that I felt myself yearning toward the emotions they represented. I slid into a seat and listened, until the constriction around my heart began to loosen a little its tight, strangling hold. True religion makes men want to be good, I believe, and something about these Mormons and their beliefs had a salutary effect on my mind. Here was no thundering of fire and brimstone, no God shrouded in doubt and mystery, but a Heavenly Father who knew and loved his children, and was anxious to help each one find his way home. It sounded almost too simple, too happy; yet if it were true . . .

Much of the sermon centered around the purposes of our mortal probation. As I listened I knew that, by any lights, by the standards of *karma*, by the expectations of all Christian religions, I must strive to do what was enjoined upon me—I had a choice, but had I a *moral choice* in the matter, if I wished to obtain salvation, whatever salvation was?

Then the speaker, as though addressing my doubts, said: "God yearns for the happiness of his children. We are not here to be punished but, rather, to be prepared—for that great and glorious life which he wishes for us. When your own strength falters, look to him in faith, let his strength uphold you. . . ."

I brushed tears from my eyes. Dr. Fielding had written, "Surely the great Maker himself would bless you for having mercy. . . ." Sitting there, amidst all those people, with my eyes wide open, I prayed and felt that, somehow, God was hearing me.

Never have I felt joy mingled with peace as I feel here, I thought. *This is what I want for my children—for Winston most of all*. He was an unusually insightful child; I felt it my duty to open up the powers that lay within him. Life which lacks a spiritual dimension is narrow and petty; I had seen it so often in the men and women I knew. Winston deserved much more—I was certain of that.

Seth Taylor said nothing further concerning the challenge that was facing me, but when he helped me into the carriage he put his hand over mine. "I will be here, if you need anything, anytime . . ."

I nodded. We were so close in the frosty stillness that I could feel the warmth of his breath on my cheek. His eyes held mine for a moment, and I wondered if he saw the desire there, but he did not kiss me again. With a word to the driver and a pat on the horse's flank, he sent the carriage away. I closed my eyes and tried to gain back the feeling which the speaker's words had given me. Instead, I saw Karan's face, more clearly than I had in a long time. His soft eyes were smiling at me, sadly; had there ever been a time when that gentle, resigned sadness had not mingled with every other emotion that trembled there?

I reached beneath the folds of my bodice to touch the ring—his mother's ring which Karan had given me when I turned eighteen. "Nothing can separate our spirits," he had said. And later, in Calcutta—what were his words? "Adversity has only deepened the impress of God's mark on your features." A tremor of anguish shot through me. I should think of him as dead to me, as he had once said he must be! And yet, all that was good in myself was inextricably bound to him; nor could I wish it to be otherwise, in spite of the pain.

"I will not fail God. I will not fail you," I whispered. The stillness did not answer me, but I did not require an answer. What I needed existed already within my own heart.

CHAPTER TWO

𝔍

IT WAS THE MAJOR'S AGENT, Mr. Longhurst, who accompanied me into the house, and the boys who greeted me. They were young men now, and though I could see in them the children I used to tumble with, their rough edges had been refined by age and education and, yes, by the trials of their lives.

"Lottie, you look smashing!" Hugh cried, and flung himself at me, wrapping his arms round my waist.

Arthur, who had now reached the advanced age of sixteen, held back a bit and surveyed me, as young men do, with an eye to my feminine qualities. His gaze made me blush. He would be a good-looking man, as the major was, yet possessing his own gentler charms.

"Mother is resting," Hugh offered, to fill an awkward silence which was building.

"Would you like tea?" Arthur remembered to ask.

"That would be nice," I answered as I removed my bonnet and traveling gloves. This house where the major and Constance were living was a bit on the small side, as such country houses go, but I liked the feeling of coziness about it. "Have you been here long now?" I asked.

Arthur frowned, but Hugh answered, "This place belongs to Aunt Alice. Father owns a house not too far off, but Mother says it is too isolated, and refuses to go there."

"Ah."

Nancy brought the tea, and we were occupied a few

moments, pouring and stirring tea and buttering hot scones.

"The last time I had tea with Mischief in the house," I remembered, "he snuck close and pounced—you remember his way?—upsetting both the cream and the sugar. It was an unsightly mess!"

"Mischief! You left him in India, didn't you?"

It was as I had hoped—their words tumbled around and over each other's, and we were back with the monkeys and lizards, the hot winds, and the creaking tatties that cooled the air.

"It seems so long ago," Hugh sighed.

"I shall go back soon enough, once I receive my commission," Arthur boasted.

"You wish to be a soldier?" I asked.

He nodded emphatically. "I could not stand business," he retorted. "I'm already a crack shot and a most promising rider—that is what I've been called."

"High praise," I replied, smiling at his irresistible swanking. He flushed, but held my gaze steady. "How is your father?" I asked.

The tension was immediate. Hugh shrugged his shoulders and looked at his brother. Arthur shifted his eyes. "The doctors give him weeks, and Mother pretends it is nothing." He, too, shrugged. "Our holiday is over quickly enough, and then we'll be packed off again. After that, who knows?"

It was their way of concluding the matter. At length I let Nancy lead me to the room where I would be staying, and she insisted on remaining to help me unpack my things. My mind was in a turmoil already, and I had yet to face the two encounters I dreaded. I wished to rush at them headlong and find out my worst possible fate.

I should have known Constance would never allow that. I took a stroll round the small gardens that ran to open, cultivated fields, with scarcely a woodland in sight, and when I came back she was ensconced in my bedroom, going through my wardrobe with casual expertness.

"These will never do, Lottie," she scolded mildly, not even turning round when she heard me enter the room. "We are in proper society now, and it is nothing like back in India."

"Geoffrey had these made in London," I parried.

"When you first returned, I'll warrant." She gave a short, harsh laugh, so unsympathetic, so like her. "They are sadly outdated, my dear."

They are good enough for May Skinner, I thought to myself, *and I doubt London fashion suffers in comparison to that of the country.* But perhaps May's very eccentricity, her penchant for being herself and pleasing her own fancies, contributed to a certain disregard to or lack of concern in the minute particulars of my wardrobe, and fittings as well.

That was to be it, then. No formal greeting, no chance to even skirt the intimacies that hung like black clouds, heavy with rain, just above our heads. There was no way round her; that much I knew. If I pressed the issue, she would spit out something sharp and cruel, and stalk off to her brooding. How could I have forgotten how powerful her presence was?

It was much the same with the major, though in a somewhat different fashion. My first glimpse of him was when he came in to dinner that night, being helped to a chair and seating himself rather shakily. It was true—he looked ghastly enough, his strong, well-toned body ravaged by disease, his skin loose and hanging, his eyes sinking into the wrinkled spread of his face, where every line revealed the pain he was suffering. I avoided those eyes, remembering only our last encounters, his implacable coldness, his unfeeling betrayal of both me and my father, the friend who had trusted him.

Why does he want me here? I wondered as I choked down my food and listened to Constance either mildly scold him or talk round him, as though he were not there at all. *There is madness here which no one dares acknowledge, yet all can feel.* The boys may have appeared inured to it, but I did not believe that. I know what madness can do, as well as cruelty under the pretense of normalcy.

The very next day I found a trio of tailor and seamstresses waiting for me in Constance's sitting room when I came out of my own; first thing in the morning I was being measured and fitted, pinched and pulled at their pleasure.

"The society luncheon is next week," Constance explained. "We have no time to spare."

15

The gowns Constance was having designed for me were matchless indeed, with the shoulder seam dropping down in the back and the skirt line set low, between waist and hips, as was the latest fashion. The sleeves were to be full and long, so that they would wrinkle across the bend of the elbow. One dress was to have a dark bow at the small, rounded collar, and a small cap with ribbons at the ears to accompany it. My favorites were a dove gray gown trimmed with elegant shirring, with a pink- and blue-flower-trimmed bonnet which would sit well back from my face, and a pale blue gown with a yellow palatine embroidered all over with roses and tabbed rosettes.

When the day for the grand affair arrived, my hair was dressed loosely, in long, flowing curls. I felt elegant, and yet as though I were play-acting, dressing up like Roselyn and I used to, pretending we were something different and finer than what we were.

In a panic of insecurity and pride I had taken one measure before leaving May's house. Upon her advice and with her consent, I had spent half an hour with her solicitor and begun the process which would change my name legally from the hated appellation of Hillard to that of my father, the name with which I was born. Now, therefore, I wished to be presented to Constance's refined acquaintances as the person I was: Charlotte Simmons. Would she brook me on this, or turn a frosty, cold ear?

Arthur accompanied us, as some male escort was desirable; he would be ensconced for the space of our frivolities with the menfolk in the game room, which was not an unattractive prospect to him.

In cowardly fashion I waited until we were in the carriage to explain about the change of my name and request cooperation from them. Arthur's enthusiasm made all the difference; Constance would appear more than niggardly to make a fuss for no obvious reason.

"It is neither here nor there to me," she concluded with a shrug of her shoulders, and Arthur encouraged me with a smile.

As he was handing me out of the carriage he drew my arm through his and whispered, "You are really quite stunning, Lottie. You shall be the envy of the entire assembly."

I thanked him with a quick hug and took the risk of asking, in a low tone, "Why does your mother want me here in the first place? Why does she put herself to all this trouble?"

"It is her way of pretending, running away from what she does not wish to acknowledge. She is living some pretense which exists only in here." He tapped his finger against his forehead. "Your presence actually aids it, helps to fill it out a bit. She has been like this ever since Lucy died, you know."

"I see. I believe you have the gist of it, Arthur." A sudden tenderness for him swept over me, but I could do nothing to show it, save a little squeeze of his arm and a warm smile of encouragement as we parted.

That fine, formal luncheon was to be the beginning of a round of such nonsense, which safely marked the perimeters of my relationship with Constance. The major I saw only in the semiformal setting of the evening meal. I let it go; I could not contend against the inevitable. I spent what time was my own in playing lawn games with the boys, or taking walks through the fields to the cool of the trees, or perhaps into the village, where Arthur, Hugh, and I would scour the shops for what interesting trinkets we could find. Thus passed my first week with them, and then the time came for the boys to return to their schools.

It may sound a bit nonsensical, but I felt ill at ease, even fragile, after their departure. Save for the servants, I was alone in a house with two people who, for all intents and purposes, I considered as enemies to me. And I had not even discovered the true reason for my being there.

My second evening after the boys left, I had retired to my own room early, written a note to Winston, and then attempted to read. But a storm was building; cool winds and dark clouds tumbled through the low valleys, churning the air, tearing at the heavy-leafed branches of the few exposed trees. I felt the churning inside my own being, felt the trembling efforts of the storm to build, to peak, to unburden itself. My attempts to ignore it were as nothing, though I changed resolutely into my bedgown and lay against the plump pillows, with only a small table lamp burning. Sleep would not come, nor would any of my books divert me.

I shall go down for a cup of hot tea, I concluded at last. *With any luck that will make me drowsy.*

I crept down the stairs, aware of each shadow along the walls, each creak and groan in the boards at my feet. It was later than I had realized; I heard the clock in the hall chime a solitary and ominous one. The windows, loose in their frames, rattled like old bones shaken up in a gourd. I started down the long hall to the kitchen, then froze at the sight of a thick yellow light pouring from a half-open doorway. Should I go on? My pulse was racing as I tried to remember the placement of the various rooms, and with a sinking heart realized that the glow came from the major's small study, the sanctuary where he spent most of his time. With a horrified fascination I could not resist, I glided closer. Then the thought came to me that he might be ill, or in need of assistance. So, despite the apprehension which thickened my breath in my lungs, I stepped forward and stood with uncertainty within the arch of light.

I had not expected what I saw, and it stunned me into the stillness of a statue as I watched. Major Reid sat at his desk with his head thrown back and a bottle of what looked like very costly Scotch whiskey pressed against his thin lips. He appeared to be literally pouring it down his throat, as though it were some life-restoring elixir, when in truth it was the pitiless poisoner of life, which would lead only to death. I knew enough from my experiences with the fever in India that spirits were the most dangerous, the most forbidden of substances to introduce into the systems of the ill and I knew beyond doubt that the major fully realized that. His jaundiced skin, already yellowed with the poison, appeared like a thin gray wrapping stretched over the bones of his face. His fingers, clutching the bottle, suggested more of bone than they did of flesh.

He moved his eyes, only his eyes; I felt them before they turned upward and attempted to focus upon my face.

"Have you come to gloat, my dear? Isn't a pretty sight, is it?"

The muscles of his face twitched as he continued staring at me. "What you are doing is wicked," I said.

"Wicked?" He repeated the word as though tasting it. "No more wicked than what Francis did when he went out looking for death, when he gave himself over to it with nary a thought for the living."

A shock ran through my system with the force of lightning striking, for I could not deny that his words were true. In the eyes of the old warrior this method of death, repulsive as it may be, appeared less disgraceful than the humiliation of life as he now was living it. In his eyes his reasons were as legitimate as my father's when he ran away from the loss of my mother by volunteering for a campaign where the odds were terrifyingly against survival.

"I am reduced," he muttered. "Nothing to fear here any longer." He ran one hand through what remained of his once dark, luxuriant hair.

It is a pity, I thought. But I could not say the words aloud to him, nor offer any form of sympathy.

"Away with you," he growled, like an old shaggy lion, wounded and sick in his lair. "Leave me."

It was a command, as much as any he had ever given during his long and powerful life. I had half a mind to remain standing there, in grim defiance of him. But instead I turned at once and moved back into the shadows, which, even in their ominous, trembling suggestiveness, were kinder than that light. It was a capitulation of sorts, allowing him this last little, empty triumph; it was also the only way for me to rise above what had passed between us, and walk free again.

CHAPTER THREE

I HAD RESIGNED MYSELF TO AN ABSENCE of at least a fortnight, but as my stay passed into the second week I wondered what good I did here. The boys returned to their respective schools, and Constance filled many of our hours in receiving and returning social calls and attending teas hosted by neighboring ladies. But these occasions lacked the luster of their Indian counterparts. For there, far from home, the wives of the officers, lonely and desperate not only for diversion but for purpose, engaged themselves in worthwhile and charitable endeavors, although in India the Englishwoman's scope was limited. Here time and energies were shamelessly wasted, frittered away on the most tedious, useless activities. I had almost forgotten my old abhorrence of the English upper classes and the way in which they viewed life. So I found myself chafing against the pattern of my days and longing for London and my little ones.

I had not yet seen this madness which had been rumored, which even Dr. Fielding seemed certain of. Was Constance doing a good job of concealing it, or did my presence truly make some kind of difference? I could not say.

Since the evening of the storm Major Reid had not come down to dinner; it seemed he wished to avoid me as much as I wished to avoid him. Constance never commented on his absence and did not seem to miss him. Was this part of the madness, this appearance of too much sanity, as it were? If I thought about it, it did seem surprising that Constance endured my presence as well as she did, that she seemed to enjoy having me near her, and even made what to her were concessions to keep me content.

At last I ventured what I knew I must and returned to the library, that lair where the old lion lay, licking his wounds and waiting to die. I made sure this time that I went in broad daylight and there were others about, and I left the door open a crack so that they might hear me call.

He knew it was myself, but he did not look up or acknowledge me.

"Sir, I have come," I began, "but to no seeming purpose. It was Dr. Fielding's letter which brought me." I paused, but he remained immobile. "You must tell me what it is you want of me when you are gone."

Silence closed around my last words, but I stood patiently, determined to wait the man out. At length he spoke, still without moving a muscle.

"I wish you to be a friend to my sons. They will need someone normal and sane in their lives. You are young enough to be their advisor and confidant. They have only an old bitter aunt and an old deranged mother. They must not lose sight—"

He could not continue without some emotion escaping. I found myself coming to his aid.

"They must not lose sight of the proud heritage which is theirs, and the strengths they carry inside. I will teach them that they can be anything they wish to be, and that life can be good if they choose to make it so."

He seemed to relax, yet he still had not moved, or even lifted his eyes.

"And Constance?"

For a long time he did not answer, and I began to wonder if he had dropped off to sleep.

"There was a time when she was as good a wife as a man could wish for, despite her faults. . . ." His words fell like burning stones into the cavern of silence that seethed with the unspoken, unspeakable things which made up both our lives.

"When I am gone, no one else will endure her. Even servants will spurn and despise her."

"Has she means?"

"She will have means enough, but not to squander! And she is unable . . ."

He shook his head, and for a moment the sun, fractured into a hundred golden shafts by the high, mullioned window, caught the ravenlike sheen of his hair, and for one heartbeat I was a girl again and he a respected officer, virile and handsome and in control of his world. Then the light faded, and I shuddered, and it seemed that his shoulders sagged.

"There must be someone strong enough to look out for her interests, keep her from ruining herself. . . ."

"Do you think even I can do that?"

"You or no one!" His look at last pierced me and I felt myself shrink.

"What do you wish for her?"

"I wish that she might remain here. It is a modest yet suitable situation, and the folk hereabouts know her, at least."

"Yes," I agreed. "But I am in London—"

"You need not be."

I was shaking my head, even as he spoke. "I could not live with her, sir, I could not expose my children—"

"I do not ask it. But I own property not an hour's drive from here—"

I put out a hand as if to stop him. "I could not! Not now . . . not after . . ."

It seemed we both paused, fearful of snapping the delicate thread of communication that allowed us to be civil with one another.

"Think upon it," he said, conceding the moment. "It would surely be a better environment for your children."

But it would be taking from you, I thought. *Leaving me beholden to you for the rest of my life, and that cannot be.*

"Whatever else does or does not happen," he said, with a tenor to his voice which had not been there before, "she must not be allowed to interfere in the lives of my sons, to shame them, to blight their prospects."

"I understand." I took a deep breath, sensing the solemnity of the moment. "On that, above all else, you have my word."

He nodded his head, as if to indicate, *It is enough.* Was that gesture my dismissal as well? I felt an irresistible desire to say something—to do something more—but I could not! I turned and left as quietly as I had come, shutting the door behind me, leaving him alone in the prison he had made for himself.

It came that night—I should have foreseen it—in the darkest, premorning hours, when the spirits of the unjust and the tormented yet roam the earth, when one shrinks from the sensations of eternity which move in tremors, like cold mists, along the ground. It was not an easy death, because in the last moments he fought it, with a terrible gasping for air and a grinding of teeth. The spirit within him, once strong and noble, reared up in defiance of the beastly betrayal of self against self, and in that horror of body and spirit he drew his last breath.

I was there. I could not avoid the watching, I could not avoid Constance's fever-bright eyes fixed in wild astonishment upon him. "Go to your husband," I urged.

"My husband!" she protested. "He has long since renounced that title." She threw her arm out in a wild gesture. "See the empty bottle—it has served well his dark purposes." She turned suddenly upon me. "Do you think, missy, you are the only one who has caught him in the middle of the night drinking himself to madness? He wants no part of me!"

"It is *you* who left *him!*" I entreated, unthinking. "He is dying, Constance! For mercy's sake, go to him!"

She drew herself up visibly, and it was as if she drew an invisible shutter down over her eyes. "This is what he wanted, this is what he has been seeking. What cause have we who are spurned to mourn?"

I stared at her, fascinated and horrified. *Sand in the head!* I thought, that dreaded Indian malady which British wives suffer and which she had avoided for years, until Lucy was born, and concern for this new daughter pushed her into some shaded area of danger and dislocation from which she could no longer escape. I thought of my own period of darkness after suffering a miscarriage and being trapped in the blackness of Dacca, and learning of the true tragedy of my father's and mother's lives. Had I sprung back because I was stubborn, more resilient? Because of something strong in my nature? Because of nothing more than youth and good luck?

He died, for all intents and purposes, alone, with no one who loved him beside him, with no hand in his, no soothing voice speaking words of tenderness and comfort.

I walked out into the gardens and through them, as fast as I could, stumbling over the unfamiliar paths, unseeing, uncomprehending. For the realization had come to me that, in their separate ways, thus had my own father and my husband died! My father in the lonely agony of battle, with my mother's name on his lips. My husband in the twilight misery of debauchery, sinking in the morass of his own weaknesses. I was trembling inside, frightened and exhausted, and longing for Winston's arms around me.

In the end, do all people die thus? I wondered. *Will Karan die like this, at the end of a narrow life of denial and emptiness? No! It must not be so!*

I realized I was crying, great sobs that took my breath away. Behind a row of yew bushes I dropped to my knees. "I will pray for you," Winston had said before I left London. Was he praying for me now? I closed my eyes, trying to draw upon his pure, childlike faith, trying to draw upon Karan's mature faith, sure and steady. I had vowed not to fail, promised myself and God and the shade of this man who had loved me.

I knelt on the cool English earth and pleaded for God to listen to me. I do not know how long I was there. But at length a peace stole through me, and with the peace a sensation, almost an image, of God as Seth Taylor had described him—his quiet yet incredible Mormon God. And this is the image I kept with me when I rose to my feet.

It was Simla all over again. Even when the boys returned for their father's funeral, Constance did not let up. Her icy imperialism, her biting criticisms were mercilessly applied; I watched both friend and servant wither and retreat before her. Her effect on her sons was the hardest to watch. Struggling between boyhood and manhood, as they were, she further weakened and confused them, and I saw with my own eyes how men can be hardened, how the wells of their natural feelings can be sucked dry by necessity—if they are to survive in this world they must develop a resilient, impenetrable shell. They cannot crumble and give way as a woman can, if she must, for then all the world as they know it would come tumbling around them, and they may never be able to stand square on their feet again. I watched, feeling helpless, wondering what was the best way to help them, if help I could.

A considerable number of friends came to pay tribute to the major, many distinguished colleagues, among them men whom I recognized as past friends or associates of Geoffrey's, but none came forward to pay their respects to me—none but Colonel Miller with his gentle wife on his arm.

"I am happy to see you, and looking so well, my dear."

He spoke the words with a kindly solicitation, and she put her hands out to me. "Do not let Constance wear you to a shadow," she whispered. "Even duty has its limits."

I nodded, grateful.

"Are you living now in these parts?"

"I am in London still, in the house of May Skinner."

The colonel nodded, but his wife smiled. "As eccentric as women come, I've heard. But big-hearted. Is that not so?"

"She has been the salvation of myself and my children," I replied with candor. "I have no complaints."

"Good." Mrs. Miller's kindness was the first warmth I had felt, though the day was bright and the sun seemed to shine down as mercilessly as in India, mocking the solemnity of the occasion. "If anyone deserves a chance at happiness, you do, Charlotte."

I met her gaze reluctantly, expecting to find pity there, and was surprised by the quiet respect that looked out at me.

"Thank you," I murmured, squeezing her hands, knowing she understood all that trembled behind those small, inadequate words.

The day passed so slowly, the hours seemed to be cruelly stretched and extended. When the last well-meaning relative left, when the servants retired, I was too exhausted to lift my head from the couch where I rested and find my way up to bed. Constance had long since retreated with a sleeping draught, but her presence hung like a pall on the household, the unexpressed awareness all had that, with Major Reid's passing, there would be no influence, no authority to counter hers.

I was just struggling to my feet when I heard footsteps in the hallway and felt a rush of fresh night air as the front door opened. I reached the doorway in time to see Arthur head down the lane that led to the fields and scattered copses of trees that dotted them. On an impulse I went after him. The night was warm, retaining some of the intense heat of the day, but tempered by a cool wind that ranged freely, gathering the sharp fragrances of new grass and freshly turned earth, and the lighter scent of spring flowers: lilac, campion, wild hyacinth and daffodil. I followed his shadowy figure, drawn by the gentle beauties which seemed to enfold me, relax my muscles, and loosen the tightness that throbbed behind my forehead. I nearly forgot my purpose as I gave myself up to the pleasurable sensations, until I saw Arthur's head bob a few yards ahead of me and suddenly disappear. I stopped for a moment, then proceeded more cautiously, and still nearly missed him, as he had thrown himself down on a mound of soft moss and field grass at the foot of a giant oak.

When I dropped down at his feet he looked at me a bit vaguely, but unabashedly. "Oak, ash, and thorn, the ancient trees of Britain," he said, as though reciting lines for a school lesson. "They embody all the mystery of our ancient races—the very key to our souls."

I listened to the wind stirring through the supple spring branches. The sound was musical and low.

"Every human soul is shrouded in mystery," I said, "no matter when he is born. The burden of existence is solitary, despite the crowded generations of living and dying it carries."

He put down the bottle he had been drinking from and swore at me. "If you have come here to mouth pretty words at me, you may go straight back and the devil take you!" he growled.

His words were not slurred yet, but his eyes were definitely clouded. I relaxed beside him and said nothing at all.

At length he began to take note of me again, with a bit of a shock. "What are you doing here?"

"Enjoying the evening," I replied, and I meant it.

He snorted in an attempt at disgust, and with some effort lifted himself on one elbow. "I don't b'lieve I can make it home."

"Lean on me," I said, standing as he did, and steadying him with one outstretched hand. "That's what I'm here for."

"Never had anyone to lean on," he mumbled as we started off, a bit shakily.

And more's the pity, I thought. "You once had me," I replied. "You have me again, and this time you shall feel it, I promise."

He glanced at me sideways, and I hoped he was too intoxicated to see the tears in my eyes.

When we reached the house I halloed for Hugh, who came down yawning and half-asleep still, but with enough presence of mind to help me deposit his brother in a heap on top of his bed. If the servants heard, well, there was no help for it. We pulled his shoes off and covered him with a spare eiderdown.

"He'll be just fine," I assured Hugh. "You can go back to bed."

I smoothed the rumpled hair back from Arthur's damp forehead and planted a kiss on his cheek, then went reluctantly to my own solitary room.

The following morning Major Reid's solicitor, Garrett Longhurst, called the family together for the reading of the will. It was the first time I had seen the man since our arrival together at this place. His very presence seemed to bode dismal, entirely unpleasant things. He had asked that I be present and, since Constance did not object, we all went into the close, dark room which had belonged to the major. We sat stiffly around the small table where the major had instructed that the event should take place, as though his influence, felt here more than anyplace, might have its lingering effect upon us. But when this odious agent revealed to us the workings of the major's mind, not one of us was the least bit prepared for it. We sat, stunned to dumb silence, so that he had to clear his throat and put voice to the response we were incapable of making.

"Seems extreme, even to me, an outsider—I'll admit that, right enough. But he was tormented with fears, tormented . . ." He coughed into his big, rumpled handkerchief when the silence awkwardly continued. "Have you questions, then? Any points I can further explain to you?"

Arthur raised eyes that burned with a cold light. "I believe my father was altogether precise and clear, sir." He raised his hand and pulled the bell rope that stood nearby, and one of the house girls seemed to materialize out of nowhere. "Nancy, would you kindly show Mr. Longhurst out?" There was the slightest emphasis, a hint of disdain as he pronounced the last word, and to me he appeared five years older than he had yesterday.

We four fell into silence again, and when the atmosphere became close to unbearable Constance raised her head. There was such a fire of hatred in her eyes that I felt myself shrink from before it.

"Malice can work two ways," she said, and, though I was used to the coldness in her voice of late, she sounded like a stranger to me. "He will rue the day. . . . He will yet rue the day!" she muttered, and I think we all knew, instinctively, that she was talking to herself, not to us.

What has angered Constance the most? I wondered, watching her. He had taken so many steps to offend, to estrange her. The boys were placed legally under the protection of his solicitor, who would hold sole responsibility for dispersing funds and monies until each reached the age of eighteen. He had divided his estate up in three equal parts, leaving her only enough to get by on, not bequeathing all to his widow until the time of her death. Many of the provisions of the will seemed expressly contrived to insult her, though I knew they were not; I knew he was looking with a ruthless eye to any possible extremity her imbalance might call forth and, in his own mind, taking actions which were protective only, no matter how cruel they might seem.

Oddly enough, he had reinstated me, so to speak, to the status of daughter, at least by adoption, and even left a small bequest of money to me. In turn, I was to be granted "rights of interference," for want of a better term; I had legal rights to the boys and was to be accorded the status of counselor or advisor; any actions or decisions I recommended and the young men agreed to were to receive the sanction and cooperation of their legal guardian. In this, as in all things, Constance was left painfully out.

"Since I am no longer needed here," Constance continued, her indifferent eyes resting in turn upon each of us, "I shall now take my leave."

It was not only her tone of finality but something inexplicable about her which sent a shudder of foreboding along my frame. I felt the misery of the two young boys who sat before me, and I thought my own heart would break. As she quit the room, I hesitated, then rose, determined to follow her, feeling that my duty and my compassion, for the moment, lay there. And in that decision so much in my future began to be faintly, but surely, etched.

I found her in the front drawing room, pacing back and forth like a panther, lithe and deadly, ready to spring. I hesitated on the threshhold of the room.

"I have no need of you, missy," she said, "and no desire for your company." Her mouth curled in an expression I could not read, but whose cruelty was evident. "I have never entertained much fondness for you, Charlotte, and now I cannot endure the sight of you. Go your way, as I intend to go mine."

I hesitated. "Constance—"

"One thing only I warn you," she said, bethinking herself. "Keep away from my sons! They are not yours to dally with, Lottie, think what you will." She threw her head back and an evil light came into her eyes. "Other women's sons—that's all you will ever have, Charlotte. First the pathetic child of poor little Judith Hillard, then mine—perhaps next the sons of your Sikh lover."

I must have started, for the gleam in her eyes fanned into a flame. "Ah, yes, he is married—did you not know, my dear? So much for his protestations of undying love and devotion." She was watching me intently, like the predator she was.

"I do not believe you," I managed to say.

She shrugged her shoulders. "Believe what you will, but that is the truth of it. She will bear his sons and thus hold the key to his heart, Charlotte—this other woman, not you."

She did not have to gloat and rub her hands, or laugh demonically; nothing else was necessary to make her triumph complete. Somehow I stood and faced her gaze for a moment longer, then turned in slow motion away. Somehow I made it up the stairs, which seemed as steep as a mountainside, and as tedious to climb. Somehow, sitting alone in my room, I survived the pain that broke over me in wave following ravaging wave.

I awoke the next morning to find my clothes set out for me, and the remainder of my belongings neatly packed and waiting. Before I could ring for her, Nancy slipped into my room, her face pale, her eyes distressed.

"Carriage arrives in half an hour, mum, and mistress says you're to be on it."

"She does, does she? Where are the young gentlemen, Nancy?"

"She sent them off hunting, with sandwiches and their father's brandy, and sweet endearments."

"I see." I was beginning to be frightened.

"Dress quick—please, miss!" Nancy said, wringing her little red hands.

I did as she bid me. When I walked out of the room, Constance was waiting.

"Nancy, bring the remainder of the young lady's things downstairs, quickly now."

"I am not leaving yet," I said, my voice calm at least, if not ringing with conviction.

"Oh, but you are," Constance replied, and before I could form an answer I saw the heavy form of Jack, the gardener and man-of-all-work, ascending the stair. "Jack will see you to the carriage," Constance continued, her smugness obvious.

She stepped aside to let him pass. He slipped his arm through mine and began to half-lead, half-tug me down the long staircase and out the front door. I was stunned, my mind in a turmoil of confusion. I could feel Constance at my elbow, breathing down my neck, as it were. I remember that there were low gray clouds streaking the horizon and the smell of rain in the air. As Jack began to hand me into the carriage which stood waiting, Constance put her hand on his arm to detain him.

"We will no longer require your services here," she said to me. "Not now, not at any time in the future. Do I make myself clear?"

I did not deign to reply, to respond by the slightest gesture. I stared back at her, digging my nails into the palm of my hand in my effort to contain myself.

"I will explain to the boys," she added, and the velvet in her voice was like the velvet in the paw of a tigress under which her gleaming, sharp claws are concealed. "They will be disappointed at your thoughtlessness, but they will get over it."

"You will not get away with this, Constance. It is futile, foolish."

She grinned, and her eyes took on that shine which others must have interpreted as madness. She nodded to Jack, who shoved me firmly inside. I heard the door click shut behind me, I heard the thud as Jack threw my bag up on top. I was pressed roughly against the seat as the coach lurched away. I remember sitting for a long time, my hands clenched, my eyes wide and sightless, my mind uncomprehending. But, even stunned as I was, my heart had the power to ache within me, to imbue every cell of my body with a dumb, nameless pain, and a rage—just, but entirely helpless—save in its power to wrench and devastate me.

Chapter Four

🍃

"Mata! Mata!" It was the Indian word for "mother" which Winston lapsed into now and again. The joy in his voice spread like a tonic through my veins. I gathered him up in my arms.

"Yes, I am back, my dear," I whispered against his hair, fighting the tears of relief that misted my eyes.

"Tell me of the country," he pleaded. "Tell me of the things you saw. Were there elephants and monkeys?"

"Not in England," I reminded him, and he put his little hand to his mouth, embarrassed by his forgetfulness and the eagerness of his anticipation.

"Never mind," I assured him. "The country is lovely without them. Lots of white, woolly sheep and long-necked geese with terrible honking voices, and little woods creatures like rabbits and hedgehogs."

His blue eyes relaxed into pleasure, and I beguiled him for the next half hour with all the pleasant things I could think of until I felt my head nodding with fatigue and his nurse kindly drew him away.

May came into my room with Tabby in tow and insisted I lie down to rest.

"In India," I murmured sleepily, as they both fussed over me, "we had dozens of servants to a household; Winston would have possessed at least two of his own. But in our miserable London rooms I had no one to help me. If I was ill or exhausted it did not matter. . . . I had to do all . . . all myself."

I noticed that Tabitha's eyes were wide, and I did not know why I was carrying on so. May pulled the covers under my chin and motioned for Tabby to darken the windows. "More's the pity," she muttered. Then, with a firm cheerfulness, "But you are in my care now, remember? Sleep well, my dear."

Gratefully I closed my eyes, feeling much like Winston; I had a desperate need for someone older and wiser to lean upon. I remember wondering, as sleep dulled my thoughts, if May Skinner ever felt as I did—lonely and frightened, and in need of someone to turn to when no one was there.

The thought that I had failed in my sacred trust haunted me. As the days progressed, falling back into their safe and usual routines, the sensation did not abate. Dr. Fielding had trusted in me; I had made a solemn vow before heaven. In frustration I shared much of what had transpired with May, and I was surprised by her response.

"You have done more than most would," she assured me. "In terms of duty you have acquitted yourself nobly; in terms of human compassion you have gone far beyond the mark."

"Yet I have failed," I persisted, "for it was meant that I aid and assist my young brothers, not leave them under her influence, and helpless."

May pursed her lips—an expression I had come to recognize as her way of showing annoyance. "You have done all you could do; you are not in control of others' behavior. Much as it distresses you, my dear, you cannot control the wheel of life as it goes round."

She spoke the words in a kindly way, and I knew they were justified. It was a weakness of mine to strive to make all things right, or as I thought they should be. *A naive outlook,* I chided myself, *for one so experienced as I am in life's coarse realities.*

So I kept still, but my discontent did not lessen, nor my conviction that Constance was certainly up to something. I knew her too well to think she would settle into any sort of complacence and acceptance. I felt she was capable of almost anything.

Thus went the conflict within myself as summer ripened around us and the plucky English songbirds braved the city smog to fill the parks and streets with their song. I was happy. No longer did want, like a stark, leering skeleton, stalk my days. Security and comfort with their gentle arms upheld me. But I knew they were in truth insubstantial, merely lovely mirages; if I scratched beneath the surface I found nothing there that was really my own.

Charity. I lived by charity as much as did the destitute and homeless in the poorhouses of London. Where was my own life? Where did I belong? There were no answers, but the questions mocked me, their shadows dimming even the sweetest and happiest of my days.

Although I was loathe to admit it, I had missed my association with Seth Taylor and his people while I was away. I shrank from analyzing just what I missed most; it was an interweaving of many things: I liked the hymns they sang and the way in which they sang them, with longing or joy or even faith in their voices; I liked the things they taught about God and the purpose of earthly life; I liked the way they prayed, as though speaking to someone they trusted and loved. Of course, I was drawn to Seth himself; that was only natural. I liked his looks, though there was nothing extraordinary about them. But the line of his jaw was strong and his gray eyes were gentle, and he seemed to possess a discernment—a spiritual quality which at times astounded or alarmed me. I had called him a poet the first time I met him, because he told me I was beautiful and had a voice like a mourning dove, soothing and low, and sweet to the ear. I smiled at the memory. But it was more than that, much more. He discerned deep things about me which no one else seemed aware of, understanding my loneliness and the extent of my difference, my sense of isolation from Londoners, and Englishmen in general. He believed I had faith; he saw great things in me. "You carry truth within you," he once said, "and light cleaves to light."

I loved that phrase—I had repeated it over and over again; it had the power to encourage me and lift up my heart. Yet now, after what Constance had told me, I felt only darkness within. Could it be true? Could Karan love another? The idea of it turned my blood cold. And yet, what real love had I for him if I wished his whole life to be a dark plain, stretching empty and bleak? I desired more for myself. If we could never have one another—but the contemplation was too much for me, and I always retreated before carrying it out to an end, thus stumbling, prey to my own weakness, confusion and doubts.

I tried to relax. I let the summer days take me in their own gentle way where they would. Winston, Sarah Elizabeth, and I picnicked in St. James Park or in Hyde Park's Kensington Gardens, which lay just across the street from us. Sometimes we walked as far as the grand new marble arch constructed as the royal entrance to Buckingham Palace. Often we would take May's carriage as far as Richmond Park, where Charles I, in 1637, enclosed 2,470 acres of countryside into a park which boasts the most stately, majestic oak trees and stretches of bright rhododendrons and other spring flowers. Here Winston could catch glimpses of the wildlife, which included the shy, graceful fallow deer, roaming freely. He missed his monkey and still mourned the loss of Shadow, my little flying squirrel, whose death had seemed to snap the last thread which bound us to India. Winston and I were both set adrift in this new world which we had neither asked for nor wanted. We still were homeless and purposeless wayfarers on English soil.

I passed many an evening in the company of Miss Skinner and her friends, attending dramatic productions, concerts, and even literary readings. I found them to differ only slightly from the activities indulged in by British women in India, the sophistication and level of affluence of the participants serving but to further gloss over true communication of spirit and heart. Everything was done for ulterior purposes which involved show and prestige and social standing. There was no real interest in the strains of a fugue by Bach or a Beethoven concerto. The magic and power of a line of writing which made my pulse race seemed as nothing to them; they smiled upon me with a wise, benign indulgence if, impulsively, I attempted to share my inner reactions with them. I had always chafed against such a shallow use of one's days, even as a girl—this more than anything made me question the mixture of blood that ran through my veins. I had no taste for common British pursuits. Yet I had never lived as an Indian; my mother's blood seemed to lie dormant within me, serving only to dilute and mix and confuse, and render me neither here nor there—really, nothing at all.

"She yet has much to recommend her, my dear. We shall marry her well!" I heard one of May's friends whisper with the air of a conspirator, when she thought I was out of earshot. Why did the thought of that prospect make my heart freeze within me?

After leaving the major's house, I had attempted to write to the boys, but my letters were returned unopened. At last the thought came to me to attempt mailing my letters to their respective schools. I was jolted into re-awareness when these, too, were returned, per their mother's directions, I felt sure. I then wrote to the solicitor, but when I received no answer from him I began to be worried, indeed. Surely he was concerned that the terms of the will be complied with, that his late employer's desires be carried out as strictly as possible, despite opposition. I pondered the matter and it continued to eat at me, acting as a constant irritation, like the fleas of India, or the terrible winds, white and hot and never silent, that blow over that vast, faraway land.

One evening as Winston was kissing me good night he said, "I remember to pray for Hugh and Arthur every night, Mother. I do so hope they're all right."

I kissed his little forehead and tucked him under the covers. Although he had a nanny to see to him, I had not given up the practice which had established itself as a habit during our garret days—so Winston and I called them when we talked alone together, or in the company of others made any slight reference to what we had been through. I returned to my room and sank into the rocker which I had brought from Major

Reid's house when I married. I felt ashamed of myself. Before Geoffrey's death I had been concerned about the neglect of the boy's religious education, but for a long time now he had left me behind. His faith was real and his consistency admirable. What a lazy, indulgent creature I was! Winston's prayers always made a difference—was that because he believed they did? Surely not that only, for the power was not in the boy; it was not Winston who brought Seth and his friend to our house Christmas morning. It was the power of the God he believed in—the God the Mormons believed in. I had felt it myself. How could I deny what I had experienced so deeply? How could I continue to ignore the basic issues of life?

I knelt that night beside my empty bed, and attempted to pray. Nothing seemed to happen. I knelt a bit longer, trying to divest my mind of how hard the floor was beneath my knees, how cold the drafts that ran along the old, loose-fitting boards. I felt tired and preoccupied. For a long time I knelt, my eyes closed, thinking of nothing at all. Then I realized that I was thinking about the early days in India when those little boys had, indeed, been like brothers to me. I began to talk about them, silently, in my mind, and if the vague image to whom I addressed myself was a hazy mixture of Karan and Seth Taylor and Dr. Fielding, I could not for the moment help that. I relaxed as I opened my thoughts and concerns to whatever power may be listening. "We are his children," Seth had told me. "He is concerned about every one of us." I knelt there and "talked" a long time. And when I arose, snuffed the lamp, and slid between the covers, I felt almost happy inside. "Light and life to all he brings" the Christmas hymn says. "Risen with healing in his wings. . . ." He had healed Sita's little body; I had seen that with my own eyes. *Perhaps* . . . These thoughts were the last that trembled across my mind before all grew numb and I slept.

I heard her voice; up a long flight of stairs I heard it, and came tumbling down into her arms. "Emmer!" I cried. "I feared you had forgotten me."

"Shame!" she scolded, hugging me to her. "Have ye no

more faith 'an that?" Her blue eyes sparkled and her round cheeks still blushed red, like the shiny skin of an apple. "I've brought 'ee a present," she beamed.

I maneuvered her into the parlor and told Tabitha to lay a hasty tea for us. But Winston must have heard us, and before we could fairly settle ourselves he had flown down the stairs, canary, cage, and all, with Sita trailing behind. Then, for a spell, Emma forgot about me entirely as she fussed over the wee ones and she and her "little man" compared notes on the care and encouragement of their feathered pets. As I stood watching, it struck me how lonely my little Winston must be. He had privilege here, yes; fine clothes, rich playthings, large elegant gardens to wander through. But no one his age to play with, and less of me than he was used to. He and Emma had been such great friends—and he had had a *purpose* in life before, of which he was well aware. I would not have survived without him. He had learned to clean our rooms, small and sparsely furnished as they were, he cared for Sita, and even cooked simple meals for me. He kept the fire stoked, ran errands—I found myself astounded as my mind went back over the list. *How simple life had been then,* I could not help thinking. Few demands beyond the necessities of living; no servants to see to, no money to spend. Nothing to separate us from one another— and oh, how sweet the association had been. Wealth and the restrictions of class put such a distance between children and parents. How strange that poverty carried blessings with it—

"Penny for your thoughts, Lottie," Emma said with a wink and a playful poke in the ribs.

"They're worth more than that," I smiled. "Are you two through cooing over each other yet?"

Winston giggled, and the pleasure in his face was something palpable that reached out to me with fingers of light.

Dandling Sarah Elizabeth on her knee, she reached into her carpetbag and drew out a length of lace which she handed to me. I caught it up with eager reverence, and as I unfolded it, I realized that she had fashioned an exquisite collar, layered and finely scalloped. I put my hand to my mouth. "It is too dear a gift," I breathed.

Emma grinned. "Ye won't think so when ah've told you the whole of it."

"Go ahead," I urged. "I know you have something clever in mind—your eyes are a-sparkle with it."

"You do wear your clothes to advantage," she began. "Ladies will take note of my handiwork when it graces your shoulders. If some should happen to ask where you came by such an excellent piece, well . . ."

I clapped my hands. "You are clever, Emma. Why did not I think of that?"

Emma shrugged her shoulders. "You b'lieve it might work, then?"

"Of a surety! We shall *make* it work—and you shall become not only rich, but famous!"

She was pleased, but not any more so than I. To return a favor, to do a good to this kind-hearted woman who had helped to save me—I shivered with delight at the thought. So we dreamed and planned, and ate all the bread and butter sandwiches and every biscuit Tabby could find in the house. When May came in and found us giggling like schoolgirls, she made haste to join us, and when we revealed our aspirations to her, she pledged her support. Under the rosy glow of fond expectations, we retired to dinner in the dining room, all sitting in a cluster at one end of the table—Winston and Sita as well. We sent Emma home late, with a loaf of bread and some of the preserves which Jean, the cook, was famous for. And even when we closed the door after her, happiness bubbled around us, like the echoing sound of our laughter. I had sent Sita upstairs with her nanny, but Winston still clung to me with a small, sticky hand.

"I think I shall tuck Winston in myself," I told May. Then, impulsively, I leaned over and hugged her quickly, planting a kiss on the delicate, powdered skin of her cheek.

"I cannot thank you enough," I cried. "You have been so generous—you have made us so happy."

She fluttered her small, delicate hands. "No matter, my dear, next to what you and your young friend gave me."

I paused with my foot on the bottommost stair, my gratitude obscuring what I should have recognized. "Life and unspoiled enthusiasm," May murmured, placing her light, finely shaped fingers on my arm. "Sometimes I forget and settle for so much less."

"Don't we all," I whispered, half to myself.

"Now, off to bed with the both of you," May purred. And I thought, as she gave us a gentle shove with her fingertips, that there was a misting of tears in her eyes much like those that warmed and blurred my own sight as I let Winston lead me upstairs.

May was as good as her word. During the flurry of the next week's social engagements we secured many a pleased, eager customer for Emma, with prices negotiated by Miss Skinner that seemed princely indeed.

"She will not know what to do with such fortune," I assured May. "Oh, I can't wait to see her face!"

I intended to take the list of orders to Emma myself, Monday-week, first thing. But early on Sunday morning, before we were properly attired and ready to receive, there came an urgent pounding at the door, and the voice of a stranger exchanging low greetings with Tabitha, and then the dreaded sound of a summons for me.

I remember only that the man was small, like a midget or an overgrown child who had eaten too many sweets. His eyes were set deep in his face, and appeared small and glassy and devoid of all feeling as he made his announcement.

"Sit down, Miss . . . Simmons, is it?"

I nodded, wondering vaguely how he came by the use of my former name, which I had requested Constance and my brothers to use. I knew something grievous was coming; I could feel it close around me, thick and smothering. "Please . . . sit . . . yes . . . very good." He did not smile or alter his expression, but he took a deep breath which seemed to puff out his entire body.

"I am sent from the firm of Longhurst and Willis to inform you of the death of Mr. Garrett Longhurst."

I gasped, but he seemed not to note it. "Whatever—" I began. "Was it an accident—" But something stiff and sickly pale in his face stopped me.

"Poisoning, I fear," he replied, almost biting his words off.

"Poisoning?" I repeated, as my mind wandered, striving to recall something it might fix upon. "Are you certain?" I asked.

"Indeed," he responded. "We have tragic but certain evidence of the murderer—or, I should say, murderess."

It was something in the way he looked at me, in the careful cadence of his words as they fell carefully, one by one; or perhaps it was a sixth sense that brought the full horror home to me, before he spoke the name I could never have brought myself to utter aloud.

"The widow of the late Major Reid had been to visit Mr. Longhurst. There was an ugly disagreement, which was not of itself unusual. . . ." He spoke the words with such caustic malevolence that I cringed, feeling as though he were pointing the long finger of blame at me, too. "But the poison which had obviously been slipped into the drink which he finished, in agitation, following the departure of his unpleasant visitor—a vial containing that selfsame poison was found among the lady's possessions when she and her chaise were fished out of the river."

I was vaguely aware of shaking my head back and forth in angry disbelief.

"Oh, I do not suppose it was suicide," he continued, watching me closely, with that terrible detached coldness. "The conveyance was small, and she had been driving her animal a bit mercilessly, and it seems a board in the bridge, loose and warped, caught one of the horse's hoofs and set him off balance—that, and the excessive speed, and the lady's lack of judgment . . ." He shrugged his shoulders, and I again felt his contempt crawl over me.

"I see." I could feel myself straining to maintain my composure, almost unconsciously holding my head a bit higher, though my hands were clenched in the folds of my skirts so that my knuckles ached.

"I regret being the bearer of such tidings," he concluded with unconcealed insincerity.

"I regret that tragic occasion has placed you in such a role," I responded, nodding my head ever so slightly. "I assume . . ." I paused.

"Yes. The executors of the will, as well as the late Mrs. Reid's surviving sister, request—nay, beg that you attend them for—"

With a wave of my hand I brushed the rest of his pompous statement aside. "Of course. I shall leave as soon as possible."

With practiced skill my hand slid over the bell rope, and Tabitha, who must have been waiting nearby, appeared just as swiftly and smoothly to show the gentleman out.

More revolting than his late partner, I thought grimly, shuddering with relief as the door closed upon him. Then I sank into the satin loveseat that stood to the left of the broad doorway, as a sudden spell of weakness drained all strength from me.

May found me there, moments later; she, too, had been waiting to learn the ominous errand of my visitor. Her delicate brow knit in a mingling of concern and distaste. "Nasty business, my dear," she muttered, pursing her fine lips. "I do not wish you to go there alone."

I blinked up at her.

"I shall send Tabitha with you." Then, seeing my expression, she added, "The matter is settled, dear. I shall feel much better that way."

It *was* a gracious gesture on her part, and eased my apprehensions a little. But how I disliked the prospect of leaving Winston and Sita again. And the boys—what possible means could I find of helping them through a nightmare of these proportions? Not only pride, but dignity and self-worth would be entirely shattered, and how, in English society, would they ever live down their shame?

So the tentacles of the past closed around me once more, and I was made to leave the comfort and security of my own world to buffet the storms and shadows of another.

"You need not go," May said, her eyes sharp on my face.

"No," I said, "a promise is a promise. The dead will be watching me." And I was not thinking of the miserable and calculating major, but of my green-eyed English father whose native land I now trod. I felt, somehow, that he would expect me to exercise stoic resolution as well as compassion. He had done so before me, and left an example I found myself desiring to emulate.

CHAPTER FIVE

❦

THE ENGLISH SUN HAD THE DECENCY to hide its face the day we buried Constance. There were not many of us to stand dismally beside the scar torn through the green earth, that intrusion into the gentle English soil which would hold her remains. For all intents and purposes I had spoken to no one since my arrival; Alice refused to meet me on anything but a most formal level, and she had made all necessary arrangements before I arrived. The boys, perhaps through the intended kindness of their respective headmasters, had been kept at their schools until the last moment. I could have wished for an interval in private with them, before they faced this public ordeal; but it was not to be. Yet, as I looked about me, I wondered how many of these mourners, neighborhood folk and distant relatives, knew the truth of what had happened. A tragic accident—that is all that had been told, and that was sufficient. Surely the family and the firm of Garrett Longhurst were immersed in their own grief and horror, for the time being at least. There was no one left upon whom they could wreak their just wrath. I believed even they would be decent enough to leave the boys out of it. Hugh and Arthur would carry the knowledge of what had happened for the rest of their lives—that was nightmare enough.

Perhaps it was natural, as I stood beneath the gentle drizzle, that my thoughts should turn to Roselyn and that other grave which rested in a distant garden, beneath the strong gnarled arms of the Banyan, where a stone angel spread wings as tender as gossamer, and the air trembled with the fragrance of jasmine and the scarlet semal petals that littered the ground. Was Constance with her now, and was her other daughter, poor Lucy, restored to her? How vain and trifling are the efforts of mortals. We cannot alter the course of the gods, no more than we can alter the course of the seasons. We tear our hearts into tatters attempting the impossible, blinded as we are to that work which God means for our hands to do here. Heal and soothe, strengthen and lift. We seldom see it that way. Karan did. Karan was one who knew how to move in harmony with the forces of life. Was he truly lost to me? Had he found room in that great heart of his for another? *I shall never love another woman as I love you, Charlotte. Nothing can separate our spirits; my heart is yours, my faith . . .*

I shuddered and looked up to see Arthur watching me, his eyes burning cold as gray ice stretched over a winter pond. The sky that stretched from horizon to horizon was gray, and seemed to press down upon us with the weight of the universe. I raised my cold fingers to my cheek, and realized I was crying tears as thin and silent as the rain.

"The colonel has settled the matter," Mrs. Miller said, in a voice so sane and normal that I had to blink my eyes at her. "He and I are appointed the boys' legal guardians. I believe Ralph would have wanted it so, Lottie."

"But I promised to look after them—"

"And so you shall, insofar as you are able. But you are young, my dear, and have your own life to live." Something in my face must have betrayed me, for she came closer. "I mean it, Lottie. We have the time and the means, and will be happy for the diversion—for the purpose they will lend to our days. Colonel Miller has the connections necessary to enable the boys to advance. Give them your love, as you always have, and leave the rest in our hands."

That is precisely what Dr. Fielding wrote, I thought.

"You have done all that has been asked of you—demanded

of you, Lottie, and more. Go home to your babies and leave these shadows behind you, where they belong."

If only I could tell her that the darkest, the weightiest shadow was the one Constance had thrown over my heart, like a net of black tentacles, as poisonous as the sting of the scorpion. My heart was smothering beneath it.

"Lottie, you look quite pale. Are you sure you're all right, dear?"

"I shall be fine," I assured her. "I think I should like a bit of fresh air."

"Fresh air? It's still weeping out there, Lottie. I believe you'd be better off here."

"Just a few moments . . ." I moved toward the small garden exit, where my hooded cape hung beside the doorway. The pall of evening had deepened the gloom of the day and blurred the sharp outline of things, but I could still see my way. With no thought or intent, I let my feet find their own path, which led inevitably through the meadows to the sparse stands of trees.

I heard nothing until I felt a touch at my elbow and looked up to see Arthur beside me.

"I frightened you," he said. "Your eyes are as wide with surprise as a child's. Did you expect fairies—or worse?"

I tried to match his mood. "I was too deep within myself to take note of anything," I admitted.

"You look like a lady in green yourself, risen from one of the ancient mounds that arch restlessly under our feet."

I placed my hand on his arm.

"You're going back to London, aren't you?" he asked.

"Can you think of anything better?"

"No, I cannot. That is why I came after you. We'll be all right, Hugh and I; truly we will." He held his hands out, palms upward. "No bottle tonight," he said, and for a moment his voice sounded very old and very tired. "I want no more of that, not after what has happened. Whatever darkness she has bequeathed me can stay buried deep where it is."

"Your father was a good man, with many notable qualities, for which he was justly respected," I began, and when he tried to shake my hand off, I slipped my arm firmly through his.

"Constance, too, had qualities of spirit which were admirable. I remember—"

"This is not necessary, Lottie. I told you we're all right. We—"

"Hear me out. This is not only necessary, but important. Whatever weaknesses your parents struggled with were theirs, Arthur. Let them lie with them here. Winston and my little Sarah were born of a father who was cold and narrow, calculating and cruel—yet I see nothing of him in them. They are free from the taint of his spirit. . . ." I paused, unable to go further. Arthur was silent for a moment, and the close, heavy air seemed to envelop us.

"What beasts we are, Lottie," he muttered, "dragging you down here, demanding your loyalty, your pampering, and never thinking one jot about your life or what you've been through." He turned suddenly boyish eyes upon me. "You must think ill of us, indeed."

"One of the finest things we can do in life is sustain one another. I came, you know, of my own free will."

He was thinking deeply, he was really seeing me for the first time. "Had it been awful, then, Lottie, your life with that man?"

"Yes, worse than I would want you to ever experience. But there are compensations, you know, to the hardest existence, which it seems God builds in."

He did not understand me, but he wanted to. "What of now, what of the future?"

"For the present, I live amidst comfort and kindness. The future is a blank to me still." I attempted a smile. "Much as yours is—perhaps even more so, for you have plotted your course."

"That is true. I hope for a commission to India in two years, if I am lucky."

If you are lucky! I thought with a shudder. *Poor, misguided thing, walking into the teeth of life with head thrust bravely forward, in true British fashion—*

"Lottie, you're off by yourself again! You've always been like that, you know."

We talked of lighter things then, and ended with my promising to write him and his promising to return my letters faithfully, as all well-intentioned people who care for each other do.

"Colonel Miller is a decent chap all round," he assured me. "Don't torment yourself on our accounts."

I promised him not to, and leaned up in the darkness to kiss his cheek. "Don't forget our talk," I whispered. "Be true to the best within you, no matter what others are doing, and you will never go wrong."

For some reason I believed that he would. I could see in his eyes a resolution that had risen from the ashes of pain and tenderness. If it had been built upon resentment and fear it would have been altogether different. *He is made of finer stuff*, I thought. *He will come out all right.*

It was late when we came in, but I arose early next morning and helped Tabitha pack our things. The boys were packed off on the early coach, and I left an hour later, anxious to put that sad place forever behind me, and make my way home.

I was, of course, delighted to be back with the children again, but a strange restlessness, almost a discontentment, clouded my hours as I fell back into the expected routine: walks in the garden, teas, lunches, late dinners after the theatre; all pursuits which sapped one's energies to no purpose at all. I found myself drawn more and more to the weekly meetings with Seth and his people. I did not think May particularly noticed, until one evening she said sharply, "One of your Church acquaintances was here while you were out with the children, prattling on about some sewing project you are involved in, wanting some—"

"Good heavens!" I put my hand to my mouth. "I forgot altogether."

"Well, I told her you had plans for the evening."

"But I must go. I have pieces to the quilt they'll be needing if they hope to finish in time."

May pursed her lips and drew her small body as straight as she could. "Do you mean to disappoint me then?"

"I do not mean to, but it is through my own stupidity, and I fear that I must. . . ."

She accepted as gracefully as she was able, once she had made certain her displeasure was unmistakably communicated. I joined with the small group of women who were piecing quilts for Beth Osbourne, who had three small children and no husband to help in the support of them since the accident which had claimed his life last spring. I liked these women who chatted freely together, changing the nappies and wiping the noses of whoever's child happened to be near. Janet Dibble was one of my favorites—a large, solidly built matron whose eyes brimmed over with merriment and whose voice was as resounding and bright as a bell. None of these people had been blessed with much in the way of the world's goods; the gospel of Jesus Christ drew in those who were looking for it, who were aware of an obvious lack in their lives. May's friends could not qualify; they had long ago lost touch with their own spirits, and seemed not even aware of a master spirit who could move through and upon all of us.

"These people are the salt of the earth," Seth liked to say. "The Lord knows his own, and picks them one out of a family, here a few, there a few, as they respond to his voice." Once, when he was going on about it a bit, he stopped quite suddenly and confronted me. "Look at yourself. You may well be the first Indian woman to hear the restored gospel of Christ."

His words made me think. For days I could not shake the effect of them. *Light cleaves to light,* he had once said, and I knew I was more than a mere coward; I was being untrue to myself, untrue to the noble natures of the man and woman who had given me life.

When I told Seth that I wished to be baptized he responded slowly, as though he were savoring the moment.

"I could say 'this was inevitable,' or 'my prayers have been answered,' but that would be diminishing it, Lottie. For your sake I am happy, because I think I know what this decision will do for you, how you will bloom under the touch of the Spirit." He placed the tips of his fingers gently against my face. "Welcome home, Lottie."

I thought for a long time about the various things he might have meant with those words.

When I came up out of the waters of baptism, with Seth's hand on my wrist and his gentle gray eyes holding mine, I felt a sense of wholeness—that is the only way I can express it; a balance, a wholeness inside. So real it was that I expected it to show in my face, in my voice. The impatience I had felt melted from me. Seth had once said, *God will take you in hand and provide* . . . That is what I felt, that my life would move differently from this moment forth.

"The Dibbles are leaving? What do you mean they are leaving?" I snapped at Seth, who was walking so calmly beside me along the shaded paths of May's garden.

"Taking passage to the States. The ship leaves the tenth of October, and there will be nearly two hundred on it."

I was astounded. That many? "Why would the Dibbles want to leave England? They have lived their entire lives here. Do you know they have five married children and nearly a score of grandchildren—do they plan to leave their whole family behind?"

"They want to gather with the Saints, to—"

"I do not understand it!" My irritation was too great to conceal.

"You left India."

"Not of my own volition, and not for noble purposes."

"Exactly," he pounced. "You must see it, Lottie. There we can live in harmony and brotherhood. We can own land, in communities of brothers and sisters—"

"It sounds too ideal to be true. Besides, what if we did not like it there? It is so far away from . . . everything. I think it is too much to risk."

We let it drop there, and I intended to speak to Janet Dibble myself concerning the matter on Sunday. But the chance did not come to me; not then, not for a very long time.

I remember that the coolness of early morning still clung to the rooms and Tabitha had thrown open the French doors which led into the gardens, so that the dewy fragrance of rose, hyacinth, and honeysuckle mingled subtly in the very air we breathed.

"An unknown visitor for me?" I asked when Tabby came with the message. "This is getting to be an unpleasant pattern, isn't it?" I smiled at her, but my mouth felt stiff with the effort. Why was a hard lump of fear forming inside me? Was this more bad news about Constance unearthed, or something amiss with one of the boys?

The man who rose to greet me was tall and slender, and carried himself like a gentleman, and there was a kindness in his eyes when he spoke my name and greeted me.

"Miss Charlotte . . . Simmons? Am I correct?"

I nodded. How had he found me, and how did he know this was the name I was now going by?

"I am Ernest Fleming, factor to Miss Marion Elizabeth Simmons of Baddenwell." He paused briefly, and when I said nothing, he continued. "I am sent to extend you a most urgent request, nay entreaty, to accompany me back so that Miss Simmons might meet you, and you might have the pleasure of visiting your family's ancestral home."

"How is this?" I demanded. "Are you privy to the fact that I at one time wrote seeking information concerning my father, and your mistress replied in a very different fashion?"

The muscles of his face twisted in a very brief expression of mingled contrition and sympathy. "That is regrettable, my dear. But at times one must make sure. . . ."

Must one, I thought. "What is it she wishes of me? And why . . . why now?"

"You attended a society luncheon, it seems, at Honeydale, the estate of one Lady Ruth Irwin, some months ago. One of Marion's oldest, most trusted friends met you there, and took a liking to you, speaking very highly of you upon her return."

"And thus piquing Marion's curiosity?"

The tall old gentleman winced again.

"I sincerely regret the circumstances you refer to, my dear. But could we not leave them in the past? Are you not anxious to meet your aunt, and see the home of your father's child-hood?"

"As the 'unfortunate circumstances' suggest, indeed I am. But what is it your mistress is interested in, Mr. Fleming?"

"I cannot wholly answer to that."

How schooled he was in the subtleties of social maneuvering!

"I can only assure you that her interest to meet you is quite sincere. I hope you will find her a gracious and gentle lady." He paused again, and when he continued I could detect a note of entreaty in his voice. "Will you so honor us, my dear?"

He must have been relatively sure of my answer. For, in truth, I would risk any unpleasantness, or even unkindness, for the chance he was giving me.

CHAPTER SIX

ERNEST WAS A CONSIDERATE and interesting travel companion, and the hours sped by as he pointed out sites of unusual beauty or note. I had believed my father's family to live in the midlands, but the house actually sat in South Yorkshire, deep within a long, grassy parkland, bordered all round with a gentle girdle of green, leafy trees. The house was stone, gray stone with a soft, rosy hue to it, showing as streaked lavender when the surface was moist. To the left of the house the woods opened up to reveal a large pond that sprawled toward the manicured acres and was as blue as Winston's eyes. It was not quite September, but the days had turned cooler, and on the morning of my arrival crows cried through the thin air and circled above the dark woods. Had my father been drawn to the birds, or not even taken note of them? Surely he had seen no omen in their sleek purple feathers, the predatory curve of their beaks, no foreshadowing of the tragic role the Crims, or the Crows of India, were to play in his life.

The house was large, the main rooms cavernous and formal, save for the mullion-windowed morning room tucked into the southwest corner, where the sun seemed always to fill it, and the fragrance of lavender, as subtle as the scent of sunlight, seemed to filter the air.

"This was *her* room," Ernest told me when he first took me there.

"My grandmother's," I guessed. But before I could entreat

him to tell me of her, I heard someone come up behind us and turned to see a woman I assumed was Marion, for she looked very much the feminine counterpart of my father.

"Ah, you are here." Her voice was too thin, and the note of triumph in it disturbed me. We stared at one another. Upon closer observation her hair, though laced with strawberry highlights, was a rather ordinary color, and her eyes more brown than green, with no lights in them.

"Yes, I can see him in her," she said, addressing Ernest, I assumed. "But, of course, the fair English complexion is forfeit, and her hair and eyes are so dark."

"But the green flecks are there, ma'am; you cannot miss them." Ernest's kind eyes smiled at me, though the rest of him remained quite proper and staid.

There was little conversation that first day, really. I was shown to my rooms, and came out to be told that the mistress of the house had previous obligations and would be absent for the rest of the day. I did not mind. I was free to wander, to imagine; to try to hear the old memories whisper through the silences that surrounded me. *How much of my father is here?* I wondered. *How much of his heart, the sinew of his personality, is woven into this place?*

I was not to find out from Marion. In her own way, she was much like Constance, cushioning her insecurities with a layer of social activities. Besides, she was subject to headaches and never came down for breakfast. So the first two days at Baddenwell I was left very much to myself. That evening I determined to engage her in conversation to some purpose, but she was a master at evasion, and I ended up feeling frustrated and depleted. "Your father enjoyed a happy childhood. . . . He was a bright child, even somewhat precocious. . . ." That was the most she had said of him, and less of everyone else. Again, I wondered why in the world I had been brought here. She was so cautious with me, and determined to keep a safe distance, and I wondered what could possibly come of beginnings so tentative and cool.

I was wasting my time, and the thought not only maddened but depressed me. I had wandered the library and sitting rooms, staring up at the family portraits that lined the walls, wondering what kind of people my father had come from, and what had enticed him to leave. Here seemed not only comfort, but solidarity for the future. Continuity—that's what the sense of generations gave one. What had broken the thread for him?

I gazed at my grandmother's portrait, but her composed face seemed closed to me, and I could only guess at the secrets her proper countenance shrouded. She was easily one of the prettiest of the women whose portraits marched up and down the walls and corridors of the place. Her hair was dark, with a veritable halo of soft, tumbling curls, which I must have inherited from her, and the thought of anything so directly connecting us made me glad. *If my father had brought me home, would she have received me? Would she have loved me?* Something elemental within me yearned dearly to know.

I could stand it no longer. After a few false starts I found my way belowstairs to the kitchens. When Ernest saw me standing in the doorway his eyes registered something very near to horror before he composed himself and rose from the tea laced with brandy he had been nursing, to see what I could possibly want.

"Do not distress yourself," I pleaded. "If this is considered improper, you must disregard that." I smiled, sensing the wistfulness of my expression. "I have lived in apartments which, placed all together, were smaller than this marvelous kitchen in which you sit, having little to eat and sometimes a cold fireplace, and certainly no one to wait upon me."

The white-capped maid sitting at the opposite end of the table registered the shock she was feeling in the startled expression on her face, so I purposefully turned my eyes now on her.

"Yet there was a time I commanded a household of four, perhaps five times the number of servants you manage here. So, you see, I can handle a variety of circumstances." I must admit I was enjoying the enigmatic nature of my behavior, and I suspect Ernest was beginning to see the humor in it, too.

"Would you be so kind as to come with me, Ernest," I

addressed him. "I am very much in need of your services at the moment."

He raised a quizzical eyebrow, but his flawless training came to his aid now. "It would be my pleasure, Miss Simmons." He swept his arm down in a rather grand fashion. "After you."

"Will the library do?"

"The morning room will be less chilled and, I trust, more comfortable."

"Yes, I should have thought of that, Ernest. How considerate of you."

"Not at all, miss."

I was enjoying myself, the delightful parrying between us, yet curiosity was burning a veritable hole through my brain.

I sat down, stretching my legs to reach a plump, cushioned ottoman. "I can bear no more," I admitted. "Tell me of my father, Ernest. You know you are the one who must do it. Tell me of my father, and of Elizabeth Simmons."

He made no pretense of objection; he had seen through to the core of me, and was not of a mind to toy with me, as a cat with a mouse.

"Very well." His eyes took on a faraway expression as he began to tug at the old memories, well concealed with moth balls and tucked safely away. "There were two boys in the family, as well as Marion, your father being the younger. But his brother died in a boating accident when he was a lad of fourteen. After that, your grandfather turned his attentions to his remaining son; and, of course, this delighted the boy."

"What of Elizabeth? What was she like?"

"A lady in every true sense of the word." The response came quickly, almost automatically. "She balanced your father's competitive training in sports and outdoor skills by disciplining his mind, channeling his native curiosity into the awakening of his spirit." His eyes grew soft with remembrance. "Her own sensitivities were well refined. Mother and son shared a natural understanding."

"What of Marion?"

"Marion was both shy and pampered, and spent most of

her time in the nursery in the company of her nanny and her dolls. To be fair, Elizabeth preferred Frances's company to hers."

I leaned forward. The stage had been set and the characters drawn. There were things to tell beyond the ordinary—I could sense that much.

Ernest sighed, as though resigning himself to it. "Your grandfather was a man of high spirits and great charm, and he had an eye for the ladies which, well, which he could not control."

"Which he chose not to control?" I ventured, and his silence confirmed me. "And Elizabeth. Was she aware of his ways?"

"He could scarcely conceal them from her, though she married him in good faith, as innocent and hopeful as any young bride could be."

"And she stood for it?"

"Women in her time and station had little choice, my dear."

I had momentarily forgotten how long Ernest had been a part of this family—some forty-five years. He had seen nearly everything, and possessed a long-range perspective.

"And my father?"

"At first the son looked to be a carbon copy of his sire. He enjoyed the flirtations and the sense of power it gave him; he thought it all great fun. And he was desirous of pleasing his father, so I don't believe he thought beyond that."

"Did this estrange him from his mother?"

"Not at all. Their closeness was too genuine, too deep for that. You might say that he went blithely along, unaware and unseeing, until one day." A troubled expression clouded Ernest's eyes, and I felt myself begin to dread what was coming.

"The Master was in the habit of going up to London quite often, staying over a night, perhaps two there. During one of these times young Frances happened upon his mother in an unguarded moment when . . . well, quite by mistake, a costly locket had been delivered to the house by a local tradesman. Delighted at the unexpected gift, Elizabeth tore open the wrappings, only to discover that the initials carved into the gold oval were not her own."

I gasped a little as a sensation of sickness swept through me.

"She was here, in the morning room, sobbing uncontrollably when he came upon her and the evidence of his father's guilt which she had no time to conceal. Her pain was so stark, so exposed—"

I shuddered and glanced quickly around me, as though a shadow of what had happened here had suddenly trembled over my heart.

"He could not bear her suffering. And from that moment he could not endure the company of his father. This placed him in a very awkward situation. He dared not openly defy the old man, nor take his mother's part against him, and do them both more harm than good. He was trapped, you see."

I realized that I was twisting Karan's chain round and round my cold, clammy fingers, until the fine strands of gold bit into my skin. I could imagine too well what kind of agony they both were suffering.

"That is when he determined to seek a commission. Of course, Kenneth was delighted, never guessing at the motive behind the action." His eyes came to rest on my drained face, and he spoke very slowly. "Of course, *she* understood and gave the boy her permission freely."

I nodded. "Gave him his freedom, though he was the only strength and comfort she had."

Something like a quiet pride crept into the old man's eyes, and I sensed his whole figure relax. "I thought you would understand."

"Her sufferings made him the man he was," I reflected. "Capable of giving his love and devotion, his entire soul to a woman, and thus suffering a hell of his own."

Ernest was watching me carefully. "What of Marion?" I asked, turning the subject, because I was trembling inside.

"She adored him, and was hurt by the abrupt nature of his leaving. I do not think Elizabeth ever took the pains necessary to make her understand."

That explains much, I thought. *Chances are she believed he was still on the same path as his father, and thus struggled against a mixture of devotion and resentment toward him for the rest of his life.*

"You do not look well, my dear. I am sorry. I feared this."

"No," I hastened. "You have set me free with this knowledge. The pain . . . is necessary."

I felt suddenly weary, as though every muscle in my body had turned to water. "Go to bed, Ernest. I'll be all right, really I will."

"I should rather see you safely to your own room first," he attempted.

"Please."

He nodded in resignation and left me alone in the morning room, peopled now with shadows I longed to make corporeal, to make real! Here in this room. My childhood memories of my father flickered before me. It was so easy to imagine him flirting, audacious, full of life—I had seen men behave thus many times at the officers' dances in Simla and Barrackpore. Yet the sight of him on his knees at his mother's feet, his shining head cradled in her lap—this sight was painfully more vivid, more real.

"So unfair!" I said aloud. "Why do the best people suffer the most?"

I arose and began to walk randomly, only vaguely aware that I was prying open the small French doors and going out into the night. I fancied I felt my grandmother moving with me through all that had once been hers, truly hers, bought with the coin of her own pain and tears. She had become so real to me— real as a young woman, much like myself, and I longed fiercely to reach out and alter the events of her life, to comfort her, love her, redeem her from what should not have been. Yet it was my father's name I cried out when I reached the dark pool, and the dim features of my own lost mother that wavered dimly before me as I knelt there and wept.

I slept late the following morning and awoke feeling fuzzy in the head and heavy with a weariness which sleep would not cure. Marion was no match for me when she found me in the library, scouring the long musty shelves.

"I've called round the carriage," she announced. "I had no idea you planned to sleep late this morning." Just a touch of remonstrance sharpened her voice. When I made no reply, she continued. "We're to call at the milliner's and my dress-maker's—" stressing with intended emphasis the syllable *my*, "and, well, half a dozen other important places. Perhaps we can eat a late luncheon in town."

I closed the book I held in my hands and turned slowly to face her, but she had already started in again.

"I assume the clothes you have with you are a result of the influence of that lady—what was her name?—who was killed just recently. Wasn't there some scandal associated with her?" Marion shuddered visibly. "Regrettable. Her taste is . . . simply off, my dear. We shall have to begin again."

She moved as she talked, replacing volumes I had pulled off the shelves to examine—anything to keep her hands busy. "And I've been meaning to ask you about this woman you live with in London. Assuming the nanny you have for your children is competent, would May Skinner consider keeping them for the next several months? They would be so much in the way here."

She had succeeded in astonishing me a little, but she was unaware of this. "Sooner than we know the season will be upon us, and we have so much to do."

I sighed, loudly enough that it gave her pause, and she turned her mild, inquiring eyes upon me.

"None of this is necessary, Marion," I said, as gently as I was able. "I appreciate your concern, but I have no intention of remaining here."

"I can do better by you than any other." Her pride had been wounded; she remained still blind to my true intent. "This Skinner woman cannot find as fine a husband for you, not in the city."

"And once I found a suitable husband?" I suddenly could not resist following the thing through to its conclusion, learning what was in Marion's mind.

"Then you would be in a condition to take over Badden-well when the time comes."

I believe she had expected a great response, a mingling of delight and gratitude, and I disappointed her bitterly.

"Is that your desire, Marion?"

The directness of my question took her aback. "There is no one else," she replied, skirting a plain answer. "When I am gone—" A visible shudder ran over her. "We have distant cousins in Derbyshire. I should not like to see this place fall into their hands."

"I see." And I did, at last. She had chosen the lesser of two evils. She had swallowed her pride to call me here and acknowledge me, believing it her duty to keep the Simmons property in the direct line of her father's blood. Despite her confusion and disappointment with regard to me, I had met with her approval sufficient enough to recommend the course she felt, by duty, to follow through to its unsatisfactory, if not bitter, end.

Unexpectedly a great wave of compassion for her swept over me. How frightened she must have been when she was a young woman and men came to court her. How intently must she have searched for signs, telltale hints which would warn her away from a life such as her mother had suffered. *A proper match.* That delusionary condition, both feared and longed for, had somehow eluded her.

Very carefully I placed the book I was holding on the long, leather-covered table which stood beside me. "I am very touched by your great kindness," I said, in all sincerity, and no little amazement, for this is not what I had planned in my mind to say. "You are more than gracious and more than generous, but I am not yet ready for . . . for any of this. May I beg off for . . . a season?" How I despised that British term, whose tentacles of power reached all the way to India. The social season, an "institution" more revered in England than the church or the crown. "My children are young; I cannot yet abandon them. The impact of my last marriage and my husband's death has . . ." What dare I say to her? How far should I go in expressing myself? "It would not be to your advantage. You would be wasting your faith and efforts—"

I reached one hand out and tentatively rested it upon her

arm. "Could you bear with me? Would you be too awfully angry, or disappointed, if, for the present, I declined?"

I had succeeded in thoroughly astounding her. She stood speechless before me. "You jeopardize everything by declining," she replied with an unmistakable note of warning in her voice. "Surely you can—"

"No. I must do what I must do, Marion, especially where my children are concerned."

I could not, did not expect her to understand. But, with myself it was as if a light had snapped on in my head, a lovely light, warm and golden, capable of illuminating everything. I began to see clearly, for the first time, what I truly desired in life. The wheat from the chaff, the gold from the brass, I could distinguish them, and judge between.

"The decision is yours, of course. I can only go so far in influencing you."

"You have been marvelous; you have made me so happy," I said upon sudden impulse. "Thank you for allowing me to come here."

The genuineness of my gratitude disarmed her, and I was able to conclude the interview on a positive note. Nor did she protest, that evening at dinner, when I announced my intention of leaving next day.

"May I write to you?" I asked her the following morning, when Ernest was seeing to the strapping of my reticule onto the carriage and we were making our formal good-byes.

"Of course." She did not yet know what to make of me.

"And will you reply?" Her eyes grew wide at my straightforwardness, at the liberty I was taking. "It would mean an awfully lot to me."

"By all means—naturally, I will answer your letters."

For some reason tears welled up, choking my throat and reddening my eyes. Marion saw; perhaps that is why she allowed me to lean forward and plant a hasty kiss upon her cheek before I climbed into the carriage and Ernest clicked the door shut behind me, and she stood watching us canter down the long lane, past the pond and the pleasant meadows of grassland, and out of sight.

CHAPTER SEVEN

🎵

IT WAS NOT LONG AFTER MY RETURN TO LONDON that Seth Taylor asked me to marry him, and because of what had happened at Baddenwell, I was able to respond as he had hoped that I would. But that was not the extent of the matter. Seth was as good a man as any woman could ask for, and I believed that he sincerely loved me; but what of my feelings for him? I had already married once where my heart did not lie, and though this was different by far, I yet worried about the risks I would be taking, as well as the injustice I might be doing to the man who wanted to live with me for the rest of his life. I knew I must face the matter squarely, in the open, before any marriage could take place. But it was not easy, not easy at all, to broach the subject with him. Yet, as it turned out, the whole thing came up very naturally; almost, it seemed, of its own accord.

We were walking in May's gardens, and he had been telling me of a row house he had come across in the course of his daily wanderings, which he believed we might be able to let.

"It will be a step down in the world for you," he teased lightly, but I knew he was concerned at reducing me to a level of living starkly below that to which I had become accustomed of late.

"That is of small matter," I assured him. "But there are other things—things that must be settled."

"Aye, for your peace," he answered, and I realized he had taken my meaning, and I could feel his tenderness reach out to me, like a wave of sweet air.

"What of yourself?" I cried, for it struck me quite suddenly that I had never told him I loved him.

"Myself?" he echoed. "I have no concerns on my account. I consider myself the most fortunate of men."

"You know very little about me."

"I am acquainted with your strengths and your weaknesses, and I believe I know your heart. What can there be beyond that?"

"I was married before. You know something of it; you know that I did not love Geoffrey—"

"I know he was cruel to you, beyond what you will tell me." The anguish in his voice was real. "And I know that you have loved before, Charlotte; I am not a fool."

My breath caught; my fingers sought the touch of the ring that rested beneath my bodice, cool against my throat. "I loved him so deeply; I do not believe I can ever stop loving him, Seth. If he were here—"

"But he is not here, Lottie—and I am."

"It is not so simple!"

He moved very close to me, though he did not attempt to touch me; I could feel his breath on my cheek.

"I love you, Lottie, and I know, despite your fears and reservations, that you love me. It is sufficient, it is more than enough to build upon, as long as you know that I want to take care of you—that I will never betray you or hurt you for as long as I live."

It was the most solemn of pledges, spoken from a heart whose integrity lent it the power of the eternities which, in awe, I could feel but could not understand.

I realized that I was crying, trembling with great sobs that shook through me.

"Come, Lottie," he said, opening his arms to me, pulling me gently against him. "You will never have to cry like this again, my dearest. Not ever again."

Suddenly it happened, as though by miracle, as though by the most natural and easy transition: we became a family, the four of us, more of a family than I had ever known in my life.

May was not pleased to have us leave her, though she sent me off with as much of her blessing as she could muster. The living quarters which Seth had secured were clean and cozy, and sufficient. I did not miss the opulence, but I missed the garden, all the things of beauty which had surrounded me. And I did miss the pampering. How quickly one moves on and forgets. It was not easy to alter the pattern of my days so drastically, to do all of the work myself. Winston loved having me with him, and was as eager to help, to ease my burdens, as he had been during those first dark days on our own. Seth was of the labouring class, the job he worked being a steady, secure one, as such things went. He was known as a "bill sticker" or "ladder-man" which brought down higher wages of one pound to a pound fifteen shillings per week for those cool of head and steady enough of foot to climb to the high places; bills, brush, and paste can in hand; to secure the advertisements on the sides of buildings for all to see. Seth enjoyed the work, and his hours, from seven in the morning until seven at night, were shorter than some. He liked being out and about and meeting people, and taking opportunity when it came to proselyte his own wares of a less ephemeral nature. Indeed, I had difficulty keeping him from proselyting Mormonism whenever he could, night or day. We spent many of our evenings in meetings or in visiting members; his expansive nature made it difficult for us to hold on long to any advantage that came our way.

"Those squash and turnips May delivered yesterday are enough to feed half of London," he would say. "And we don't want 'em spoiling, so how about divvying them up? I know half a dozen families at least who could make good use of them."

So it would go. He saw nothing out of the ordinary in his behavior, but I caught frequent glimpses of the nobility of spirit behind the acts of generosity. And I learned. I shall never forget one particular evening when he came home from work and asked apologetically if I had any old frocks I had grown particularly tired of, or that perhaps ill fitted me. "I believe Beth Osbourne could make good use of another dress, if she had it," he explained.

I went into our room to select one, and was impressed to catch up a shawl and a pair of half-worn slippers which had always been too tight for my feet. We went together to the small rooms she shared with her children, and I felt myself shrinking back a little, recalling too vividly my own experiences with squalor and despair. But there was no despair here, I could see that in the children's faces and in the calmness behind Beth's tired eyes. Yet, when we presented the dress to her, tears rolled down her cheeks.

"What a boon this'll be," she said, catching it to her. "I shall save this for the Sabbath and not worry about washing me other one out every Saturday night. What a burden off my shoulders that'll be."

I sat stunned, and was quiet as I walked back with Seth. Nor did he press me until I said quietly, "I had no idea."

"Of course you didn't."

"Why did you not have me bring two?"

He chuckled softly under his breath and slipped his arm around me.

"I am so petty, Seth, complaining over the difficulties in my life, when women such as herself go—"

"Hush," he said. Then, "Bas! Bas!" as I did with the children, to make me laugh, and I realized for the thousandth time how fortunate I was to have the love of a good man. I had never before known what it was like to repose total trust and confidence in a husband, and bit by bit I could feel myself begin to let go, begin to soften deep inside toward him. He felt it, too, and responded, and gave even more to me, so that all of my days were blessed with this light.

Autumn made itself felt in the streets of London, where beggars and street vendors and ragged, barefoot children jostled one another for existence. In the London parks the leaves of the elm and plane trees turned yellow and red, and large black crows circled over tree and tower, stirring the gray air into commotion with their cries. I would stand and watch them in a torment of longing, as their haunting voices drew from the depths of my soul all my loves, all my fears.

At the time of my marriage I wrote to my brothers and also to my father's sister, with a note for Ernest tucked in. The boys were simply boys—both curious and happy for me. When at first Marion did not respond I felt a keen disappointment. But as I had much to occupy me, most of it of a happy nature, I pushed all thoughts of her aside. I also wrote once again to the last address Vijaya had given me, and to Dr. Fielding, at the address I had copied from the letter Garrett Longhurst had shown to me. And, all in one week of rain and a fierce, biting wind that drew the first shadows of winter with it, my answers came.

The Hindustani, scripted in a small, cramped hand, came from Vijaya's sister-in-law, who succinctly informed me that my old ayah was no more. *Nothing remained to hold her to this world*, the woman wrote. *She has gone to her husband, where the peace of Allah awaits her. Distress yourself no more concerning her.*

What was it Vijaya had said? *You carry my devotion with you, as long as life breathes through your veins—see how much, indeed, you shall be.* "You live as long as I live," I said out loud, "and I shall yet do honor to your memory."

To my disappointment, the reply which bore the doctor's postmark was written by a young assistant, a Lieutenant Brown, who kindly informed me that Dr. Fielding was working in the hills above Simla, among the native peoples, teaching and training the best of their men. So like him. But when I thought of his frail constitution, his burning, exhausted eyes I wondered if he could survive the ordeal of it. Would I ever hear from him again? Or would he, too, fade beyond reach, as all that had once been dear to me seemed to do? I felt shut off, as though someone was slamming doors shut behind me, forcing me, like a horse with blinders, to face in only one direction: forward, always forward, to where I could not yet see.

When the envelope with the Sheffield postmark arrived I did not want to open it, shrinking from further disappointment. But I had to laugh softly when I realized that it, too, was written by a substitute, a less concerned party once removed.

Marion is not well, but she sends her best regards to you, Ernest wrote. *It is truly so—she requested that I answer your correspon-*

dence and express her regret for the obviously unwise action you have taken, yet at the same time her concern for your well-being and future happiness. . . .

She could not bring herself to write—that would be acknowledging too much. But neither could she ignore nor dismiss me altogether, and that was good—very promising, as I looked at it. Someone seemed to be sweeping the past up behind me, clearing the broad, undefined path of the future where I must venture forth. And that realization made me very uneasy indeed.

Winston had been eight years old for these past several months and, therefore, of an age to be baptized. This pleased him well. On a mild, mellow day in early November, shortly after my twenty-second birthday, we went far down the Thames, toward Gravesend, where the noise and smog of the city could not reach us, and performed that hallowed ordinance. It did not surprise me when he came up out of the water, dripping and shivering, to give me one of his golden smiles and say, "Look at the light, Mother. Look at the wonderful light."

I hurried toward him, with my arms held open, and a soft blanket to wrap him in. As I moved I sensed, almost felt, someone moving beside me, someone whose gentle yearning made itself felt to my heart. "I will take good care of him," I whispered. "With God's help I will return him to you as pure and magnificent as he is now."

As I thought the words it seemed a sunbeam burst directly over my head, encasing me in a feeling of love which seemed to seep into the very pores of my being. And I knew this was at least part of the wonderful light Winston had felt.

Christmas in London. Christmas, when the love of the Savior had rescued me, literally, from the depths of despair, when a young man with quiet gray eyes had told me that I, too, had light in myself. This year when the snow came, weightless and soft as fairy puffs floating through the thin air, we all four went out into it together, Sita riding happily on Seth's shoulders,

Winston laughing and carefree for once in his life. *We have a warm fire to return to,* I thought, *and plenty to eat. And companionship, love and companionship.* I felt nearly giddy with joy. On Christmas Eve we coaxed Emma and her quiet husband over, and ate roast goose with plum pudding and Scottish trifle, with roasted chestnuts and Christmas crackers, with laughter and carols, with mistletoe and candles, and warm mulled wassail to ward off the frosty air. On Christmas Day there was an elegant dinner at May's house, with elegant gifts, Sita sparkling, and Winston smiling into my eyes. And Seth ever beside me, the kindliest presence of all.

But on Boxing Day came the last, best gifts of the season, in a small brown paper package marked Baddenwell and addressed in Ernest's most even and proper hand. Carefully wrapped in an old length of cotton was a small, framed photograph of Elizabeth Simmons, my grandmother, her black curls like a mist of dark gossamer framing the delicate lines of her face, her eyes gentle, enigmatic, patient.

I found these quite by accident, in an old box containing, among other things, some of your father's childhood belongings. I believe the oval of Elizabeth should, by all means, be yours, and one day, by rights, your daughter's.

I wiped a smudge of tears from the corner of my eye. "There is something else in here!" Winston cried.

I let him tear off the wrappings, and watched as he lifted out a very small, very perfect model of a sailing ship, perfect in every detail from the lines of the rigging to the sweet-faced figurehead sweeping before. "Let's see what Ernest says," I told him. He waited, breathless and expectant.

The ship should by all accounts be Winston's. I remember it as one of your father's favorites. I helped him sail it in stream and pond many a day.

Winston ran the tip of one finger gingerly down the graceful curved line of the hull. "I shall take good care of it for him."

"I know you will, Winston."

"Do you think your father . . . likes me?" His blue eyes could look so solemn.

"I am certain of it." I felt a catch in my throat, but continued nevertheless. "I believe he is grateful to you, for the care you have taken of his daughter."

Winston's smile lit his whole countenance and darkened the blue of his eyes. "You mean, like my mother up in heaven is grateful to you?"

"Yes, like that."

He went off to play with his treasure, and I sat in the gentle stillness for a long time contemplating mine.

CHAPTER EIGHT

I HEARD SETH WHISTLING MORE MERRILY than usual up the front stairs. He burst in the door and planted a quick kiss on my cheek. "There's a ship leaves for New York in April. Would you like to be on her?"

I glanced up at him quickly. "Don't talk nonsense," I said.

"Lottie, please, do not put me off like that. You know how deadly serious I am."

Reluctantly I met his gaze, which told me all I had longed to avoid. I had not learned until my return from Baddenwell that his parents and sisters had taken ship, along with the Dibbles and others, while I was away. I believe he would have been on that vessel with them if it had not been for me.

"Why, Seth? Why is it so important? What's wrong with staying here?"

"You must understand what it is that draws us."

"But America is so far away, Seth, from everything that is loved and familiar."

"You left India."

"Not for any noble reason, and not of my own accord."

"That is precisely it!" he pounced. "It is not America, but Zion we go to, where we can live in freedom and harmony and raise our children up unto the Lord."

"It sounds too ideal, too good to be true. What if we were to discover we hated it there?"

Perceiving how real my fears were, his eyes grew gentle.

"Lottie, you more than anyone I know desires that kind of existence, especially for Winston. Cannot your faith extend this far?"

"Not April," I hedged. "I must have time to think about it."

I could see him already begin to relax. "Do you realize that last year nearly two hundred Saints left for Zion? This year they anticipate three to four times that number."

"So many," I marveled. "I do not understand it, especially considering how costly it is."

"We'll find a way, just as they have. What of September, Lottie? There's a vessel sailing for New Orleans in September."

"Perhaps September," I said.

He left it at that, pleased at the progress he had made. But I brooded inside, feeling trapped and afraid, at times even angry at what was being required of me. All our possessions would have to be left behind—even the few precious things I had managed to bring out of India. At length I knew I must face it squarely and make it a matter of prayer. And, to complicate everything, I knew what Seth only suspected—that I was with child. I had already given birth to one baby aboard a rolling vessel; I did not particularly desire to do so again. How vulnerable tiny infants would be under those crowded, unsanitary conditions.

Beset by a myriad of swirling fears, I approached the Lord, struggling as though a vapor or a thick, unseen obstruction separated him from me. Time and time again I attempted, until at last I was able to pour out my heart and hold cupped in the hollow of my remembrance the truths I had learned. That was the first night in many that I slept undisturbed and awoke feeling rested. And that very morning my answer came.

I remember feeling apprehensive as I held the long envelope in my hands. *Longhurst and Willis*, Major Reid's solicitors. Were the tentacles of Constance's evil deed reaching out, resurrecting shame and horror? I slit it open and very tentatively pulled out the thin sheets.

Then I stood staring at the bank draft made out in my name, laughing out loud, because it simply could not be true. *The small inheritance the major had left me in his will!* I had given no further thought to it past the first few weeks, reasoning that, if it existed at all, Constance had made certain that it would never be seen by me. Now it sat staring at me, black letters and numbers that appeared very real. *One hundred pounds*—a princely sum by my reckoning. As soon as the first shock abated, realization flooded over me and I was amazed.

At the first notes of Seth's whistle I went flying to meet him, delighting in his own shocked disbelief at such bounty. "You are a spoiled one," he teased. "You see, even God cannot resist blessing you, Lottie."

I remembered his words. I kept them like a precious amulet close to my heart. I wrapped myself in the warmth of them whenever I felt chilled and frightened—then, and for many, many years yet to come.

We paid fourteen pound thirty shillings for passage—four pound a piece for us and three pound fifteen for each of the children—aboard a vessel named the *Tyrian* which was scheduled to leave Liverpool harbor on September 21. Joseph Fielding was to be the company leader, and that pleased me well. But when Seth told me he had handed our money over to an agent by the name of Norman Dobson, I questioned him a little.

"I do not know this man. Are you certain he can be trusted? You should have paid the agent from the ship line yourself."

"He is handling all the reservations from our conference, Lottie. No one else seems to question him. I'm sure it will be all right."

The remainder of our precious hoard was safe in Barclay's bank, which made it seem all the more unreal now it was out of our hands. But we spent many happy, foolish hours talking about what we would do with it once we reached Nauvoo. *Nauvoo . . . Illinois*—such foreign-sounding words to my ear. Would they ever become common reality, part of the pattern of my everyday life?

Neither my fears nor my curiosity were much allayed by the letter we received early in March from Seth's mother. They were "settled in," she assured us, but conditions in the city were horrid. They had been beset with either mud or ice all winter long. *Too cold for human flesh to endure,* she wrote, and I shivered at the thought. Too many people, people pouring in daily, and no place to put them, she complained. I raised an eyebrow at Seth, but he only grinned back.

"She has always been one to see the dark side of things," he assured me, "and to cry before she's been hurt."

I had not yet met the woman, and his words did nothing to assure me. "You are not like her," I said.

His smile widened. "No, I am like my father's people, soft-spoken and gentle, and hopeless dreamers."

"And we are all blessed by those qualities," I said, a bit shyly. But he knew that I meant it, and left his chair to come over and kiss me in a long, lingering fashion, and discomfit me more. I was happy with Seth, so happy that at times it frightened me, so happy that at times I forgot India and was able to look at my life here as being what it should be: belonging to me, fitting, feeling familiar, and heading, at least vaguely, where I wanted to go.

Summer came slowly, with many false starts—it happens often this way in England. At times I longed for a bit more sunlight as days of gray, weeping skies continued, week following week. *This is my last spring in England,* I remember thinking, *my last summer . . . my last walks along the Serpentine or through Kensington Gardens.* Sometimes a voice within my own head would ask, *What is England to you?* And I wondered myself at the love I had come to feel for this green, compact country where so much had happened to me in such a short while.

In late May, Seth brought me the large, succulent strawberries which are usually out of season by the tenth of June. But this year, perhaps because of the cooler weather, he was able to keep the supply up 'til nearly the end of the month. Hardly a day passed without a halfpenny lemon ice for a treat, and fresh vegetables sold from Covent Garden, or brought to our doorstep by May's man, Joseph, at no cost whatever. That, along with cheap fish from St. Giles, became the mainstay of our diet, save for an occasional Indian delicacy thrown in. Slow, mellow days, the last we were to experience together for many a year. Long evenings with Seth, walking in the parks or reading by candlelight, making plans for the future of this yet-unknown child I carried, boldly putting words to the fragile dreams we nurtured within our hearts.

It was a July day when, even round the London window boxes, bees contrived to hum, and Winston's canary sang with them. I remember fancying the smell of jasmine floating in the soft air about me. I remember three round melons, firm and ripe, sitting on the kitchen drainboard, a surprise Seth had brought home with him the evening before. I remember how slowly I moved to answer the brisk rat-a-tat knock at my door, thinking, as I walked, how low and uncomfortably this baby sat. I remember all that, as though it occurred in slow motion, as though the horrors which followed froze the short inconsequential prelude within my mind.

The man who stood at my door had broad features, well roughed by wind and weather, with tiny wrinkles, like the squiggly patterns of sand crabs, framing his narrow blue eyes. He held his hat in his hands and twirled it round and round, with an unconscious nervousness, the whole while he talked.

"My husband is at work now. Is the matter serious?" I asked him, sensing from his awkward manner that it was.

"Indeed, that it is, and more's the pity that I must bring it to your attention, mistress, but 'twas your husband's name scrawled across the agreement form."

"What is the trouble?" I asked.

"We need the remainder of the fares settled." I must have blinked stupidly at him. "Yourselves and a dozen others, ma'am, who've reserved berths on the *Tyrian* for September."

"I thought those reservations were paid for in full."

He crushed the stained felt hat beneath massive reddened fingers. "Deposit only, with the amount outstanding due weeks ago. Mr. Dobson—"

"Norman Dobson?" I gasped the words out.

"Land sakes, mistress, I didn't know 'twould distress ye so. You look white as a sheet."

I put my hand to my throat. I could feel my pulse throbbing against Karan's ring.

"Truth is, we can't hold them much longer without riskin' them altogether, and we can't make no profit sailing with a half-empty ship."

I managed to nod. "My husband will not be home until this evening. Could he come and call on you then?"

"Be much obliged if he would, miss. I'll take no action 'til I hear from him then. But it must be soon, mind you." He thrust a limp, rather dirty card into my hand, closing his big fingers for a moment round mine.

"It's right sorry I am to have upset you, right sorry."

I smiled at him weakly, and the effect seemed to only increase his fears.

"Sit down wi' a bit of tea, you hear, and rest yourself. You look terrible pale."

I nodded agreeably. And once I had closed the door on him, I did sink into a chair, feeling weak all over and a little light-headed. *So my fears concerning Dobson were well founded! What in the world were we going to do now?*

I sat for a long time brooding over what had occurred when I realized something was happening, something that startled my scattered attentions back to the moment. Surely this baby could not be coming—right now?

Struggling to remain calm, I called for Winston and sent him with a message to Emma. "This is most urgent," I told him, with my hands on his shoulders. "You must run all the way, and stop for no one and nothing."

He promised me, his blue eyes as round and solemn as still, deep-water pools.

"I shall say a prayer as I run," he added. "That will help, too."

Bless his heart! It would take him close to fifteen minutes each way. I changed Sarah's nappy and sat her in her cradle with her toys and a handful of crackers. Then I set about getting ready the things I thought we might need. Each pain that came seemed longer and harder than the last, and I had to stand still, with my hands clenched, trembling and perspiring, until they passed.

"Emma will be furious," I thought. "Does she know

aught of these matters? I will surely be of little help to her."

I tried to push my building fears aside and concentrate on the necessities at hand.

By the time Emma arrived I was a little bit groggy with pain; it seemed like hours since I sent Winston away. I managed a weak smile for him, then almost cried out in relief when I saw that she had brought a midwife with her.

"Go watch yer wee sister, laddie," the midwife told Winston, giving him a gentle shove. "We'll take care of your mither just fine."

Her soft Scots served to soothe me nearly as much as her ministrations. I closed my eyes and tried to draw deep breaths as she instructed. Why was each birth so different? It seemed that Sita had been easy compared to this.

"You must push a wee bit harder—and longer, if you can, lass. Her face is turned up, so we must work her round a little—"

"Her?" Emma demanded, her tone as loud and protective as it had ever been. "How do you say that, when there's of yet no way to tell?"

A smile, like the gentle sparkle of sunbeams, flickered over the woman's features. "I'm an old hand at this and I say 'tis a lass. Are ye taking bets?"

Emma snorted, but I was too weak with concentration to even smile at her. Every muscle in my body was trembling with fatigue when I heard Emma cry out in triumph, and the midwife chuckled under her breath. "A perfect girl bairn," she murmured.

"Give her to me," I begged, too weak to even hold out my arms.

"We'll clean her up a bit. You just close your eyes and rest now. She'll be here waiting for you when you wake up, aye, and for a long time to come."

I remember almost nothing of what took place after that. When I awoke in May's house, with the yellow room wrapped comfortably around me, I struggled onto my elbows in weak protest. Then I heard Tabby's voice, "The baby's sleeping peacefully, Miss Charlotte. Everything's taken care of; rest a bit longer yourself."

I remember falling back onto the pillows with a sense of relief. Tabitha's voice came, as if through a dense fog now, "She's a real beauty, she is."

"Seth. Where is Seth?"

"The mistress has sent for him. Rest yourself now."

I remember thinking dreamily, *I have a new baby girl. It's all over. I am happy, so happy.* . . . Yet something hidden behind the swirling mist mocked me, something I could not quite remember, that sat like a small smouldering stone in my heart.

I heard his whistling on the stairs, a sound so bright and real amid all the smothering quiet, that I nearly called out to him, just to hear the sound of my own voice. Not until he sat with his arms around me did I realize how incomplete things had been without Seth. Now I could rest, now we were whole again. Tabitha brought my baby to me and laid her into my arms.

"Look at her, Lottie. Have you ever seen anything so beautiful?"

I touched one smooth, rounded cheek with my finger. "Indeed," I answered honestly, "I have not."

I could not remember Sarah being this fair when she was first born, though I did remember the dark, fathomless wonder that shone out from her eyes. This child had masses of light curls, so long I could wrap my finger around them, and eyes that already looked gray.

"Most infants have blue eyes," I told Seth. "But look at the gray in hers already."

That pleased him. "I want to name her after you, Lottie."

I shook my head. "Remember what we agreed?" I wished to name this first daughter after his mother, as I had done with Sarah. "Victoria, after your mother," I reminded him. "Victoria Grace."

He was not entirely pleased, but he gave way to my wishes. "It is by the grace of God that I am here—that she is here." I explained in a hushed whisper.

"Yes," he agreed. "Grace it shall be."

And Grace it was; I can never remember a time she was called Victoria in all her growing up days.

❦

I forgot entirely the source of my unhappiness; that evening all shadows fled, only the wonder of birth and renewal, of love and family wove around us with gossamer threads.

Not until some time the following morning did it come back to me, rushing through my consciousness with the warm, sickening force of the monsoon winds. Then I began fretting, lest the messenger from the ship line had become disgruntled and dissatisfied with Seth's failure to make an appearance as I had promised. What if, even now, action had been taken, all that had been anticipated and sacrificed for by so many had been snatched away?

Seth's countenance grew as gray as his eyes when I told him; I could see his shoulders visibly slouch.

"It is all my fault," he muttered bitterly. "If I'd have listened to you—"

"Nonsense," I retorted. "It is true what you said, that everyone trusted him. How were you to know?"

"By acting on your fears, however slight they were."

"And how might you have done that?"

"I made my decision according to my own counsel and wisdom. I did not seek the confirmation of heaven, did not take the time or trouble over a matter as vital as—"

"Seth," I soothed. "You expect more of yourself than you do of anyone else."

It was true; he was lenient in his appraisals of others, but harsh and unbending in the expectations he laid for himself.

He gave me a grim, twisted little smile. "I am right in this, and you know it. Now you, and heaven knows how many others, stand to suffer because of me."

"We stand to suffer because of Normon Dobson," I replied emphatically.

"I must go see this fellow right now," he said, running his fingers roughly through his tangled brown hair.

"By all means. Go at once."

"I dislike leaving you, Lottie."

I smiled bravely. "Heavens, I am in good hands here. Go, and God go with you."

He kissed his fingers to me from the open doorway, and I returned the caress. More long hours of waiting, hoping and praying. How I disliked that all-too-prevalent aspect of life. Action, even action ill taken, seems always preferable to the grinding, wearing effect of helpless, frustrated idleness, especially where one's life, the core of one's very existence is at stake. *Perhaps that is why my father, in desperation, did what he did.* The thought was no comfort to me; rather, it further depressed my spirits with a sensation of gloom that even Grace, in her endearing innocence, could not efface.

Seth did not return for hours, and when I heard him on the stairs, there was no whistle to mark his coming, no bounce to his step. He sank into the chair placed close to my bedside. I reached for his hand.

"It is Norman Dobson, all right. With the cunning of the serpent he went about among the groups of Saints, using the connection with his sister as reference." Seth shuddered. "Edith Dobson was a member of the Church, and she did take ship with a group of Saints, but she died on board. Her brother has hated the Church ever since then. So, you see, he did this for spite."

I felt suddenly cold inside. I rubbed Seth's limp hands. "How many were involved?"

"Twelve from our group, nearly a dozen more from various locations. The agent has already been in touch with them; they had pieced together the gruesome puzzle before I came along."

"Has he given us time?"

"Five days. He must let the reservations go up for public bidding then; he must see to his own interests."

"Of course. He has been more than generous with us." I could feel Seth's misery reach out to me. "Twelve," I mused. "And how many among those are children?"

"Five, I believe, counting ours." His eyes avoided mine; he knew what I was thinking, but he did not approve. He would not ask—he would not even suggest it.

"Comes to a little over forty pounds. We can manage that, Seth, and have nearly half our original sum left us, more than—"

"No! It is money you earned through years of suffering. I will not allow it."

"Do not be silly, Seth. You're not thinking properly about this. Years of suffering? People are not wont to be paid in hard cash for the things they endure in life. I gained what I was meant to gain from those experiences. This has nothing to do with anything, it is neither here nor there—it is only money!"

He shook his head stubbornly. There was still a dull torment clouding his eyes.

"What greater use could it be put to?" I asked gently. "This would ennoble it, sanctify it, Seth, for our good."

I was pleading. I could see a slow comprehension creep into his gaze. "Who knows? Perhaps this is the very purpose for which it was given us."

He could not gainsay me; his own spiritual wells ran too deep. "I knew you for something extraordinary the first time I set eyes on you," he breathed. Nothing I said could convince him otherwise. The devotion in his eyes was to me—though you may think it strange—a shining evidence of the reality of God and of the existence of His goodness in the hearts of men.

CHAPTER NINE

𝔍

DURING THE DAYS FOLLOWING THE BIRTH of my child I found myself living a very odd existence. May brought in a professional nurse and insisted that I have at least two weeks of rest. The efficient, uniformed woman had both Grace and me well in hand before she had been an hour in the house. Between the two of them they rather squeezed Seth out of the picture. After all, he worked long hours. Why not have the care and company May could so lavishly provide? Tabitha and Joseph seemed overjoyed to have the vivacious, if noisy, children back again; even Jean, the cook, made much of them, somewhat to my surprise. We were definitely wanted here; Seth must not be selfish about us. So, without much choice and no discussion, we became rather firmly ensconced. At first, I must admit, I enjoyed the sheer pleasure of being waited on and fussed over, with no grinding, recurring responsibilities or tasks. *Relax and get your strength back.* That, and that alone, was to be my only concern. Seth fit in where he could—always there for the evening meal and to kiss the children good night. Many evenings he had meetings and church work to attend to. A small room was prepared for him just down the hall from mine, but often as not, he went home to bed. *Just to keep an eye on the place,* he would say, *and make sure the wee bird does not starve to death.* But I knew he was uncomfortable being in May's house. At first I simply let it slide by, having no will or desire to resist or complain. But as the days passed, each one grew longer and longer. The lack of him began to irritate me, like sand in the shell of an oyster. Then the irritation deepened into a sense of loneliness that made me feel hollow and uneasy inside. With the loneliness came a sharpened, unwelcome awareness of the subtle forces at work here. And with the awareness came a small, prickling sensation of fear.

At length one morning, unable to resist any longer, I found my way early down into the small, sunny sitting room whose French doors led into the garden. The doors were flung open to catch the last of the morning coolness, and the air was saturated with the mingling scents of half a dozen ripe blossoms. I threw my head back in delight.

"You appear to be in fine fettle this morning, my dear." May chirped the words in her usual high, clipped fashion. I gave her a vague smile and said, as casually as I was able, "I shall miss this spot more than any other. You know what your gardens mean to me."

She glanced up sharply, her eyes bright, her whole attitude tensed.

"Well, a few minutes in the fresh air, Lottie, but do not tire yourself."

"I am quite recovered, May, capable of returning to the responsibilities of my own household—though I shall always cherish these blessed days and your wonderful generosity."

The words carried the ring of sincerity, rising, as they did, from the depths of my heart. For I was coming to realize that I might, in very truth, never set eyes upon her again. Even yet, her next words came as a shock to me.

"Consider well what you are doing, Charlotte, consider well."

When I did not at once answer, gathering my stunned senses and trying to determine a fitting response, she continued.

"I realize that Seth is a good and a kind man. But what can he offer you, my child? Ten years from now, what will your lot in life be?"

I was beginning to feel hot all over, save for a cold spot somewhere near the pit of my stomach.

"You have so much to offer—you could achieve whatever situation you desired."

"He is my husband. Would you have me abandon him?"

The words were too blunt. She winced, but more at my lack of finesse than at what I was saying.

"Think of your children," she pressed. "This young man, in his misguided zeal, will lead you and them on a merry chase, Lottie, and when he is through—"

I put my hand out as if to stop her. "Please. This is wicked. I will listen to no more—"

"Better now, my sweet girl, than later, when you are used up and disappointed, when—"

I placed my hand on her arm, thin and wiry beneath its shroud of fine silk. "May, dear May, please stop. You distress yourself to no purpose. For me there is no regretting, no turning back."

She shook my hand off as though the touch of it burned her.

"Your loyalty does you justice." Her tone was terse, offended. "But you are young yet, and you set your sights low, too low—"

"I have seen much of the world; you forget that."

"And because of what you have suffered you seek safety in obscurity. You deserve better than this life you live." She pounced on her supposed advantage with the tenacity of a small, wire-haired terrier. But these last words had an abrupt, calming effect on my spirit. I smiled at her, and I could feel the serenity in my own expression, for all the tension and combativeness had left me.

"May," I began, very gently. "Please listen for just one moment. Let me try to explain. . . . You must not worry over me. I have chosen this life—wholeheartedly. It contains all I wish for, all I long to be worthy of and attain."

She did not understand. Understanding would have been difficult even if she had desired it; it was nearly impossible now.

She shook her small head at me and pursed her thin lips.

"I do not wish to distress you," I said. "You have done so

much for me; you have cared for me as truly as any woman has—at least any woman I can remember," I added wistfully.

The shrouded reference to my mother appeared to touch her. She placed her hand over mine. "Consider well, Lottie. Will you do that much for me?"

I promised I would. And she knew that, against her best judgment, that promise would have to suffice.

That evening when Seth came I was packed and waiting for him. He said nothing until we were back in our own small house and the children tucked in their beds.

"I thought I had lost you for awhile there."

His words startled me, came close to wounding me.

"Did you truly? Did you doubt me?"

"It wasn't that."

"Yes, it was."

He was struggling within himself, I could see that. So I held my own tongue and waited. " 'Twas myself I doubted, I think. Doubted my ability to make you happy. Felt unworthy of you. I always have."

I was dumbfounded. "You are so much better than I!" I cried. "Kinder, more pure of heart."

"That's how you see me. But you don't see your own strengths properly, Lottie. You never have."

I smiled, feeling suddenly happy all over. "I shall try to see myself through your eyes from now on," I promised, "if you'll do the same."

His smile came slowly, like a light gently building, until all around throbbed with the golden warmth of it, laughed and sang with it, as though sorrow could never again exist as long as such irrepressible love prevailed.

For all intents and purposes we had lost May's friendship. She enjoyed the image of being a friend to struggling causes, to the new, avant-garde, anything that stirred her blood into feeling young, clever, or vital again. But we had committed the unpardonable offense of carrying the whole matter too far, carrying ourselves into her affections, thus making a personal inroad, which entirely changed the rules. I felt the loss of her as a sad, gentle impression that lingered for days, or would come over me in sudden, unexpected moments, with a feeling of sorrow, heavy and drear.

Seth settled the matter of the passage money and preparations for the long journey went forward. It was now August, Grace had arrived but a few weeks early, and we had scarcely over five weeks until we must leave.

In the midst of all this Emma came to me one day, her eyes red and swollen, everything about her sagging. I had never seen her this way.

Some tragedy has struck, I thought, pulling her in the door and forcing her into a seat. "You look like death warmed over, Emmer. Tell me what has happened."

"Me man has flitted, that's what."

"Flitted," I repeated as comprehension came to me. "You mean he has left you?"

"I do. Gone back to the country where his sis can take care o' him. Says this black city air is no good for his lungs. Ah told him he couldn't say, since he'd never been out in it over half a dozen times a year, an' then only to ride like a gentleman across town in a cab."

I thought of the Christmas days she and James had visited his sister, with gifts for the six little children, all purchased from Emma's earnings. "What of his sister in London?" I asked.

"She's neither here nor there," Emma shrugged. "The sister in the country has a rich husband, ah'm told. She's moved to pity on her poor, suffering brother, and who is my James to refuse such an offer as that?"

"And yourself? Haven't you been invited to go along with him?"

She shook her head. "Ah'm too much for him; ah'm too much for the lot o' them." She blew her red nose on a hanky as large and unkempt as a man's.

"Then it is certainly a good thing I secured your ticket to America months ago," I smiled. "Though it appears that James won't be needing his."

Her bloodshot eyes stared at me. "Ye did no such thing! Don't tease me about this, Lottie."

I gave her the baby to hold, and produced the papers from Seth's desk; that was proof enough for her. "I'm not sure why I did it," I tried to explain. "I just had a feeling . . ."

Emma gave out a shout as curdling as the Scottish highlanders must sound going into battle. The sound brought Winston running, and soon we were all shouting and laughing together. When Winston learned that his beloved Emmer was coming with us, he misunderstood and jumped to conclusions a bit.

"Jolly good," he cried. "Emmer's to be a Mormon same as we are."

Her ruddy face blanched at that. "Not so fast, laddie," she blustered. "I've no mind to be dumped in the stream just yet."

But all else was settled, and I was secretly as happy as Winston to have her coming along. Grace was a fussy baby compared to what Sita had been, and I fretted myself concerning her. Emma's help on the dreaded journey, as well as her companionship, would be of great value to me.

"I'll traipse up to them grand houses again and sell a few more lace collars to pay you back the price of the passage."

I shook my head emphatically. "Those are wages in advance," I assured her, "for the services of nursemaid, cook and companion for the duration."

She grinned back at me, and a memory of the first day I had met her came flooding back to my mind: my birthday, alone in a miserable tenement, without means, without husband, without friends. She and Winston had planned a surprise for me, and from the beginning her frank, pleasant manner had won my heart. I brushed a tear from the corner of my eye and gave her a quick hug. Our eyes met briefly, yet they spoke all that words could not ever express.

I wanted desperately to see Baddenwell again, to say goodbye to Ernest and Marion, but it seemed an indulgent expenditure of funds we were sure to have a dozen uses for later. I wrote to the boys asking if they could take the train down to see us, perhaps over a week's end, and when they agreed I was all aflutter with excitement.

They arrived late on a Saturday morning and stayed through most of the following day. At first there was an awkward strain. They had not expected to find me in such modest quarters, on a level of living so obviously lower than any they, and they believed myself, were accustomed to. But Arthur took at once to Seth, who endeared himself to the lad by listening attentively to his boyish boasting, his talk of plans for himself. Hugh fell in well with Winston from the start. Watching them play, heads bent close together, made a lump rise in my throat. *Son and brother, neither one of my blood, yet as surely mine, as inextricably bound to me. How strange this mortal life is.*

I wrote out the address from Seth's mother's letter and gave it to Arthur: *107 Mulholland, Nauvoo, Illinois.* "You can write to me at this address," I told him. "As soon as we have a place of our own, I will let you know."

"Sounds like a great adventure to me, Lottie," he grinned. "But I think you're a bit afraid."

I struck at him playfully. "I did not even wish to come to England, remember? It . . . it just seems so far away."

"Aye, and with me bound soon for the Province myself. Thousands of miles will separate us."

I shuddered as his words struck me like so many sharp little stones. "Nothing can separate our hearts," I said. "You won't forget . . . anything?"

"I won't forget, Lottie, I promise."

It was so difficult saying good-bye. They were miniature Englishmen—stiff upper lip and all that—but I cried unabashedly. Seth put his arms around me and I wept long after the carriage that carried them had rumbled into silence. England was an extension of India—or, actually, it was the other way round. Life, customs, speech and manners were largely the same among the British here as they had been at home. America I knew, by mere instinct, would be different. And, once I put foot on that ship, all this would remain behind me forever. I knew, but I could not comprehend it, much less accept it as truth.

Two weeks, only two weeks remaining. Then one evening Seth came home whistling, as usual, whistling and humming, his eyes sparkling with some secret he was nearly bursting with, and I realized the hour was five, not seven, and my supper not even begun.

"I'm here to help you," he grinned. "You'll have washing to do, and packing."

"Not this soon. Have you gone daft, Seth? We do not leave for two weeks."

"*You* leave tomorrow morning," he said, "you and the little ones. Joseph will accompany you." He could contain himself no longer. "You're going to Baddenwell!"

"You have taken leave of your senses," I muttered. But he was laughing, reaching for my waist, twirling me playfully round.

"Our surprise; mine and May's."

"Seth—you didn't." I grew instantly sober.

"Ask May for favors? I'd walk across the ocean to America before I'd do that. Nay, she came to me! Wanted to do something for you—came herself to one of the meetings last week. I could think of nothing, then this popped into my head, so I told her."

I was backing away from him, disturbed still.

"No, Lottie, she was so pleased—seemed almost *relieved.* Strange, but that's what I felt from her. She wanted to do *something,* Lottie. Would you deny her that chance?"

There were tears in my eyes as I shook my head. I did not deserve such rich favors when there were those with so little they would have difficulty scraping together the foodstuffs and provisions required for the sea journey.

"It's all right, Lottie," Seth soothed. "Make the most of the moment. Enjoy what has been given you. 'Twould be a sin to do less."

His words, simple but wise, released me, and I flew to the first of a dozen tasks that would consume the short hours until the following morning when May's carriage arrived.

England in the rain, with black crows circling like an omen above our heads. England green and wet, weeping with beauty, and a stillness that seemed to mirror the stillness of the soul at rest. England, where I had been only a sojourner—which, like my father, I would carry in my heart forever, though my footsteps would never bring me again to her shores.

Winston was in a veritable fever to be in the country. Nor did his own active imagination allow it to disappoint him after such a long wait. Songbirds and water birds, clouds and meadows, gamboling sheep and grazing cows—each was a wonder to him.

Word had been sent ahead, so we were expected. Ernest met the carriage. A young maid with crisp bobbing skirts whisked the baby from me. Other kind hands lifted the sleeping Sarah from her cramped nest in the corner. In a matter of minutes the children were safe in the nursery, and I sat in Elizabeth's morning room with a hot cup of tea in my hands.

"Marion, thank you," I said, to the still-faced woman who watched me. "You will never know what this means to me."

"I will never know why you are abandoning it, leaving all prospects for security and advantage behind."

I sighed. I was too weary, far too weary to try to explain. I picked at the small frosted cakes on the platter, but my eyelids were drooping, even my head felt too heavy for me to hold up. I was only half aware of being helped up the staircase and into my room, half aware of the feel of cool sheets beneath me, and the dim arching canopy overhead. *I am home again,* I thought drowsily. *Home one last time, Father.* And then I slept.

It happened naturally, as if some former fate had decreed it. Winston went off to explore the next morning with Ernest, and Marion took Sita in hand. She was as endearing as any three-year-old can be, but she could try one's patience as well. How was it she went so meekly, hand in hand with this thin, austere woman? How was it that I observed them from a distance, as they moved through the gardens or sat by the lake, giggling together, even skipping along the pebbled paths, or feasting on sticky concoctions the kitchen had managed to produce? I was dumbfounded, but too pleased to disturb them, so for many of the daytime hours I kept pretty much to myself—

which was a kind of heaven of its own. I haunted the library, becoming familiar with at least half a dozen of the old, thick volumes which my fingers had itched for the first time I was here. I napped in Elizabeth's morning room, closing my eyes and in the stillness trying to find some shadows, some whispers of her. The house and grounds became familiar to me, and I found marks of her everywhere: in pantry and keeping room, in laundry and kitchen garden, in the stately dining and drawing rooms. Even in the nursery I came across a book which had her childish scrawl written across it, and wondered if my father had turned its pages when he was a boy. I tried to picture him here, brimming over with life, confident, sure of his powers. Then I would reverse the image, to imagine him wounded, brooding, angry, suddenly uncertain of which way to go. I walked with their memories but, in the way of my people, I walked with their spirits as well.

Marion did not tire of Sarah's company. When our brief stay came near its close, she approached me. It was late in the evening, and we found ourselves alone together for the first time. She was as nervous as a fox surrounded by a circle of hounds, so I smiled at her warmly and said, quite honestly, "I have never been happier than I have been these few days."

"Then you do not mind my monopolizing your daughter?"

I realized for the first time that she had expected me to resent her attentions, her marked preference for the child, as if it posed some threat to me. I could not tell her that she had been giving me what I had prayed for these many years.

"It pleases me more deeply than you know."

My response so disarmed her that she added before thinking, "She is very like both of them, Frances and Father. Yet I believe she has Mother's sweetness."

As soon as the words were out she regretted them, until she glanced over and saw that my eyes were spilling over with tears. "I remember him," I said, "but only with a child's memory."

"Perhaps that makes you fortunate," she said.

On a sudden impulse I took a step closer. "He remained

true to all the noble things he vowed as a boy, vowed when he saw his mother's suffering—"

Her head came up and she gazed at me sharply, but with an interest, terrible and burning, in her eyes.

"You would have been proud of him, Marion, proud of the kind of man he became."

She had no idea how far my knowledge of her family matters went, nor could she bring herself to ask me. Yet I could tell my words pleased her, so I hazarded a little bit more.

"His green eyes were sharp as a cat's and as sparkling as a wizard's, but he had a kindly air about him that drew both men and women. He was always very gentle with me, and with my mother—that is the first thing that endeared her to him."

She wanted to protest, but something would not allow her.

"I have one of his early journals," I proffered. "Would you like to read it?"

She froze, poised on the edge of pride and longing. At last she nodded and said softly, "I would like that, Charlotte, very much."

And it came to me at that moment what I must do. "I will send it to you if you will hold it in safekeeping for me, and for Sarah Elizabeth. Who knows where we shall be going, and I should hate to see it come to harm. Would you do that?" I asked.

"Of course. Yes . . . thank you, Lottie."

"Oh, Marion, will you please write to me once this whirlwind settles us . . . someplace."

"If it is . . . so important to you," she replied, and I wondered what my face revealed.

At that point Ernest entered the room to ask if we would like a late tea, and the moment was lost. But it was enough; I would not push Providence in asking for more. Sufficient to the day was the wonder thereof.

CHAPTER TEN

𝓙

LIFE IS MADE UP OF STOPS AND STARTS, little beginnings and endings, like so many small deaths fragmenting the sense of wholeness.

I had dreaded coming to England, but I dreaded even more leaving her. No word had come from India, no response from Dr. Fielding concerning himself or Karan. The mists refused to part, to allow me one glimpse, one sigh, before turning my back forever on the land of my birth. I could not complain; many were in the same condition we were, with a good number worse. Less than a week before we were to leave for Liverpool, Louise Bell knocked on my door early in the morning. She had never made a personal visit to our house before. She and her husband, her two children, and her young sister, Jean, were sailing to New Orleans with us.

I invited her in, noticing how red her eyes were, how pale her face. But we were all doing more than our share of crying these past days, so I thought little of it until she blurted out suddenly, "You should not have done it, Sister Taylor!"

"Done what?" I questioned, my mind blank.

"The fare!" We've no way on the earth to repay you, seeing as we've sold everything we own just to meet the expenses of the journey. But I did save out these—"

With an embarrassed sniff she thrust her hand out. In the open palm lay a pair of pearl earrings set in a filigreed pattern of leaves and rosebuds, so beautiful that I caught my breath in admiration.

"They should fetch a good price, or if you took a liking to them . . ."

"They were your grandmother's."

"My great-grandmother's."

"Wear them the entire way across the ocean—make certain nothing happens to them," I said, annoyed by the tremor in my voice. "They are too dear, too precious for your little Clara and those children coming after her." I placed them into her hand and closed her fingers around them. "It was only money, Louise, and money, at that, which I did not earn, or even deserve necessarily. You must think nothing of it from this moment forward. Put it out of your mind."

"How can we?" There was astonishment in her eyes, glistening through her tears.

"Because I have told you to! Because you will hurt me if you do not. Please! Why will people accept anything at the hands of each other except that one thing?"

My words had set her thinking, despite herself. "We can never—"

"There you go again! I mean this. I will never change my mind. You need not glance askance at me ten years from now wondering what I am thinking. By that time all of this will have gone out of my mind. It is a good, noble use for anyone's money. Now, go to Zion, and God bless you."

She put her arms around me, very gently. "God bless you, Charlotte Taylor. God bless you."

When she had gone I went into our bedroom and shut the door, then dropped down onto my knees beside the bed. "Help me to remember," I prayed. "Help money and material means to never be so important to me that they stand in the way of people, in the way of love and compassion."

When I rose to my feet I felt as light as a feather, as clean and sweet inside as a newly filled rain barrel. It was a feeling I wished to keep with me all the way to Zion, if I could.

We traveled by train to Liverpool on a morning of blue mist and sweet English air. When we reached the city, a gaggle of blue-black crows followed us down to the wharves.

"That is a good sign," I said. "If the crows go with me, then I know I am protected. I also know that part of my spirit will always remain here with them."

Seth said nothing, though he looked at me strangely. I found Liverpool to be a city where the very air was charged with the seething emotions of commerce, where tradition contended hand in hand with invention; where dreams and wild victories rose on the same breath as tragedies and the bile of lost hopes. Energy—there was more energy in this city than in London. I felt it breathing down my neck, churning around me. Two hundred thousand people here, half of them struggling along Pier Head, it seemed, behind which hundreds of masts rose along the crescent-shaped harbor: graceful ships— such as we would be traveling on—barks, brigs, sloops, tugs and small private fishing boats that plied the broad Mersey River in search of the common man's trade. The flags and pennants that rode the proud breeze were so brightly colored and so varied that they made the docks look like a carnival. Winston caught the sense of excitement, but I felt heavy and leaden inside. We boarded our ship the night of our arrival. She was the *Tyrian*, American-made. Maine was the name of the North American state where she had been crafted. I did not think American names and terms as colorful as the English, and certainly not as beautiful as the Hindustani, except for *Nauvoo*. That word did not sound American, it sounded ancient, and rich with unstated meaning. Captain Jackson himself greeted us as we came aboard. Steerage, located between decks, where the two hundred of us would stay, was rudely furnished with tiered bunks ranging along each side, with long board tables thrown up along the center aisle—eating, sleeping and living all would take place in these dark, airless chambers. I scrambled up to the deck and stayed there till the stars broke through the heavy black sky, reflecting their cold light in trembling patterns along the still, glassy surface that bore us up. Though I was shivering in the moist night air, yet I lingered, loathe to go down below. Seth and Emma would settle the children for the night; I knew that. I should feel guilty for abandoning them, but I could not bear to return.

"You'll get used to it in time, miss."

I jumped at the voice, seeming to come unembodied through the quivering night. When the kindly, pocked face of the second mate, Mr. Jones, appeared in the glow of the lantern he carried, I smiled in relief.

"I have done this before," I said. "I came all the way over from India."

"Ah, then, that's yer reason. You know what you're in for more than those blissfully snoozing below."

It did me good to laugh with him, to chatter idly for a few minutes. When at last I turned, reluctant still, to join the others, he called after me, "You ever need anything, miss, you holler for me now, you hear."

"I will, I promise. And . . . thank you, Mr. Jones."

He tipped his sailor's hat to me with a touch of gallantry that was truly endearing. "My pleasure," he said.

I filled my lungs with a cold draft of sea air and descended the ladder slowly, pretending that the stars were following me, helter skelter, to scatter like bright bits broken from the ceiling of heaven at my head and feet.

We sailed down the Mersey past the Rock Lighthouse and Fort until our sails filled with the sea wind and we were out on the open water, with England truly behind us. I did not look back, save to lift a hand in tribute to the careening crows that were now no more than black specks against the bleached, cloudless sky. We were forty-nine days on the ocean; such a voyage could be a story in itself. We had squalls and storms of frightening proportion when we huddled together, "hatched down" as prisoners in the belly of the heavy, shivering ship, shut out from light and air and, at times, from hope, with nothing but faith to sustain us; we pushed slowly through fogs too thick to breathe, as dense and dirty as seaweed; we sat through calms that were more maddening to the senses, more eerie than fog and storm together. We subsisted on barley, potatoes, and rice, with careful rations of beef and pork, sugar and tea. We had an abundance of salted herring and sea biscuits, but never an abundance of light, sharing less than a dozen lanterns to stretch the full length of our quarters. But the crew were, by and large, decent men, and treated us well. I found little to compare to my voyage from India. There was no drinking, no gambling here, no jaded women and decadent men. The Saints were organized into wards headed by presidencies, and careful rules were observed, with attention to sanitation as well as health. We held meetings, sang hymns, joined in prayer. We were Saints of God, bound on a holy journey to the promised land; and the kingdom of God, as our leaders reminded us, must exist in our midst. It was not a vague scriptural term, elusive and symbolic, but a manner of living, a condition of the heart.

Statistics—I can quote the unfeeling statistics that marked that passage. Three babies were born during those seven weeks, two marriages were performed, one brother was lost overboard, and five children died while a dozen others hovered near the edge of death with serious cases of the measles. Grace, not quite two months old yet, was one of these.

We worked tirelessly, Seth and Emma and me, spelling one another when exhaustion overtook us. For some reason a black and terrible fear closed around my heart. *The sea granted me one life,* I would think; *now it claims one in its turn.* I grew pale and shaky, exhausted with the efforts to care for Grace, unaware of the concern both Seth and Emma felt.

One evening when the baby's fever was high and she was particularly fretful, Emma drew me aside. "You are exhausted, love," she said. "It is a beautiful evening, why don't you go up for some air? That nice second mate, Eddie Jones, has been asking after you." She gave me a broad, comical wink.

"I am staying here," I snapped back at her.

"Please, lovie," she crooned, as if to Sita.

"How could you be so uncaring?" I cried. "Do you think I want to be above deck, taking the night air, when my baby dies?"

Emma took me by the shoulders hard and wrenched me around to face her. "Listen to me, Lottie, we are well ahead of this thing. Grace is not going to die."

I did not realize that I was crying, that Winston's blue eyes were wide with fear, that heads were turning thoughtfully away from the scene.

Suddenly Seth was beside me, half pushing, half pulling me up the narrow ladder. The cold air struck me like a slap, and I shrank against it. Seth tugged at me mercilessly and I stumbled after him until we came to a deserted corner of the deck, where he stood at the railing and drew me close to him. "The sea is lovely tonight."

"The sea is dark and rolling," I cried. "Can't you see how angry and greedy she grows?"

He stared at me much as he had that morning we arrived in Liverpool. "Greedy for what?" His voice was little more than the moving of his lips as he formed the words.

I tried to pull away from him, but he would not allow it. "Why do you fear the sea?" he asked, his eyes as calm as his voice.

I would not answer, so he asked me a second time, and at last I cried pathetically, "The sea gave me one child; I think it wants to take this one, Seth. . . . I think it wants to take Grace away from me!" My voice ended in a choking sob.

"Lottie!" Seth entreated, with his hands on my shoulders. "You poor, tormented thing!"

I choked on my tears and took the handkerchief he offered me.

"Lottie, listen, listen carefully." He cupped my chin in his hand and tilted my head to face him. "The sea did not give Sarah to you, the sea had nothing to do with it. You had a fine, healthy baby who was born during a voyage, and that is all. Nor has the sea desire and a will of its own to snatch this new child from you."

His words made me tremble; I wanted to hush him, but he went resolutely on. "Where does this black superstition come from?" He shook me a little, wanting an answer.

"I do not know," I said, thinking suddenly of Dacca, then of the Crims and their methods, secret and ruthless.

"Lottie, my darling." His voice was low and gentle. "Your fears are groundless; put them from you. Remember the truths you believe in, and trust in him who did, in reality, return your child to you."

His words stopped me. The verity of them flooded through me, like a wash of cold sea water. I remembered well that Christmas night when I had despaired of Sita's life, when I had waited, dreary and hopeless, for the black powers to close over her. I remembered what it was like when Seth and his friend placed their hands on her head. I remembered the light and peace that flowed through me.

"Let us resolve the matter," Seth said. His eyes had been studying my face, his eyes as gray as the cold sea, yet as warm as the sun. "I will get Brother Bell and we will administer to her. We should have done so before."

I clasped his arm with trembling fingers, fighting a sensation of panic. "What if the answer is no this time?"

How unhappy and clouded his eyes were. "Then the answer is no," he replied firmly. "She is my daughter, too, Lottie, and whatever happens, I want to place her in God's hands."

I nodded numbly. I knew he was right; I felt much the same way myself. But these fears, these terrible fears—

"You are beset with the false traditions of your fathers, Lottie." His voice was still patient, persuasive. "Give me your hand; come with me. Please."

He held his hand out and just stood there, waiting. I fought the dark thing that had me in its grip and put my hand into his. His strong fingers closed around mine, and his strength seemed to flow through me. We went back down together. We found Brother Bell, and I watched as the two men anointed the damp little head and called upon the power of their priesthood in her behalf. It was not my faith, not this time, not yet. Perhaps it was the faith of her father and the will of heaven combined. I saw her features, stiffened with suffering, relax. I saw her sink into a normal, peaceful sleep. And I was there by her bedside next morning when she awoke, smiling and rested, with no fever remaining, and a healthy color seeping back into her skin. Seth said nothing. Not by glance or word did he criticize or remind me of my weakness, my ignorance. I felt nothing but kindness from him. The tender effects of his love did more to free me from what he called "the false traditions of my fathers" than all the sound doctrine on earth. For, after all, is not love the highest of doctrine, the most sacred force within us, and within him who created us?

We reached New Orleans on the ninth of November as the year 1841 drew to a close. Here, in this shifting, dazzling, exotic city I felt at home. Many dark-skinned, even black-skinned people roamed the wharves and streets. Many languages were spoken, in anger or laughter, and the air was warm, warm and languid like the tepid, flower-strewn water of a soft, sunlit pool. We were to stay an extra night aboard ship while the brethren arranged for river passage. The confinement ate at me and I paced the cramped quarters like a caged beast until Emma drew her thick arms out of the laundry suds and dried them on her apron.

"I'll be back before sunset," she announced. "Seth, help your wife with this washing, and then start packing. We sleep tonight in New Orleans!"

"Do you believe she'll pull it off?" Seth asked as he bent over the tub good-naturedly.

"If it were anyone else, I would have my doubts. But Emma? I think I'll start packing."

We laughed together; I wanted freedom too desperately to anticipate it. But I did begin organizing and packing our things, wishing desperately for even one of the dozens of bored servants that had swelled my Indian households. Winston, who knew me well, helped. "Emma will do it," he assured me. "Anything she sets her mind to just seems to happen."

"You're right," I said.

My back ached and I felt hot all over. It seemed so dull, so commonplace to pull into the busy harbor and then merely sit here. True, we had walked out in the city for an hour or so, just enough to whet our appetites. This was America, but only one small fragment of her. She was as vast and diverse as my India—more so, they said. This Creole city, founded by the French and Spanish, bore little in common with New York or Boston or Philadelphia. Their inhabitants did not speak or dress or behave like one another; they did not even eat the same foods. And, where we were going—very few knew anything about it. The prairie—that's what I heard some people call it, talking of sweet-smelling grasses that grew as tall as a man's shoulder. No mountains, but woods in plenty, and the broad Mississippi to water the acres of cultivated soil which produced the food to feed this vast continent. I had no pictures to call up in my mind. Each time my eyes lighted on something new, I tried to store the sight there, to make it, even in a little way, a part of myself.

Emma did not return by nightfall. Dark sky met and merged with the line of dark water; still she did not return.

"Has she met with some accident, even foul play?" I asked Seth.

"I don't think so," he replied. "I think she has most probably forgotten all about us."

I put the children into their bunk, whose mattress had been aired on the deck all day and smelled of the tangy salt air and the warmth of the sun. Winston was bitterly disappointed.

"Tomorrow," I promised him.

When Seth and I walked up on deck it was largely deserted. Many of our party had boarded a riverboat that afternoon. Some few, with means, had taken rooms in the city. The remainder were crowded down below. Two days, perhaps three, and there would be a boat for the rest of us.

I looked up at the stars. *Are they really the same,* I wondered, *that stand over India, that glitter above the Thames?* I heard a commotion over to the left of us, and a high feminine voice bellowing out with the force of a fog horn. I lifted my head and saw Emma swaggering toward us, her strong arms flailing in all directions, her red face sagging. "Is she—"

"Drunk as a lord," Seth laughed.

When she reached us her breath nearly bowled me over, and I could not understand her slurred speech. She waved a fistful of money about, which I at last pried from her and stuffed into a pocket of her dress. She kept repeating one word again and again, amid a tirade of chuckling over some joke of her own. *Creel* or *crow,* it sounded like. Second mate Jones helped Seth get her down the gangway and onto the lowest bunk, where I normally slept.

"She must'a had one roaring good time," he grinned. "Now, if you could spare the pretty missus for a couple of hours—" He winked at Seth, but his eyes besought mine with such longing that I shuddered and turned away, busying myself over the still warm kettle, with the excuse of pouring a strong brew for Emma. He understood and did not press me.

"Jones would never harm a hair on your head," Seth said after the man had clambered back up the stairs.

"I know. But there is something in the way he looks at me—"

"He is a man," Seth said simply. "If I were a sailor, living as he lives, I'd look at you that way, too."

It was Seth's way of expressing his pride, the pleasure he felt in having me for his wife. I kissed his forehead. "I don't really want any tea," I said. "I think I'll just climb up to bed."

I glanced at Emma. Her slack mouth had fallen open and she was snoring like a man. I wondered, with no little curiosity, what she would have to tell us when she woke up the next day.

It was Emma who woke me, shaking me like a rag doll.

"Everyone's dressed and fed and ready to go. You have five minutes, love."

She meant it. Our possessions stood in a neat pile, awaiting transport. She had secured an upstairs apartment on Canal Street the first hour she had been in the city, but then her newfound friends took her to the French Quarter, where she stayed most of the night. Here there were bars, and prostitutes hanging over filigreed balconies where wisteria drooped. Here there were gambling halls, lavish theatres for the production of plays and operas, exotic French restaurants whose succulent dishes perfumed the night air. And everywhere there was music, music pouring out of open doorways. "Music is the language they speak in the Quarter," Emma sighed.

She led the way and, in truth, the rooms she had obtained for us were decent enough. When I asked her about the cost, she grinned widely, her fingers searching for the bills in her pocket. "I sold several pieces of my finest lace last evening," she crowed, "with promise for more. Oh, Lottie, this place is like a wonderland!"

I could understand how she saw it that way. When she cajoled us into accompanying her that night to the French Quarter I was stunned at how succulent and sensuous everything was: the colors, the textures, even the tropical air reflecting the handsome Creole dandies and the haughty planters clad in silk suits and ties, with fancy stitched boots and slender sword-canes at their side. And the women, the women were like exotic flowers, or rare, stunning peacocks of a dozen brilliant colors to dazzle the eye.

"Creole women are reputed to be the most beautiful on the face of the earth," Emma whispered. "But just look, Lottie! I think the men are as beautiful."

It was true, what she said. As I glanced sidelong at the handsome dark shapes that moved past me, I stopped suddenly on a note of laughter. "It was not *creel* or *crow*," I cried. "It was *Creole* you kept saying over and over again last night."

We shared a good laugh together; that entire evening in her company seemed enchanted to me. I was not surprised when she came to me early next morning and announced, in a voice heavy with sorrow and apology, her intention to stay.

"Sally Gray owns an exclusive women's shop here, and she's offered me regular employment."

"That is good news!" I cried.

"There is great demand here for fancy goods such as I can produce, Lottie. They'll fetch a most handsome price."

"As they should!" I responded, then sighed at the burden of attempting to cover my own feelings. "Oh, my dearest Emmer, I shall miss you dreadfully."

"An' what o' me?" she blustered, lapsing into broad Cockney.

"This is where you belong," I said. "Life will be good to you here, Emma, and that is what I most want."

"You won't let Winston forget me?"

"That would be impossible, and you know it!"

It was not an easy farewell. I had expected—at least I had hoped—well, no matter. I kissed my last link to England good-bye and walked with my husband to the place where the river-boat was tied up to the wharf. I did not look back; I did not wave to the substantial, vibrant figure who watched after us— I could not have endured that. But I did pray as I walked: *Look after her, Father. Keep her in your tender care, and let her be happy, let her feel your love in her life.* It was the best I could do for her, it was all I could do for her before I walked away.

Chapter Eleven

𝔍

THE MISSISSIPPI REMINDED ME of the rivers in India, long and winding; stretching, they told us, for over two thousand miles. The hazards of travel on the ocean were nothing compared to those aboard the steamboats that plied the river, their side wheels churning the brown water white, their twin stacks, crowned with ornamental fretwork, rising like sentinels above the squat craft. We had been told the horror stories of exploding boilers and bursting steam pipes, of the deaths of thousands of passengers every year. But for some reason I liked the crude, noisy boats and the lean, lithe men who steered them, sometimes poling the boats over shoals and shallows and around the treacherous sandbars, quick-eyed and quick-footed. Accommodations were poor—all but the wealthy crowded below in steerage, with no sanitary facilities, with no real beds to lie upon, and even the food we needed to live by left pretty much up to us. But the days of such privations could be counted on both hands; we would be there in less than two weeks. And we had decided to husband the little hoard we had brought with us, so that we might establish a home and some means of support in Nauvoo.

The river breezes were cold and refreshing this time of year, and some mornings we awoke to a heavy frost powdering the deck and whitening the heavily treed shorelines we slid through. The "father of waters" carried all forms of humanity along its broad back. We saw fine ladies decked in slippers and satin, Indian squaws wearing leather and moccasins, and Negro slaves, their ebony bodies gleaming with perspiration, clad in rags that scarcely covered their nakedness. We saw Quakers and soldiers, emigrants from dozens of nations, frontiersmen in buckskin with long rifles and the tight, muscled faces of hunters. A colorful piebald of human expression, a seething conglomerate of human emotion and human need—all feeding into the river, as fresh, strong rivers do, or tiny, meandering streams. Thus, I fancied that the "old devil," as the Negro folk called the Mississippi, had a life of its own, as rich and varied as the gamut of all mankind. The river spoke to me as nothing had spoken to me since I left India, and I felt somehow reassured that soon I would be making my home somewhere along her broad shores.

Sita quickly became a darling of both passengers and crewmen, and Winston, curious as a monkey, poked his nose into every corner and kept so many people busy answering his questions that he was no trouble to me at all. We went from Natchez up to Vicksburg to Memphis, into the sprawling heart of America where the towns, awkward and ill-formed as newborn calves, hummed with progress; and a sensation crackled in the very atmosphere that anything was possible here. The known history of Great Britain is over a thousand years old, of my country much older. I tried to remember how new and unschooled this United States was. I tried to respond with an enthusiasm matching that which I observed all around me, but I could not. It was something ancient in the river which drew me; I did not like the fresh, wide-eyed awkwardness of what the people were doing upon the land.

St. Louis, Missouri brought us to within three days of our destination. The weather was getting colder, with a real bite to the air when the wind was up. Despite this, we women washed and mended while the men trimmed shaggy hair and beards and polished the dull leather of their boots till they were shining again. The river was very muddy here and the prospect dreary as we headed on. Seth knew I was nervous, so he refrained from teasing me. I dreaded my first sight of Nauvoo. I dreaded what would happen inside myself if I did not like what I saw.

But with the cold came the deep, russet colors of autumn that crowded the banks and splashed along the high black bluffs where the trees grew close and thick. In a gentle curve of the river stood a horseshoe of land and, upon this graceful sweep, a city rose with row upon row of neat, orange brick houses that, at first glance, looked very much like England to me. Beyond the city stretched the endless prairie, shimmering under the touch of a breeze. The late afternoon sun stretched her golden fingers to emblazon the scene: barns and animals and tidy gardens, smoking brick chimneys; all shimmered rosy and inviting beneath that light.

I drew in my breath. "Yes," Seth said beside me. "Yes." I reached for Winston's hand, suddenly eager to step ashore. As we nosed into the dock we could see the faces of the Saints who were gathered, already waving to those of us on the deck. I trembled with excitement, clutching Winston's hand so tightly that he cried out in complaint. Seth laughed. His gray eyes were sparkling; behind them I read his relief.

"Is your mother there?" I breathed.

"I don't see her. But then, I did not inform her of when we would arrive."

I glanced at him, a bit startled.

"This is our moment, Lottie—just the two of us together. Everything else in good time."

I looked up and kissed him. Sita danced in his arms as the ship shuddered and bobbed to a stop. People began pouring down the long ramp; there was a rising wave of voices and laughter, and even the sound of glad tears. I stood and watched; the sun stretched across the broad prairie, an explosion of churning red fire with streamers of crimson and amber and palest rose. I felt Winston tugging at my hand. "Hurry along, Mother. I thought you were anxious to leave."

We went together. The crowd seemed to part to admit us; I saw the tall stranger turn and stride toward a small knot of people, bending forward eagerly as he extended both hands.

There was something about the way he carried himself, about the way others looked at him. "That is the Prophet Joseph," I said.

Seth stopped and looked where I pointed. "Yes, I believe that it is."

Joseph moved off with the others, but as he did so, he lifted his head and smiled, his expression encompassing all within reach of it with the warmth of a benediction. A thrill, like fire and ice, trembled through me or, rather, from my heart outward, as though something deep within my soul had recognized him. The spirit of song and poetry, bequeathed by my mother's blood, lifted at this sight of a prophet.

"This is a good omen," I said.

Seth neither laughed nor scolded me. "Yes, we are fortunate to have seen him, to have felt his blessing, as it were, rest upon us."

We walked in his footsteps, from the low river landing, toward the streets of Nauvoo.

We arrived in the city on the nineteenth of November. Before the month had ended we were living in a home of our own situated on the corner of Parley and Bain Streets. The sixty pounds remaining of the Major's money translated into so much in American terms. Forty pounds, or two hundred dollars, purchased us a modest home and a city lot. We secured a fine cow and the provisions we would need to set up housekeeping: bedsteads and mattresses, chairs and tables, a wringer and a washboard, and a three-legged iron bake kettle called a "spider." Meat was cheap—two pence or four cents a pound, one pence for fowl, and eggs only two pence a dozen. Vegetables were dear, but we determined to plant our own garden come spring. Flour was ofttimes scarce, so I began to learn how to cook with cornmeal: ash cakes in the fireplace, johnny-cake and other breads, and hasty pudding, sweetened with honey or maple syrup, which the women made from the tree sap they gathered in early spring.

The abundant blessings which I enjoyed at times became almost a pain to me. Many of the Saints, especially the immigrant converts, struggled pathetically. Some were so miserably poor that they dwelt in crude shelters built on the prairies outside the town, some of logs but others of sod and mud construction, with no chimneys, windows or doors, only a funnel through the roof or side wall and a quilt hung over the entrance.

"They will feel it bitterly when winter sets in," Seth's mother, Victoria, would chirp. Seth's mother—'twas she who offset my blessings and evened the balance a bit.

Victoria was, heaven forgive me for saying so, a weak, sniveling woman who judged everything in life with a view to her own interests and comforts. I believe even her looks, through the years, must have been altered by the narrow, petty nature of her spirit, which shriveled both body and soul. Her nose and chin and lips were sharp, her hair limp and lackluster, her hips narrow, her hands thin but large-knuckled, her voice lacking cadence or timbre. As though to contrast her own plainness she dressed in the brightest, most gaudy colors she could find, which only accentuated the problem. Seth's father, Kenneth, on the other hand, was a large hurly-burly sort of a man, at least to look at him; and yet he was timid as a mouse inside. His hair and beard were nearly black, so that Seth's coloring was a moderate blending of the two. His eyes were by far his strongest feature. They were a gray as warm and soft as a mourning dove's, with mere suggestions of green and blue streaks lacing through them, as a dove's wings would be. Phyllis was like her mother; thin and pale-skinned and nondescript. In Mary Jane her father's features, touched with the feminine, had become really beautiful, and she had inherited his patience without his dullness.

I believe the girls liked me and would have truly warmed to me had their mother not discouraged, almost forbidden it. I used to puzzle upon what it was that had turned her against me. I know she disliked the fact that I had Indian blood, and that that blood clearly showed. And she was always dropping hints about how large a family Seth had to support, though he had told her—without asking my permission and without naming the sum—of the significant inheritance which had

brought us to Zion and provided for us here. I know she bitterly resented *that*. Perhaps, all boiled down, it was as Seth
maintained: he was her only son, and given her nature, she
would have worried and niggled at any girl who took him
from her.

Nevertheless, she was not pleasant to deal with, and it
grieved me more than I showed that I could not win either
kindness or approval from her. Nor could my little ones, especially the two who had no legitimate connection with her. But
even little Grace, with her shy, winning ways, could not get
through Victoria Taylor's reserve. I suspect it was an almost
vicious sort of jealousy: this undeserving foreign woman had
nabbed her son, yet her daughters, sweet girls that they were,
had found no husbands as yet. Grace was not theirs, she still
belonged to me, and I was the outsider, I threatened her strict,
imposing order of things.

So things were. I could accept them because Victoria and
her family existed outside my own life. Seth was happy with
me, and I was happy with him, and we were both happy here.
He whistled his way across the city in search of employment,
something to do with people, something where he could move
and be active and hone his skills. Two days after we were into
our house, still plastering walls and painting and staining
floorboards, he came with the news that he had been hired on
at the *Times and Seasons* selling advertising, and rustling up
newsy tidbits as he went along. I was delighted for him,
though it meant more of the burden of the unorganized household would fall on me. Only once did I ask his sisters to come
over and help; when they gave some flimsy excuse and never
after showed any interest or inclination to be of service, I put
the thought of them out of my mind. If only Emma were with
me! I thought of sending for her but, of course, that was
impractical, and by the time she got here, even if she could
come, I would no longer need her the way I did now.

We got by, and each day saw improvements, each day I felt
more and more at home in Nauvoo.

Sometime in mid-December winter bared his claws and

struck, with the ferociousness of a coiled viper or a springing tiger. I had never known such cold as this. The thermometer rode well below zero, and a wind, wet and whistling, tore through the flesh and chilled clear to the bone. I dug out the mittens and wool wrappers Emma had made, but they did little more than blunt the sharpest edges of my suffering. I huddled by the fireplace whenever my tasks would permit me, using more wood in a week, Seth claimed, than others used in a month. Then it began to snow—softly at first, with the magic I remembered from London. Then the wind bethought itself and froze the soft pieces of fluff into bits of hard ice. The mud froze, the shallow river wore a thick gray coating of ice. The cold branches cracked and the very air crackled, and still the thick snow poured down.

Winston loved it. He joined the other boys, whether friends or strangers, sliding down the white streets. Seth came home one afternoon with a long wooden sled and taught Winston how to handle it on the low, ice-packed slopes. The child was growing into a young boy. Even Sita was losing her babyish ways. Seth, heaven bless him, was fair and gentle with each of them; in his actions there was never any favoring of one over another.

Christmas in the promised land was not quite the same as in London. None of the loud, gaudy displays of wares, none of the fancy rich draped in furs traipsing off to the theatre; not even crackers and roasted chestnuts. Here it was more personal and intimate, with turkey and venison, hot biscuits, roasted potatoes, vegetables, and cakes and pies as part of the Christmas feast. Emma sent gifts that were in keeping with her new, extravagant lifestyle: a gray felt hat for Seth, a length of watered silk for me, Creole puppets and baubles for the children, and rich creamy pralines to eat. We had a small reunion of sorts, all the London Saints gathering at Janet Dibble's house. We sang carols and hymns, then told stories of our trials, both in coming over and since we'd been there. Then someone started in reminiscing about "the old days back home." It was wonderful; I could close my eyes and smell London, see May's bright, tiny features, the long drive leading up to Baddenwell. Oh, how we tormented ourselves for an hour or so! Seth's family was there, but they had no part in my memories, and not much more in my affections, I fear. When we gathered round to sing, Brother Dibble playing his mouth organ and another the violin, I had to fight back the tears. Music opened up all the tender memories I held in my heart's most private chamber. Karan was with me, Vijaya and Dr. Fielding; Geoffrey and the major, even the young lieutenant, Hugh Sheldon; all moved and mingled together, as they had in my life. I wept over Emma and my little dead Shadow; I wept over the relief I had felt that Christmas morning when Seth Taylor entered our drab rooms and brought the spirit of healing with him. I wept as a girl weeps who has not yet let go of any of the strands of her life.

When we returned to our own little house Seth built the fire up to a roaring blaze. "As long as I am here to take care of you," he said, "you will never be cold, never be frightened or unhappy again."

One perfect moment—such come seldom in mortality. I savored it then, and drew it out many times over the long years ahead, that I might drink again of the pure love and gladness it held.

Chapter Twelve

"YOU COME FROM LONDON, YOU SAY, Sister Taylor? Did you live there before your marriage?"

It was the same question put to me countless times since I had arrived.

"I was born in India, actually."

"India—!" on a note of wonder.

If I felt contrary I would leave them there, dangling, too polite to ask further, yet itching to know. If a mischievous spirit o'ertook me I might add, "My father was a British officer, my mother the daughter of a Sikh princess," which, in fair truth, she was. I grew weary of the curiosity I met with on every hand. Eyes followed me as though I were some sort of an oddity.

"People admire you," Seth said. "You are beautiful and exotic; they do not know quite what to make of you."

"All sorts float up the river to Nauvoo," I argued, "musicians and trappers, bartenders, gamblers, women of ill repute—and American red Indians . . ."

He would smile. "But none of them come to meeting and present such a lively enigma as you do, my dear."

Winter took a long time in leaving. Not until late February did the ice on the river break up, cracking and thundering all times of the day and night. What a mess that was, with cold mud and sharp, rough ice shards littering water and shoreline. The children were filthy when they came in from playing, with red ears and red, running noses. In March the sugaring-off started—the tedious process of drawing the sticky sap from the maple trees. Some of the women I had become acquainted with taught me how to tap into the tree bark and secure the buckets to receive the slow-dripping liquid. Nearly twenty gallons of the precious fluid were required to produce just one half-gallon of syrup, to be used in hasty pudding or to pour over one's breakfast oatmeal and warm johnnycakes. Sunday evening prayer meetings were held in private homes throughout the city. We were kindly invited to many, partly because of Seth's convivial, outgoing nature, partly because so many entertained curiosity concerning his wife. The rooms were generally well filled, presided over by elders and following very much the pattern I had grown familiar with back in London, save for a certain informality which allowed all to speak freely if they possessed some insight worth sharing, or harbored a question on a certain gospel subject which they wished discussed. We met many more people under this practice than we otherwise would have. Most of the women were friendly with me, willing to assist when I had questions concerning how things here were done. I appreciated their openness and their quiet, though unexpressed, sympathy. After all, many of us were in the same boat, and most had come up by the same strenuous path we were climbing now.

The weather was raw still and I had to grit my teeth to go out and work with the women, but I was determined to do my share; I could not bear to think of any of them talking behind my back at how weak and pampered I was. Besides, Seth spent all his spare hours preparing the fields we had rented that they might receive crops. And some of the brethren had offered to help him raise a barn as soon as the ground was well thawed. I must shoulder my share without complaining, the way he did.

By this time I knew, though I had not told Seth yet, that I was with child. It surprised me a little, and perhaps I entertained a few reservations at the idea of having another baby to care for while Gracie was only a baby herself. I have always wondered, with my superstitious nature, if that is why it happened—if I *caused* the baby to miscarry through some secret thoughts of my own. Be that as it may, I was out in the blustery March air, shivering even when the sun occasionally broke through the high branches and filtered fitfully down. To this day I cannot say quite what happened. I felt suddenly faint and light-headed. Then a pain in my abdomen, sharp and searing as a heated blade, brought me to my knees. The sisters were quick. Capable hands lifted and carried me out of the wind's way. Then somebody's husband with a flatbed buggy took me to my own house.

I think for a time I drifted in and out of consciousness, calling for Seth, who was out peddling his wares here and there and could not be found. The woman they brought to me, Sister Abigail Haven, was a well-seasoned midwife, with large sinewy hands that were as soft and gentle as a young girl's. I began to perceive what was happening and fought it, fought it with my teeth hard-clenched against the pain and the blackness inside my head.

"Wist, child, you do yourself no favors. Let it come easy now."

The woman's voice was as vague as a whisper; it barely penetrated my consciousness. I continued to struggle, seeing only Dr. Fielding's kind, crinkly eyes, feeling the jolting rhythm of the horse-drawn gharry, then the shimmering heat of Dacca, and Geoffrey bent over me, his lips compressed into an angry line: *At least I have one son . . . at least I have one son. . . .*

When I awoke it was the strange, soft-faced woman who bent over me. "You were not with us for a while there, lass," she said. "It should be easier now."

Easier now! I shuddered and lay back on the pillow. "Was it a boy or a girl?"

She hesitated for a moment. "I believe it would have been a boy-child, from what I could tell."

"I cannot carry my sons!" I muttered. "What is it about me—or is it God's will against me?"

"Do not speak so! 'Tis wicked and ungrateful of you. Look what blessings you have."

I gave my benefactress a dark look and turned my face

away from her. I wished to grieve alone—all alone. I dreaded facing my husband, dreaded seeing disappointment seep into his gentle gray eyes.

When they first brought him to me I pretended sleep, and they left me alone. I was so weak; every muscle in my body turned to water. And my skin felt burning, as though some internal furnace was heating it. I do not know how much time passed, but when I opened my eyes to see Seth's solemn eyes watching me, I knew he was deeply concerned.

"How long?" I mumbled. My tongue felt like cotton in my mouth, and my throat was so dry that it was painful to swallow. "I'm sorry . . . so sorry—"

He pressed his lips to my forehead. "Lottie!" The compressed sound was hoarse with anguish. "I have been so worried. Please . . . look at me, Lottie. Please don't leave me again!"

I tried to lift my arm, to reach for his hand to reassure him, but the weight was too heavy. "The child," I whispered. "I am so—" I could not say the words again.

"The child?" he sounded truly offended. "There can always be children—it is you I want, Lottie! It is you that matters!"

I could not believe what I heard. I sank back and closed my eyes, for the first time relaxing—for the first time letting go of the hard knot inside. They all said, later, that I began to heal from that moment when I had opened my eyes and seen my husband's loved face.

I was not an easy patient for the quiet, persevering midwife who came daily to care for me. I was taciturn and ungracious, still entertaining grudges against Deity and life in general, when I should have been grateful, so grateful!

"You had a touch of the ague," Abigail explained one morning as she steeped water for tea, and another large kettle for laundry. "That and your own state of mind put you in some danger, my girl."

I felt she was judging me, though nothing in her manner betrayed it. But she appeared unsympathetic, and how could she begin to know all I had been through in the years before this?

Sister Dibble, bless her motherly heart, kept my children. Victoria came by once or twice to "report" on their rambunctious, even naughty behavior. I endured silently, with as much grace as I could, until she snapped, "That Winston is a lazy, willful child—a handful already, missy. Looks like you'll have a fine time in store."

"That I will," I answered, turning on her like a she-cat defending her young. "For Winston is the most obedient, most delightful of children. I have *never* seen him be rude or show disrespect—or not trip over himself to prove helpful. Do not criticize him to me. I will never listen to another word from your lips against him! Do you understand?"

Victoria drew herself up with a little wheeze and a sound of startled disapproval and, with Sister Haven's subtle assistance, soon scuttled out of the house.

"Good for you, miss, standin' up to her that way," my nurse replied upon returning. But when she saw that I was crying, she drew a chair up to the bed.

"I had one like that," she said. "A real gentle spirit, with no guile in him. And work—he could work. Skinny as a rail he was, but he worked like a horse."

Some quality in her voice made me turn my gaze to her. "Your son, how old is he?"

"Would have turned eleven this year."

My heart sank. "You lost him; I'm sorry," I said simply. "Have you other children?"

"Four sons in all," she replied, almost matter-of-factly. "All lost at Haun's Mill."

My mind went cold, and at the same time blank.

"Missouri," she added, reading my gaze. "Lost my husband and my sons. Only Abbey left"—she smiled grimly— "named after me."

I felt myself go cold, and then hot all over. I lowered my eyes from her, consumed with compassion—and shame.

She reached across the coverlet and placed her hand over mine. "It's all right, sweetie. You had no way of knowing."

"But I've been so rude and pompous!" I cried.

"Grief does strange things to people; I ought to know it. I

figured you had your own dark crosses that didn't show."

I began crying in earnest now, great sobs that shook through me. She gathered me into her arms. How I ached at her tender touch. I felt her calm love tremble through me, soothing my tightened muscles, loosening the terrible constriction around my heart.

"Poor motherless child," she cooed, stroking my tangled hair. "Cry as long as you need to. I understand."

When at last I looked up, choked on tears and taking her broad handkerchief gratefully, I asked how she knew I was motherless.

"'Twas your husband's ravings," she answered in a tone of apology. "He was that worried about you."

"I am blessed," I whispered, tears starting fresh again. "You were more than right when you scolded me. Can you ever forgive me?" I begged.

"Think nothing more of it"—her voice was husky with her own efforts to control herself—"save to remember that always, no matter what happens, you will have a friend in Abigail Haven."

"I shall remember," I promised.

When Seth came home that evening he found me calm and composed, and looking better than I had for days.

"I am all right now," I assured him—and I was. "Will you go to Janet's and bring the children back?" I asked him. "I want them around me."

He was happy to do as I bid. Perhaps I had rushed it a bit. For the next four days I fell into bed exhausted and shaky, but the contentment was worth it, and the growth I could feel, a new strength building within me which I considered to be well worth the price it exacted from me.

Spring made the difference; the renewal of spring precipitated a renewal within me. The prairies were smothered with flowers—the air was redolent with the wild scent of them. The rich Illinois soil, black and sticky when turned by the plow, smelled as pungent with life as any green, growing thing could be. Seth sowed flax for the loom as well as wheat, some corn, and a plot of vegetables for home use: potatoes, onions, radishes, cabbage, beets, lots of greens and lots of tomatoes. At the end of a long day we would sit together and watch the sunset, across the Mississippi into Iowa, where the blazing sun would at last sink behind the far Iowa hills. If we had energy enough for it, we would climb the temple hill where the view was unobstructed, breathtaking in its grandeur; I had never seen anything quite like it before. Later in the night the heavens would catch fire again, picking up the weird glow from the prairie fires, ten to twenty each night set to burn the straw and refuse grass in preparation for putting in crops. It was an eerie sight which frightened Grace, though Sita jumped up and down clapping her hands.

"It looks as though the gods are angry and have begun to burn the whole world up," Winston commented one night.

"So it does," I agreed, wondering how such thoughts came to him. "But we live beyond the earthlings, in a blessed sphere, close to the eternal realms where the gods' wrath cannot touch us."

He liked that. "It is such fun telling stories with you, Mother," he said, and I wondered how many times, since that first terrible night when his mother died and I sat by his bed, how many times we had used make-believe and imagination to chase the shadows away. I shuddered to think of that brief spell in London when, in despair, I had drawn so far within myself that I had left him alone and comfortless; it was not magic and make-believe which had sustained him through that. Something deep within his spirit, something I believe he brought to earth with him, had come to his aid, and to mine. I could not help holding him precious; I could not help it at all.

The work, the work that came to my hand seemed endless, sometimes overwhelming to me. Cleaning and cooking—cooking here was a chore, not an art as it had been in India—tending the garden and fowl, even milking the cow when Seth was not around, then the churning of butter and the setting of cheeses, which could not be neglected lest the precious cream go to waste. There were candles to make against the long winter nights, and soap making—how I hated the blistering, backbending labor of soap making!

But even that was not all. The luscious summer fruits must be dried for winter use or stewed for pies. Currants and some fresh berries we made into preserves and jellies. Always something, always something, though at least the spinning and weaving could be left for the short, less stressed winter months.

Some days, when the morning still held the last wisps of coolness, I would leave the children with Winston and slip down to the river to watch the boats coming in. Here only was I put in mind of India and the great sacred river which carried all the world on its back. There was a churning in the very air here, like the white froth which the huge wheels churned up from the gray muddy water. I could feel the dreams the myriad of people carried with them; sometimes I could see hope sparkle in their eyes like laughter, sometimes I saw only despair, or a terrible weariness of life, as though the inner fires had burned too low and gone out altogether. I liked to look at the faces, the travel-worn clothing, and wonder where the traveler had been. I seldom spoke to the strangers, though now and again one would exchange a pleasant, or perhaps a shy, hesitant smile with me. At times some bold-eyed adventurer would wink from under the brim of his immaculate felt stovepipe or through the expanse of curly beard that he wore wrapped round his chin. Somehow this touch with humanity enlivened me and I could return with more resignation, even more enthusiasm, to my ever-recurring chores.

I had never seen a barn-raising, and I did not really see ours because it took place while I was ill. But I watched as neighbor after neighbor repeated the process and marveled at the lack of class barriers here in this wilderness as men and women pulled together for one another or for the common good.

Seth had taken on yet another job, which he delighted in, working mornings for a local merchant, Julian Winters, who ran a store of fine and fancy apparel for ladies. Seth thought it great fun to match his wits with the exacting customers who walked through the door, unaware of what designs he had upon them!

Summer came, and the river became slow and lazy. Clouds of mosquitoes rose up like magic from the wet lowlands, and the terrible swamp fever swept through the people like the prairie fires swept through the brown grass.

It looked to me much like the malarial fevers that laid us low in India, seeming to follow much the same pattern. One day in late June, Seth came into my kitchen and I jumped at the sight of him. Of course, I had not expected to see him there mid-morning, but that in itself had not startled me. It was the *quiet* of his approach; he had not been whistling, and that occurred only when something was very wrong.

I wiped my hands on my apron. "What is it?" I asked, trying to keep my own vivid imagination from responding before he could form his reply.

"My sisters. Both Phyllis and Mary Jane have the ague."

"Light cases or—"

"Serious. Mother says she is worn out with nursing them, yet they are not anywhere near the crisis point, and Mary Jane in particular grows worse every day."

That was one of the many things I appreciated about my husband. He did not say "Mother is worn out." His use of words conceded to the never-stated reality of how his mother structured her life. "Mother says—" that meant he understood, and was as frustrated by her selfishness as I myself was.

"Shall we have them here, or would you rather I go there?" I asked plainly.

He considered a moment, accepting my offer because he had known I would make it, because he was committed to the same course himself.

"Let us bring them here and put them in the small room at the back where you will not have to entirely wear yourself out—" He smiled despite himself at the repeated phrase. "Nor will you have to run back and forth between households."

"We must keep the children from them."

"Winston and I will take care of the children."

"You cannot, Seth, you have too much already."

"Winston and I will get by."

And so they did. He arose half an hour earlier each day and

prepared the morning meal. Winston washed up while he scrubbed and dressed the girls, who were then in Winston's hands till Seth returned to check things over at noon. In the evenings, tired as he was, Seth prepared food and finished what chores I had not been able to get to. It was an exhausting schedule for all of us. Winston, quiet and solemn, did his part and more, and I watched with pleasure as the bond between my two men strengthened. As for myself, life became a blur of bedpans, soiled sheets, medicines, poultices, soup and cool compresses, and the dull depression of sickness and suffering. If one girl did not need me, then the other did; never did I seem to stop for five minutes together. During one spell I went for days without setting eyes on my children, for even Winston was forbidden to enter the sickroom. After that Seth shooed me out every third night or so and I enjoyed the luxury of washing myself, dressing in fresh clothing, and holding my little ones to me for an hour or two.

The heat of an Illinois summer wilts the flesh like parched cabbage leaves; if it had not been for that I believe the girls would have mended much faster. I felt that I could scarcely draw breath in the close, humid air. Accustomed to desert heat, as I had been, I detested the moldy wetness in hair, clothing, and bedding, like the nightmare seasons in India which I had usually escaped. But when the crisis came and passed, and we knew both girls would get better, I was too grateful to complain about anything, at least for a while. The last few days before I returned them to their mother I grew to know them a little and found their company pleasant. Phyllis, removed from her mother's influence and subdued by her illness, was not so bad. Mary Jane was a sweetheart and would have been very like Seth if she had been left to bloom as nature intended.

Victoria never said a word by way of thanks or appreciation, but we had not expected her to. The girls, on the other hand, greeted me warmly whenever we met, and slipped away more and more often to spend a few idle moments with me and the children, and that pleased both myself and Seth well.

CHAPTER THIRTEEN

꙳

PERHAPS TOO MUCH HAPPINESS IS NOT GOOD for the soul, or at least for the soul who wishes to be sanctified. That autumn in Nauvoo was the happiest time in my life, sweet and mellow, filled with the bounties of nature and the bounties of love.

Our barn was snug and filled with hay and fodder to feed our milk cow and the horse Seth had bought. We had pigs and a few hens and turkeys; I liked the taste of turkey meat and looked forward to the time the New England Saints called Thanksgiving, when the coming of the American pilgrims was celebrated and the people ate big turkey feasts. Seth harvested our corn and wheat; I did not like baked corn and corn bread, but I did enjoy eating the fresh white ears as they were picked out of the field. We cured meat and I pickled dozens of cucumbers. Those who already knew how taught us to press apples for fresh cider; that was a taste I came quickly to like, and there were so many varieties of apples bending the heavy-bowed trees. In some fields I could smell them, as one smells the river, or the wet prairie grasses, or the faint perfume of flowers.

The whole world blossomed for us, blossomed and blazed, the trees on the bluffs and in the river bottoms aching with colors nearly too bright to behold. The first frosts nipped the dull edge of the heat, which sizzled a little and then withdrew. Seth's work was prospering, so we enrolled Winston in one of the nearby schools run by a clever and kind English woman. He did well right from the start.

"Better at writing than he is at sums," she told us. "But he possesses an excellent memory, and seems to enjoy history more than most children."

"He remembers India," I told her, "and has more of a sense of the world being large and varied than most children have."

Rather than resenting or misreading my remark, she warmed to it and seemed determined to draw him out even further. I was well pleased. The boy had been little more than a drudge since we were first left alone in London. I liked seeing him come a bit into his own, liked seeing his spirit awaken to the keen pleasures of knowledge.

I received my first letter from Marion, after sending half a dozen over the past months to her. Perhaps it was my absence that made her wax bold, but I could feel a friendliness in her words that made my heart sing. I read parts of the letter to Sita; I wished her to remember this woman who was blood of her blood, who had responded to things in my daughter that must have come from some fine ancient strain in her line. I was happy, with a gentle, contented happiness that seeped through every moment of my day, that colored the simplest task with a sort of splendor.

Now in late autumn, as in the early spring, the large black crows came calling, circling the drying cornstalks that rattled like loose bones under the breath of the wind. I loved the haunting melancholy feeling they drew out of me—wistful, at times painful, but throbbing with something that sat near the very core of the sources of life. I marveled and enjoyed, and moved in a dreamy sort of gratitude through day after day.

Winter came as it must, but I had built up some resistance and was not quite so shocked by its harshness. We did indeed celebrate Thanksgiving with some Saints of our acquaintance who hailed from Massachusetts: Alice and Stewart Hopkins, who knew Seth's uncle's family. Turkey and cranberry and pumpkin pies, and singing, "We gather together to ask the Lord's blessing." Singing as *Americans* brought strange sensations I had never experienced before. *Will I ever become an American?* I wondered. *Live in this country long enough that it seeps into the cells of my being, that I love it as I love India and*

England—that I begin to think, to judge all things as an American? The thought both excited and disconcerted me. Seth was eager; he had cast his lot with this place and this people, heart and soul, before he ever set foot here; he had no doubts, no spells of homesickness, no looking back.

"How is it that you can remove your heart from one place and simply give it to another," I asked him, "with no qualms at all?"

He looked at me as though I were a small child who had asked a simple, naive question. "I am an Englishman," he answered. "England will always be part of me; I carry everything with me that formed and influenced my life. Now I weave a new fabric in with the old—different colors to vitalize the whole, Lottie. They can blend, even contrast, but they need not be a threat to each other."

I nodded, more subdued than he realized. At times, in the common, day-to-day press of things, I forgot what amazing insights he possessed; I forgot that he had a touch of poetry in his soul.

We celebrated our second Christmas with the Saints, on the banks of the Mississippi River on the plains of Nauvoo. In the white, hushed silence of those hallowed days our thoughts were truly lifted heavenward. We listened to the Prophet preach to his people; oh, how I loved Joseph's words, the singing yet simple quality of them, the breadth of his spirit, the depth of his love. He had spent much time in hiding these past months due to the accusations his enemies had brought against him concerning the attack on Missouri's governor, Boggs, that degenerate man whose cruel order had cast the Saints from their homes to become a hiss and a byword throughout the land, as they sought helplessly for succor and protection. I had not been here; the trial by fire which many in Nauvoo had survived, some at great loss, had not come to me. But as I listened to the stories, as I pieced together what had happened, I bethought myself of India and the harsh persecution of the Indian people by the British, who consider themselves lords and masters, clearly superior to any and all things native. Though the land is not theirs, yet they presume to sweep it up in their greed and assumption of superiority.

The Prophet was home now, celebrating Christmas with his family, and I was here with Seth. I had just turned twenty-four years old, but age was beginning to mean nothing to me. I counted time differently; I counted growth and progress by different means.

The new year had to break through a barrier of ice to come into existence. Two days previous a snapping cold spell had sent the temperature plunging, forming fresh layers of ice over the river where the ice had been but spotty before. Even now it is difficult to tell it—even now, after all this time, it is so hard to look back.

The first week's end of the new year some of the children had formed a skating party in which Winston had been included, much to his excitement. I thought the weather too bitter for him to be out, and the sun much too weak. But he pleaded, as children will, and I gave in to him, planning to send Seth to fetch him home in a couple of hours, whether the boy willed it or not.

Our home was not far from the river, where we sat at the corner of Bain and Parley; Parley leads straight down to the broad sweep where the children were wont to play. Less than half an hour after Winston had gone skipping off with the others Seth came in from the barn where he had been working, dangling Winston's gloves in his hand.

"He must have dropped these."

I looked up in alarm. "But why did he not come back for them?"

"And have the others leave him behind? You know how it is with children." He smiled. "I'll run them down to him, otherwise his fingers will freeze and fall off one by one."

His smile grew into a lopsided grin; he knew what a mother hen I was where Winston was concerned. On impulse I laid down my sewing and wrapped my arms lightly round him.

"You are so good, Seth, so kind."

He planted a kiss on my nose, then drew me close, very close, and kissed me most tenderly. "You deserve every kindness, my love, both you and Winston."

His lips lingered over mine, warm and insistent. I could both melt and tingle at the touch of him. I watched for a moment as he sauntered out of the yard, whistling gaily. He turned and kissed the tips of his fingers and lifted his hand to mine.

How could I know—how could I ever have dreamed that would be the last time I would ever set eyes on my husband? Dear heaven! How could I have known?

They said he arrived just in time. A few of the older boys had been playing tag across the thin glassy surface and, in their enthusiasm, gone out too far, and some of the little ones had ventured after them, then been drawn by the branch and trunk of a huge tree protruding out of the ice. Foolishly they had skated close, grabbing for the long leafless branches, making up a game of their own. Too late they had felt the ice crack beneath them, too late they had seen the cavern of black water open up to them where the branches had broken through.

Three went under before they could stop themselves; the others drew away, horrified, screaming for help.

Seth was the first to reach them. Crawling over the precarious surface he was able, through sheer brawn and will, to pull two of them out and pass them on to their fellows, who had formed a line across the safe area and handed them across to safety. The third lad had floundered, sinking under the jagged hole in the ice which now extended much wider, as more and more chunks broke loose and floated near the surface. He could get no purchase on the slippery surface of the wood and he was losing strength fast.

Winston stood by—Winston stood close by as Seth lowered himself into the freezing water and went after the child, whose head had already disappeared below the black surface several times. He went under, only once. He did not come up again; he never surfaced at all.

Who can say what happened? Perhaps an underwater snag caught the strands of Seth's thick jacket and held him fast. Perhaps the child had been caught thus, and Seth stayed under the dread weight of water a few beats too long, working to free him, then met with some obstruction himself in struggling toward the surface. Who knows, who knows? It was talked of, talked to exhaustion for months and months after. But none of the conjecture brought either Seth or the drowned boy back. By the time help was fetched, a thick smothering snow had begun to blow in over the river, and the gray clouds snuffed out what there had been of the sun. The snow was blinding and icy cold. One man, they say, offered to go under, but the others prevented him. It was too late by this time, both man and boy had been under far too long; why risk a further death now?

At home, busy about my chores, I did not at first grow concerned. In the back of my mind I dismissed my first fears with the thought that Seth, more than likely, got caught up in their sport and stayed with the boys for a while. Not until the snow began did a feeling of foreboding come over me, suddenly, and with such power that I sank into a chair, trembling, feeling chilled all over. I clenched my fists at my side and attempted to pray and, as soon as I did, I knew in truth that something had happened, something more tragic and terrible than I would want to find out.

Abigail Haven, whom they called in to stay with me, said they told her that I fainted the moment I opened my door and saw the face of a neighbor standing there, hat in hand. I have no recollection. In my mind there exists a huge black space, empty and bottomless, that marks the day of Seth's death. I remember nothing, except that the agony made all other agony I had suffered pale at its side. Later, much later, Abigail told me that I cried out for my mother; and, from the look in her eyes, I think I must have done so often and very piteously.

The first thing I do remember is turning my face to the wall and announcing very coldly, very woodenly, that I wanted to die. Abigail could not touch me, no matter what methods she attempted. Indeed, I truly believe that I would not have endured the presence of any other human creature save her in my house.

Days passed, days running into a week. I was not eating enough to sustain myself, and nothing, not even my children, could entice me into embracing life again.

Then came a dull, leaden morning when I happened to lift my head up to see Winston pass through the room. Abigail, sitting beside me with Grace on her lap, called out to him, but he did not even pause. His head was down, his shoulders hunched in misery. He looked pale and diminished, and I could feel his misery like a palpable thing in the room.

"He has been like this ever since—" Abigail did not finish. "I'm worried about him."

I knew from her voice that she meant it. I turned my head away again, but the peace I had found in blankness did not return. A voice within my head began to speak to me, calmly, firmly, and I could not shout it down.

How many times have you left him, with his child's strength, his child's understanding, to manage for the both of you? How many times have you deserted him to whatever terrors exist in his own youthful mind? How much, in your selfishness, do you think the child is capable of bearing?

I do not know how long I lay there under the flailings of that voice, soft but determined. I do not know what at last moved me to struggle up to my feet. The house was dark, and Abigail no longer sat beside me; I believe I was dimly aware of her voice off in some corner crooning Gracie to sleep. Seth had fixed a little loft above the kitchen for Winston where he could be by himself. I climbed the narrow sagging ladder, but paused after several rungs. The sound of muffled weeping was coming from somewhere above my head. I waited breathlessly, aware that my feet were cold and my mouth was dry. When I could no longer bear the hopeless bitterness of that weeping I moved forward again.

As I lowered myself onto Winston's low bed it all came flooding back over me—everything from the death of his mother, through the nightmares of Dacca, of leaving Karan and India, of Geoffrey's death and the abandoned, pathetic state we were left in—everything, with not the slightest detail spared. Even as I shrank beneath the onslaught, something in me rose, something strong and burning. As I gathered Winston into my arms I felt as though I were gathering a portion of my own self unto me, fierce and sweet, totally intertwined with my being—

and the feeling gave me a sensation of unbelievable joy.

"Go ahead, my darling," I whispered against his hair. "Weep all you need to, Winston, I am holding you now."

After awhile he raised his head and fixed his sea-eyes on me. "I was afraid," he said, and his voice was a child's voice. "I was afraid of losing you, too."

"Forgive me for that," I replied, "and for all else which you have suffered in your love for me," and my voice was firm and still though tears flooded my eyes.

I held him, I held him for so long that my back ached and my legs became numb. At last he slept and I descended the stairs, cautiously, clumsily, my muscles as shaky as if I had risen from a sickbed which, in essence, I had. Yet everything inside me felt strong, even whole, in a way I could not understand, but which was too real to deny.

I went back to my bed and my sleep was deep and peaceful. When Abigail came in the next morning I was already up and dressed. "I will be all right now," I said, hesitant to look at her.

"Yes," she replied. "Yes you will, dearheart." She let out her breath on a sigh. "I'll pop back home then, but I'll be back tomorrow to finish that flax I've been weaving."

"Bring Abbey with you," I said.

"That would be a pleasure." There was obvious relief in her voice, but such a tenderness, too, that for a moment—just a moment—I moved into her arms and laid my head on her breast.

"Thank you . . . for suffering all you must have, for my sake."

"Bless you, Lottie," she whispered. "I'd have had it no other way."

Without saying much Winston and I lit into the house and set it to rights again. At times I even found myself humming under my breath. At the end of the day, dirty and exhausted, I poured hot water into the tin tub and bathed the pollution of my grieving away. Then I took some of the dried apples and made a pie for Winston, and we played games with the children and giggled and laughed. And not simply because I wished it to be so did I feel Seth's presence there, so vital and dear that I fancied I could turn and speak to him and he would answer me back. His yearning protectiveness encircled us all so that our small house felt hallowed and part of heaven itself. And thus I began to comprehend the love our Father in Heaven has for his children on earth.

Chapter Fourteen

※

How does one hold a funeral without a body? I had reached my own peace and could have dispensed with any and all outward signs. But Seth had too many friends who could not bear to let him go so suddenly without saying good-bye. Then there was his family, sunk in the narrow bitterness of their grief. A great compassion for them all overwhelmed me, and his mother did not entirely destroy it when, the day before the service, she snapped at me, "I hope you will have the decency, Charlotte, to at least put on a face of mourning tomorrow. All eyes will be watching you, and though Seth may have been your second husband, people will still consider it proper that you should deeply mourn."

I said nothing in reply to her; what could I say? How could I describe deep and sacred things to her mind? But Mary Jane followed after me, ashamed and contrite.

"I am so sorry, Lottie dear!" she cried, catching up my hand.

"Take no notice," I soothed. "She cannot touch me." Then I thought to add, "But remember, please remember that I loved your brother with all my soul—I did, and I always will. He was one of the most noble, guileless men I have ever known."

She smiled through her tears; I embraced her briefly and went on my way, almost fearful of this tenuous strength which sustained me, but thanking God for it with all of my heart.

I was forced by necessity to coldly calculate my assets and determine how best to continue into a future which I dared not face save for one day at a time. Many women such as myself did sewing, took in laundry, or opened small schools. I felt inadequate in all those areas; I can do nothing intricate and lovely if it takes using my hands, and there were many women with admirable British educations whose credentials far out-shone mine. For awhile, as winter wore itself out, I did little things to get by, selling eggs and the extra butter I churned—that helped meet our minimal expenses. For, in truth, we had fruit and vegetables, meat and meal, and even wood enough put by. Seth had provided well for us. I would not feel the lack of him in that way for many months yet. And I was fortunate to own the home we lived in outright; why, there was still a small reserve of pounds, or dollars, safe in the bank. And something else, something ponderous and weighty, had come along to demand my attention, to stretch the strings of my faith: I had discovered that I was with child.

At first I believe I ignored the signs, not wishing to give cre-dence to them, to believe the unbelievable. And, of course, my feelings were torn. How could I let go of Seth if I carried him constantly with me? How could I give birth alone, resurrecting my need for him and all the bitterness of my loss?

I determined to tell no one until I absolutely had to. But, of course, Winston knew and grew so solicitous of me that I had to now and again shoo him out of doors and off with the other boys his age. I knew he worried still, I knew he missed Seth sorely, and I did my best to find ways to ease and comfort him.

"Your name was the last on his lips," I told him one evening when I knew his day had been particularly trying.

He looked up at once, all intent attention.

"You see, he was taking your gloves to you," I began, real-izing too late that this was proving more difficult than I had anticipated. "And when I thanked him he kissed me and said, 'You deserve every kindness, Lottie, both you and Winston.'"

Seth had, in truth, said "my love," but I did not feel safe in trying to repeat that endearment. I watched in some surprise as the color blanched from Winston's face and he staggered to his feet. He would have run from the room if I had not detained him. "What is it, child?" I demanded, for I sensed something terrible in him, black and tormenting.

At first he would not reply; time after time he withdrew from me stubbornly, presenting a blank face to my entreaties, veiling for perhaps the first time his inner thoughts from my eyes. I did my best to hide the hurt and concern I was feeling and let the matter drop for a while. He did, indeed, on a muttered excuse, slip outdoors and away from me, but I watched after him, and he did naught but putter harmlessly around the yard and the barn.

I bided my time until the girls were tucked into their beds and there was no one but the two of us. "Tell me, Winston," I began. "You must sooner or later. Why not rid yourself of the torment now?"

The anguished response that leapt into his eyes gave me pause. He looked as if I were pronouncing a death sentence on him, as if his very existence was to be pulled out from under him.

"We are too much a part of each other," I said, keeping my voice at a gentle pitch. "I cannot bear the pain of watching you suffer so."

My words, though not intentionally cruel, made the poor boy tremble all over. Really concerned now, I reached for his hands. He snatched them out of my grasp, as though my touch had burned him.

"We cannot be part of each other, not ever again—not so long as I am responsible for killing the person you love!"

I stared at him, dumbfounded, slow to take his meaning, which should perhaps have been obvious.

"You make no sense, Winston. What in the world do you mean?

He was trembling so that he could scarcely get the words out, but he was determined now. "You are only trying to protect me, trying to make it easy for me!" he cried in distraction. "But other people see it—*she* saw it, and cursed me for it."

"Who saw it?" I asked, dreading his answer.

"His mother, of course." He would not use Seth's name; he had hardly ever spoken it since Seth died.

"You said so yourself," he continued, his voice still at a high, uncontrolled pitch. "He came to the river *on my account.* If I had not been stupid enough to drop the wretched mittens, if I had been responsible enough to go back for them myself— but no, *no!* He had to bring them to me at that moment! He had to—"

Dear heaven, the torment in his eyes was terrible to behold. I prayed in my innermost soul for guidance.

"You had nothing to do with—"

"You are saying that to protect me! You are saying that because you love me—if you do love me still!"

I sat silent. I must not blunder too many more times.

"If what you say is true," I began, "then there are many wretched, guilty souls the world over, and I myself am one of them."

His eyes became instantly sharp and narrow, though he lowered his head to conceal it.

"When I was a girl in India," I continued, "my sister, Roselyn, and I disobeyed her mother's orders and went to play beside the river, and it was I who urged her to the disobedient act. She came down with the malarial fever and died from the effects of it. But I did not die—I who, as you view it, was responsible."

Forgetful, he lifted his eyes to me.

"And that is not all. When I was a young girl and fell in love, it was with the wrong man. A native—a Sikh soldier." He raised his eyebrows. "You know how forbidden that was." I drew a ragged breath, praying for the strength to continue. "He was kinder and wiser than I was and wished to end the relationship because it would bring nothing but pain. I would not. I would not give him up. So Major Reid sent him away, and it was in this exile that he met with a terrible accident where he was attacked and dragged by a killer lion and had his leg nearly chewed off." Winston was with me, leaning forward in his chair. "This happened because of me, as you see it. Because he was maimed he could no longer remain in the service. Some would say I ruined his life."

I waited a moment before continuing. "There are others,

Winston, other times with myself and with all people living. You, yourself, remember the terrible incident in Barrackpore when the baby girl was bitten repeatedly by a scorpion concealed in her clothing." He nodded solemnly. "The poor child died, but was it the fault of the ayah who cared for her dearly, and yet was too dull to discover the insect hidden among her clothes?"

Winston said nothing, but he was no longer trembling and his eyes, though dark pools, were quiet again.

"My darling, only the cruel and vindictive, only the willfully blind view life as Seth's mother does. Such people feed upon their own misery, in part, at least, destroying themselves."

I felt him relax.

"You understand," I pressed softly. "Thus, you must let it go. Seth loves you still; your very existence pleases him. He is here—you have felt him; he will be with us both all our lives. We must do nothing to spoil that or to bring him unnecessary sorrow."

I spoke the last words slowly, uncertain again of my territory. But he nodded. "I've been so unhappy," he said. "I didn't know. I couldn't see anything but the terrible pain."

"And you think I do not understand that?"

His piercing gaze studied me. "Forgive me, Mother, and thank you," he said, in that odd, serious way of his. "I will not disappoint you again."

I smiled despite myself. "You may well disappoint me many times before you are grown, Winston," I said, almost lightly. "And that will be all right if you do. All of us—even the best of us—are human."

He took my meaning and smiled.

"But for your information, you have not disappointed me yet, my darling, not one single whit."

His smile deepened. We looked across the space at each other, but there was no longer any space between our two souls. Love had healed, love and knowledge, which is power, especially when it is used well.

❦

The first muddy, messy days of spring came and the term of school ended, and Winston informed me that he was now free to do whatever I wanted of him. I knew he desired to fill Seth's shoes, but he was just turning eleven and not particularly large for his age. I had already determined not to attempt to rent the fields Seth had rented the previous spring. Brother Wilson, who owned them, kindly offered to let me purchase what flax and fodder I needed for his price in the fall. Most people were kindly and helpful, and I knew that was partly because Seth had been so well liked. I saw a whole new batch of curious looks on faces of those who had known him without knowing me. I tried to be patient and understand, remembering the things Seth used to say. Merchants in particular I found willing to cut prices and that impressed me, for I wondered how many widows received like treatment at their hands. Julian Winters lamented loudly the loss of Seth.

"My sales have gone down, and that's the truth, mistress," he moaned. And I liked him, because he did not hedge nervously around the very mention of my dead husband's name. Then he eyed me shamelessly, with open evaluation. "I wish you would come and work for me in his place."

"That is most kind of you," I responded. "But I would be as bad for your business as Seth was good."

He lifted an eyebrow, intrigued already.

"People do not like me," I said. "My looks disturb them."

"And why is that, do you think?"

"Because they cannot figure me out. I fit no mold, and that makes them uneasy. Women in particular."

He threw his head back and would have laughed, but he caught the expression of my eyes just in time.

"Your candidness does you justice," he said instead. "And you are partially right. The women envy you your exotic beauty and your gentle ways. But many of our best customers are gentlemen."

"And you think that they respond differently?"

"I know that they do."

I let it go, because he was beginning to embarrass me, and I was uncomfortably aware of my pregnant condition, which thus far I had been able to rather successfully conceal.

"Whenever you are ready," he conceded, sensing my mood. "And do not be surprised if I plague you about it every now and again."

The more I thought about it, the more I was grateful for his offer. I *was* concerned about finances. With another child on the way I had a goodly number of mouths to feed. It would be foolish to use up my scant, precious savings when I had a means ready made of bringing earnings into the house.

Winter blustered with spring for dominance; the fields alternately froze or flooded. I had told Winston he could be in charge of our kitchen garden and make it as large as he liked. He spent hours poring over seed catalogs and the advice for gardeners printed in the *Times and Seasons*. The poor child did all things with such thoroughness, such a desire to please. Yet I wondered what price it cost him, somewhere inside.

I wondered, too, how he was faring at this point, as far as Seth's loss was concerned. I had thought myself reconciled and, for all matters of the spirit and the eternities to come, I felt I still was. But, oh, the day by day living, the countless things that brought him to remembrance, the countless times I needed him in little ways. I had my bad spells, but I saw well to conceal them from Winston's eyes. Yet he always knew, and did some little thing to make it easier, to let me know his heart was with mine. Would I could see so well into his little soul and likewise succor him.

I did not participate in the sugaring off in March. This baby had not been easy to carry and I wished to do nothing to risk it. Perhaps the lingering nausea, the backaches and headaches were connected to that other, bound inextricably with the loss of the father who would never set eyes on this child. I remember walking out one day in early March clear to the river, alone, and pausing to watch the ring of crows circle overhead. For the first time I felt chilled by their cries, the hollow emptiness of the raspy sound in the still gray air mocking my pain. I turned my back on them and scurried home like a small frightened child.

Not until April did the sun come to stay, and then it came with a will, drawing liquid out of the earth, out of the sky, so that the whole world seemed to steam. I disliked it, but could do nothing but try to ignore it and work on just the same. Some of the English Saints showed up one Saturday and did the repairs about yard and house that Seth would have done. Winston, in his thoroughness, gave them a complete list, and I had to laugh. I was forbidden to lift a finger to help them, so I baked a plain spongy cake and sugared strawberries to pile over it. Sita and I had picked quarts of the ripe fruit two days before.

The lilt and accent of their voices, the sweet smell of the fruit, brought London back to me, Seth whistling in from work with berries as large as small apples in his pack, the two of us laughing and relaxing together, making love in the still warmth of the night. My face grew stiff with the pleasant expression I forced there. Too many memories, and too glaring the obvious absence of Seth's own family from among the intimate gathering of English friends. Even Sister Dibble did not attempt to justify Victoria or make apologies for her. And though I thought I cared not a whit, yet the cruel rebuff cut deep. When they left I collapsed gratefully, not even attempting to fool Winston, whose eyes had already rested with concern on me several times.

He made me put my feet up and brought cool lemonade for me to sip and a cold cloth for my face. I did try to smile and make little of it, beyond fatigue and the heat, but of course, both of us knew.

"The garden is planted," he said, as though giving an accounting, "and everything here in order. I think you should take Brother Winters up on his offer and work in the store, Mother."

I removed the cool cloth and stared at him.

"I can handle things, you know that. I'll do all the weeding and churning, the washing and other heavy work—you don't have to be gone the whole day. I told him too many hours on your feet at one time would not be good for you."

"*You* told him?"

"I ran into him at the post office the other day."

"I see. And you two had a little discussion about me."

He blushed just slightly, so I knew my surmisal was true. "You both felt sorry for me, and thought I needed something—"

I bit my tongue, wishing the words unspoken as soon as they were out of my mouth.

"No." I could feel that I had hurt his feelings, though he plunged bravely on. "I thought you wanted to do it, anyway, and now the time seems just right. That's all."

"I agree. And I *have* given it serious consideration. I'm just a little afraid. That's why I snapped at you."

I was not sure I liked the fact that the more honest, the more adult I was with Winston, the more he relaxed and accepted and understood.

"Being in this condition, you know, what if people think it unseemly, or simply gawk at me? What if—"

"Don't worry, Mother. Pay them no mind! You are so beautiful and clever, all the men will wish you to help them. Let the women's hackles go up—you can't help it if you're prettier than all of them."

"I'll try to remember that," I smiled, loving him so fiercely that I hurt inside.

So it was arranged. Though the fear I had spoken of to Winston was real I was amazed at how quickly Julian Winters's predictions came to pass. The men were charmed by me, and although a few flirted overtly, most behaved in a proper and decorous fashion, simply appreciating, I believe, the opportunity of being waited upon by a gracious and helpful woman whose looks pleased their eye. I could have pressed my advantage and alienated the wives and other women who watched me covertly, but I was careful to do just the opposite and courted their kindness discreetly, even openly at times, as in the case of Sister Hammond, a handsome older woman who was always impeccably attired. I made a point of asking her advice concerning which bonnets to wear with which gowns, which bodices would look best with which skirts. And I praised her taste and discernment, which I could do very honestly. After awhile, bit by bit, she warmed to me. I had thought at first, naively, that I would occasion the sisters' pity, being a widow, without a man's protection and care. But I had not taken into account the dark shadow of polygamy which constantly played over their lives. I was a young widow, pleasant and comely, interesting by very virtue of my difference from the other women about. As summer drew on and my condition became more evident I could almost see the ladies relax. When Julian, who noticed also, made comment upon it I replied simply, "I no longer pose such a threat to them now that they see I'm with child."

He caught on at once. "Oh, I see, yes, polygamous marriages." He rubbed his chin thoughtfully. He was a fine-looking man in his forties with a full head of thick golden hair. "I had to sign a pact with my own wife, you know, before she would let me hire you here."

I struck at him playfully with the feathered hat I was carrying. But I wondered later if there had been any truth to his words.

Winston, of course, got on beautifully without me. And, if truth be known, I enjoyed being out and about, meeting people, seeing what went on in the city. I had never spent much time in Nauvoo, always taking my walks down by the river and, when not involved in household duties, keeping pretty much to myself. There were so many people here, and each one of them interesting, with a different story to tell, with a background humorous or tragic, or a magical mingling of the two. I wished I had skill with a pen and could draw out the passion and pathos of their lives so that perhaps someone, years and years later, could stumble upon my words and feel a whole lost reality spark into existence again. It was a fancy I entertained now and again as I became acquainted with Nauvoo.

Chapter Fifteen

𝒥

As if to try me, I had the whole long summer to live through before this baby would come. We had little rain, and the sun rode white in the heavens. Winston took to watering his delicate vegetables and the flowers he nurtured. Some of the fields took on a brown tinge, but the corn, with its glistening green leaves, continued to thrive. Brother Wilson said that if you go into the fields on a hot night you can hear the corn squeak as it grows.

Mary Jane had timidly approached me when my condition became evident. "I'm glad there's to be a baby," she said. "Will you let me come and help you when the time comes?"

I had nodded my head, then on second thought wrapped my arms quickly round her. I had not wanted my true feelings to show. So I had been my whole life, and I was learning but slowly. No one can approach a person who holds others at arms' length as I did, sometimes in timidity, sometimes in pride, sometimes from nothing more than a perverse desire to be by myself and not be bothered—and, I suppose that is a form of selfishness, after all.

Late in June there was a flash storm with winds cold enough for April and such a torrent of rain that much flooding occurred along the streams and rivers. It is always messy in Illinois after a rain. I remember I was picking up branches that had littered the flower gardens, Sita beside me gathering the little ones which were too hard to bend over for. I had been sweeping for nearly an hour already and there was a burning pain building in the small of my back. *If Winston were here,* I remember thinking, *he would insist that I sit and put my feet up while he fetched some cold lemonade.* Then, for no accountable reason, I thought, *If Seth were here he would make a game of it all, and I would not even notice the ache in my back until later, and then he would have rubbed it for me.*

After we had cleared away the bulk of the debris we headed back to the house. At first I did not even recognize the man walking down the street toward us. It was not until he called out to me and I stopped and took a good look at him that I realized it was Seth's father. His large figure appeared stooped and slumped over, and he appeared as if each foot, as he moved it, was too heavy to lift.

I waited, perplexed. Obviously he was coming for some reason. I invited him into the house and poured the last of my cool buttermilk for him, remembering randomly that it was a favorite of his.

"Might I speak with you alone, Lottie?" he asked, nodding slightly in Sarah's direction. Then I knew this was to be something of terrible import, though I could not imagine what. Grace was asleep in the next room. I sent Sita off to play with the chickens, wishing unaccountably that Winston would come back from the smithy's where he had taken the old horse to be shod.

"I know no easy way to tell you," Kenneth Taylor began. "About a hundred miles south of here, after the flash floods, they found a body washed up. No one thereabouts could identify it, but they discovered Julian Winters's trademark etched along the inside of his belt leather, so they sent word down here."

He paused, mercifully. I realized my hands were clutching the arms of the chair and I was having difficulty breathing. He heaved his large bulk from his seat, walked over and poured a glass of water, then brought it to me. "Drink this now." He pressed my fingers around the glass and I did as he said.

"In such cases they require someone to identify the body. First off they asked for the widow, but when they learned I was his father, they said I would do."

"Who . . . how did they . . ." I could not get my voice to form words properly.

"Sheriff knows me, pretty much knows the situation."

"Of course," I managed.

"I saw the body, Charlotte, and there is no doubt it is our Seth."

The way he spoke those last two words—"our Seth"— made me shudder. I dared not look into his eyes.

"You may rest assured, and in some peace, I pray, that we can lay him to rest."

What is left of him, I thought gruesomely. *Why did this have to happen?* I had pictured him, foolishly perhaps, lying at the bottom of the river, covered over with a layer of soft silt and sand—dark and protected—not fish-gnawed and bloated—

"If I have done wrong, I am sorry. But I thought only to spare you."

My attentions were drawn reluctantly back to the quiet man sitting before me. "Spare me?" I repeated stupidly.

"I did not wish you to have to see him . . . that way."

I raised my gaze to his and for the first time saw the horror that burned in his eyes. He had taken upon himself this gruesome cross *to spare me!* I thought to myself, *This man is nearly a stranger to me, yet Seth is his child. Seth is the baby he cradled in his arms, the son he pinned his hopes on, the charming, gentle infant he watched grow into a man.* I remembered suddenly Seth saying to me, "I am like my father's people, soft-spoken, gentle, dreamers . . ."

"You did the proper thing," I replied. "God bless you for it." I shuddered involuntarily. "You are right, I could not have borne it, I could not—"

He was on his feet again, with amazing agility for one so large. "Think no more on it." His voice held a pleading note. "Seth would not want it that way. It is a black shame it had to happen. Try to forget it as soon as possible."

He had placed his broad, well-fleshed hands on the arms of my chair, close to mine. I moved one hand and laid it over his. "How can I thank you?"

He was truly discomfited, stammering a little and fidgeting

where he stood. His eyes said, *I would never have considered allowing you to suffer such a horror while I had the power to prevent it.* But his reply was, "We've not done justice by you, child, and that is the truth of it, and I am rightly ashamed."

I gave the hand I held a little squeeze. "Seth understands," I said, "he always understood—certain conditions. And so do I."

I cannot say why I added that last bit, but it made a difference. Kenneth Taylor sighed and moved reluctantly away.

"Shall I make arrangements . . . ?" He was uncertain again.

I had not been thinking, but I answered instinctively. "Must this be noised about? How hushed can we keep it?" I was thinking only of Winston. "Would to heaven you could bury him out back behind that apple tree he loved—by night, with not a soul knowing . . ." I shuddered myself at the picture I drew.

"The idea is a fair one," he responded, to my surprise. "But I'll tell you how I think it should be done."

At first I was adamant, in arms at the very idea. But he won me over wholly when he said, "If you do not tell the boy, my dear, he will be bound to find out some way—through Victoria's spite, if no other. Think what harm that would do. Mark my words, this will prove good for him, this act of service, this tender office."

Hopeless dreamers . . . I gave him a wan smile. "You are right," I agreed.

"Leave it in my hands," he said, patting my arm.

Thus it came to pass on the last day of June, before first light, a small procession of friends and family formed a hushed half-circle around the hole Winston and Seth's father had dug. Brother Dibble said a few well-chosen words, and so did Jacob Bell, who had come over on the ship to Zion with us. Then Winston, to my surprise, stood and paid a brief tribute to the young man he had loved.

"He was more my real father than my own," he said, and there was a proud light in his eye. "It was love that made him mine and me his. He gave me the best within himself, and that was a lot. He gave me the chance to have the gospel in my life, and he showed me what it could do, inside myself, if I let it."

I was choking on my tears. It would grieve Winston if I cried, and what if I shattered his terrible composure?

"And one last thing," he was saying. "He made my mother happy. I had never seen her happy before—and so I thank him most of all for that."

Phyllis and Mary Jane, along with some of the London sisters, sang "Abide with Me," one of Seth's favorite hymns. I did not hear any of the verses or even the dignified strains of the music. My heart was ringing with the words Winston had spoken, trembling with pain and joy.

Those days following the burial were difficult for me. I found myself walking a lot—thinking, trying not to think, sometimes wearing myself out, my only means of defense at the moment. On one of these walks I found myself passing along "Brick Row" or "Widow's Row," a group of low buildings on the corner of Main and Kimball. I counted the doors; there were ten—ten small rooms facing into a garden plot, that was all. Haven for those who had no one to provide a living for themselves and their children. I shuddered. I could so easily have been there, huddled and miserable, like those first days in London.

As I watched, a woman approached the door nearest to me. She wore a shawl over her head, despite the warmth of the weather. The shawl was faded and nearly threadbare. I took a step or two back and began to discreetly lower my eyes. But she paused only feet away from me. "May I be of assistance?" she said.

By her voice she was at least as young as I was. "No thank you." I smiled as brightly as I could and began to move on.

I could feel her eyes following me. Uncomfortable and curious despite myself, I glanced back. She was leaning against the fence, as though she needed it to support herself. "May I help you?" I said. "Are you newly arrived here?"

"Yes. Came from Boston on the riverboat only last week."

"Do you live here?"

She nodded.

"Alone?"

"With two of my children."

"Where are the others?" The wording of her reply had made the question seem natural, though now I realized that it probably sounded rude.

"Two are with me, two remained back with my husband."

"I see."

"No you don't."

There was a warm defiance in her tone which led me forward. She looked young, my age at the most. Her eyes were a pale blue, as delicately veined as a bluebell newly bloomed. She had let the shawl drop to her shoulders to reveal a mass of red curls that appeared to reach nearly to her waist.

I turned fully round and walked back until I was close to her. Only then did I see the tears in her eyes.

"Do not mistake yourself," I said softly, "the way I have already done once or twice, making a fool of myself." I smiled wryly. "The things people have suffered do not always show in their eyes. I have been walking aimlessly, stubbornly, because I do not want to go home and face the three children who depend on me. My husband died six months ago."

"And you carry his child." She thrust her chin forward, peering at me. "Was he a good husband?"

"Yes. The best of husbands." I could see a sad, unwelcome triumph fill her eyes. "But I was married before when I was very young, in India. That husband was as cruel and decadent as Seth was wise and good."

Her gaze now reflected a cautious confusion.

"Are your children inside?" I asked.

She nodded.

"Why don't you collect them and all come home with me for a bite to eat? We can get acquainted." I held my hand out. "I am Charlotte Taylor."

She touched the tips of her fingers to mine briefly. "I am Merin Campbell," she replied. "Stay there just a moment, I'll be right back."

That was the beginning. I often wondered if I was fated to walk by the Brick Row that day. Each of us, in her own way, needed the other. I was nearly twenty-five, Merin but twenty-three, yet she had given birth to four children, one right after another, the first son being born when she was just sixteen.

"You don't look much older than my Thomas," she had said wistfully to Winston that first day we all met. Thomas, I learned, was seven, Ralph six; they had been left with their father, at his insistence.

"He didn't rightfully care that much if the girls and I left," she stated with a candid openness that was almost childlike. "'You follow those Mormons, you do it at your own risk,'" she quoted him. "'Wasn't me who changed, Merin; you're the one who got those fool notions into your head.' He liked saying that." She shrugged her thin shoulders in resignation.

"So you were acquainted with the group of Saints with whom you traveled?" I asked.

"Not really, not more than three or four of them. He wouldn't allow me to go to meeting, you see. He beat me right properly each time I attempted it."

I leaned back in my chair, aghast, trying not to show it.

"It's all right," she said softly. "He wasn't that mean when I married him; he just kept getting worse and worse." She sighed and picked up one of the scones she had buttered, plopping a large spoonful of jelly on top of it. "The hard thing—the only really hard thing—was leaving my boys behind."

"Will he be good to them?" I bit my lip, but I had to ask it.

"Fair enough. They're menfolk like himself. He'll raise 'em hard, but I don't think he'll be cruel to them." She sighed, and it was like a little shudder going all through her. For my part, I could think of nothing to say. We ate in silence for a few minutes, then Winston jumped up from his chair.

"Would you like me to take all the girls out to see the new kittens in the barn?"

"That would be wonderful, Winston," I replied warmly. Grace was nearly two, and she worshiped the ground Winston trod upon. I believe she heaped all her affections for Seth on top of what she already felt for a very indulgent brother.

"That's a fine, fine boy you've got there," Merin observed after the children had all tramped out and the silence of the room gathered companionably around us.

"Indeed," I agreed. "There is so much to him that at times it almost frightens me." I considered for a moment, then added, "He is not really my own. His mother was my husband's first wife. She died when he was only a baby of two. I've been his mother ever since."

She nodded thoughtfully. "It's a certain thing he adores you, that's easy to see."

"He has been my strength in many tight situations," I confided, "in ways that should not be required of a mere child."

"I do know about that. Some were born old from the beginning, if you take my meaning. He's most likely one of them. You couldn't change his nature if you tried to. Besides, I highly suspect you've done much the same thing for him—and will do many more times before he's full grown."

She smiled at her own words. I relaxed and smiled, too. I had not truly relaxed, truly let my guard down for these many long months. I had never in my memory, since Roselyn, had a friend my own age.

Merin and I worked together as much, actually more, than we simply talked or spent pleasant time in each other's company. I taught her the ways of Nauvoo. I shared my vegetables with her, found her a job at one of the local millineries, kept her children with mine when she had no one to watch them, provided her with eggs, cream, and a gray-striped kitten from the litter in the barn. She sewed new frocks for my daughters and pants for Winston, whose legs seemed to be growing at least half an inch longer each day. She even attacked my pile of mending and made new curtains for my kitchen windows, and she gave me the gift of song.

She had a voice as high and pure as a bird, trilling as sweetly as Winston's canary we had been forced to leave behind in London. Every time she came to the house either Winston or I would beg her to sing for us, and she always demurely obliged. She knew more songs that I thought had ever been written, lullabies like "Hushabye Baby" and "Bye, Baby Bunting"; old Scotch love songs like "Annie Laurie," "Flow Gently Sweet Afton," and "Turn Ye Tae Me." She knew songs from America which I had never heard before: "Oh, Susannah," "Down in the Valley," "Come All Ye Fair and Tender Maidens," and a dozen such more. We laughed and cried together, as the music moved us.

"I wish you had a piano," she said out of nowhere one night.

"You can play?" Winston asked in awe.

"Circles around most, my boy," she said, winking at him. "I know minuets and marches, concertos from Mozart and Beethoven, as well as songs like you've heard."

Our evenings were no longer solemn and quiet affairs. Merin sang melodically, and as Winston and I learned the songs, we joined with her. Our hours were expanding and so were our hearts, the shadows giving way before the brightness of increasing love.

CHAPTER SIXTEEN

AUGUST. AS I FIGURED IT, MY BABY WOULD be born in August, and late in the month, at that. Perhaps it was the fever that brought on the birth; perhaps it was the other way round. I remember tying the pale vines of honeysuckle to the trellis Seth had built along the south wall of the house. I remember drawing in the delicate aroma which I usually loved, but which now made me feel sick—sick and dizzy and suddenly too weak to stand up on my legs.

By the time Winston fetched Abigail Haven I was shivering and trembling all over. She took one look at me and sent me straight to my bed. Here my memory grows dim. There were days of fever in a darkened room; burning skin and parched throat followed by chills that seemed to rattle my bones; Winston wandering in and out, talking reassuringly to me in his low, solemn way; broths and juices; a back that ached to the point of burning; and a tightness in my swollen stomach that would scarcely allow me to breathe.

Abigail assured me it was really only two days before the child came. She said I rallied splendidly for the birth, but I hardly remember that. Emma Roselyn came—for that is what I was determined to call her—with as little trouble as possible. Abigail called in a wet nurse, Merin took Sita and Grace, and Abigail and Winston together began to fight for my life.

Some of that period will remain forever blank to me, days spent in that twilight region where both thought and will are suspended along with awareness. Abigail said my body fought well. She also said that I took a turn for the better when I heard that piercing loud voice that somehow combined a Cockney accent with the easy drawl of the South.

I cannot remember. When I first opened my eyes to focus them upon Emma's loved, florid face I reached out to her with both arms, and even her gentle hug caused me to wince with the pain in my head. Much later Abigail helped me sit up against the pillows, and Emma regaled me for an hour with tales of New Orleans and the colorful figures that moved in and out of her life. Days passed again before I wrapped up in a quilt against the hot August day and walked, with one on each side of me, to sit for half an hour in Seth's big overstuffed chair.

It all remains hazy still, because it was hazy in the living. It may seem very strange, but I did not even ask after my baby until the second time I was fully awake. I don't believe I realized or remembered that she had been born. When Emma blared, "I want to see my namesake! Where have you hidden the bairn?" I blanched, then colored with a flood of emotions. When Abigail laid her into the curve of my arms I thought, *She looks like Seth.* And something in her gaze, young as she was, made me think she would be like him, too.

I cried then—in relief, in sorrow, in self-pity, in joy.

"How did you know to come?" I asked Emma on about the fourth day I had been out of bed.

"I'll let you guess that, lovey!" She cooed. So I turned at once upon Winston.

"I wrote to Emmer," he said. "I thought she should be here. I thought she would want to."

She reached over and gave him a sound, enveloping hug.

I had not written her about Seth's death, and she blamed me for that a little. But putting it down on paper, attempting to explain tragedy and emotion in so blank a manner—I shrank from the very attempt. *Besides,* I had reasoned, *I will be compelled to write again when this baby comes. So I shall do the whole wretched business but once—and later, when it will be somewhat easier.*

In that I for once had judged right. With Emma there, a physical and emotional bolster, I wrote to May in London, to my brothers at their respective schools, and to both Ernest and Marion at Baddenwell house. Then I tried to forget it and what reactions might be forthcoming. There was certainly enough to divert my attentions right here!

Abigail continued coming almost daily to help me, and Emma kept us both in stitches telling of rogues and scoundrels, ladies of ill repute, naughty but wealthy gentlemen, haughty but wealthy ladies—all of whom seemed to contribute in some way to the wealth our Emmer was accruing. I thought it amazing, yet wonderful.

"I shall have me'self a husband by Christmas," she informed us. "That is, if I want one."

"Well, tell us about him," I urged.

"Him?" she blared like a Canada goose. "Bless my 'art, love, there are five of 'em."

"Five?" I cried.

"Aye, five, if you can believe it, to choose among!"

I could believe it. She may be a bit loud, a bit brash, but Emma possessed a charm of her own. That, combined with her good heart, was a winning combination. Besides, she had lost weight this past year, and I saw for the first time the comely shape beneath the bulk.

"Well, well," I teased her. "It must be true that they breed real men out here in the American wilderness! To think of *five men* who would fancy themselves capable of handling the likes of you."

She simmered with pleasure. Oh, how good it was to have her with me again!

When she was not working, Merin came and sang for us, sang till her throat was hoarse with bringing the silken notes forth. Then it would be our turn to ply her with drinks and food, to fetch a basin of cool water for her tired feet and soft sugared candies Emma had brought from New Orleans to pamper her sweet tooth. Oh, but those were the times! August melted away, but we took little mind of it. We lived in a world of our own, savoring every golden moment before reality, as it eventually must, pushed its way back in.

᳓

A strange thing happened the night before Emma left us, so strange and so real that I know it was somehow intended. I was awakened by the baby, who needed feeding; and when I could not settle her I took to walking the parlor, crooning softly, hoping to lull her to sleep. Emma came out, rubbing her eyes and wrapped up in quilts like a bear, to keep me company. We talked only softly, speaking of more serious matters under the soft cover of an unlit room in the middle of the night.

"Will you be all right, hon, when I leave?" she asked me.

"I believe so," I replied.

"What o' the future? Why don't you come back to New Orleans with me?" What a laconic slur there was to the words when she spoke them. "You would have your pick o' men there, Lottie. You could make a good life."

When I did not reply she knew what was in my mind, and it annoyed her, to say the least.

"I cannot fathom it, this blind dedication to such a harsh way of life. What is it for now, lovey? With Seth gone, what's it all for?"

I could not answer her; the terms I must use were as foreign to her as the experiences they attempted to represent. Yet her question haunted me; I wondered for the space of a heartbeat what it would be like to *let go!* To live in the warmth and ease of Louisiana affluence, or to return to England and make a life of consequence there for myself, free from the weight of this constant expectation, this constant struggling within!

I had no sooner entertained the thought, brief though it was, when I heard the first faint sounds. My head came up. "Did you hear that, Emma?" I whispered.

"I cannot say for certain; I b'lieve I heard something."

We sat in the dark room together, all our senses gathered and poised. It came again, this time louder, more definite, the notes falling like fragrant petals on water, sweet and warm to my ears.

"Saints bless us!" Emma hissed. "What's going on here?"

The clear whistling came once again.

It cannot be! I thought. Yet such a tender warmth enveloped me, such a quiet, all-pervading assurance—"It is Seth's whistle," I said.

"Do old houses have echoes?" Emma shuddered.

"This is not an old house," I replied. The whistling came once more; musical, suggestive of laughter.

"It is Seth saying hello to you, Emma, and reminding me of his love."

She stared, bug-eyed, wondering, I believe, why I was not dissolving into a puddle of tears. But *happiness* was the only sensation I was feeling, happiness like a balm, like an elixir driving throughout my whole system. I smiled at her through clear eyes. "I know what I am doing," I said. "I am staying right here, where Seth placed me." *Where Heavenly Father placed me,* I wished I could add.

She shook her head, but she was no longer inclined to argue. When I saw her off the next day she kissed her hand to me till the boat disappeared on the great tide of water, too small a speck against sky and river to make anything out.

It was my fault, my doing altogether. I had told Mary Jane that I would call upon her to help me when Seth's baby came. But I was not there in any practical sense of the term, and by the time I had my wits about me enough to send for her I received only a terse reply back, in Victoria's hand: *You have help there in plenty, and I have need of Mary's assistance myself.*

I let it rest. I had not time nor energy nor heart to fight what seemed a losing battle. Emma left and by mid-September I went back to work at the store. Ingeniously Merin and I juggled our schedules so that our hours away from our children seldom overlapped. With Winston's help we never left them unattended, and most of the time one or the other of us was there with them ourselves.

I wanted Winston to return for the winter's term of schooling, but he flatly refused. "This is where I belong," he maintained.

"Not at all," I argued. "An education is essential to any kind of a future that might prove attractive to you."

"I shall get my education," he said resolutely, and I could tell he had something I did not yet know in his mind.

It was good to dress up and go out among people again. I felt strong now, and with the cooler weather my energy seemed to return.

Every minute was busy. When I was not at the shop or caring for the children, when I was not cleaning house or cooking, milking or gathering eggs, I was preparing flax for the wheel, preserving apples, making jams and pickles and a goodly supply of candles for the long winter nights. Merin and I worked out systems of spelling and assisting each other, and the work went more quickly that way. I was not alone. As the days shortened and the gray blanket of night settled over low land and river, I did not feel that terrible aching emptiness in my heart.

After a very short while Winston's plan became evident; he could not put it into action without some knowledge of it coming to me. I thought it an excellent scheme, and I knew he could handle it. He had charmed Sister Johnson, a neighboring lady who ran a small school, into tutoring him privately three evenings a week. She had four strapping sons of her own, so there was little he could offer for payment in return. I was tickled when Merin confided the clever "arrangement": she would give piano lessons to Sister Johnson's two daughters and one of her sons, her recompense coming at last from Winston, who would tend the children and do chores for her a designated number of hours each week.

"I like the chance it gives me just to play," she argued when I raised a weak protest. "You have to admire the boy's enterprise and audacity." So I said nothing to Winston and his "arrangement" stood. My remaining concern was that his life seemed constituted of all work and responsibility; he seldom made an effort to join with his old friends in innocent sports and games.

"Give him awhile," Merin responded when I confided my fears to her. "I think he feels guilty when he plays; it is too bound up in his mind still with what happened to your husband; thus it is more punishment than pleasure to him."

I knew she was right. The best I could do right now was to

organize my own time to free Winston as much as I could. At first he seemed to sense what I was doing and unconsciously created new tasks to fill the spared time. After awhile he began to relax, then at last to look forward to this precious freedom.

As for myself, I tried to take each day as it came, grateful for what I had. Gratitude had become a real part of my life since I first met Merin and made myself face how many women were worse off, much worse than myself. I was all right, no matter what happened, as long as I remembered that.

I had learned much about fashion and fabric working for Julian Winters; of all the things I was grateful for, my association with him, and what it brought into my life, ranked high. That autumn on my twenty-fifth birthday he gave me one gift—and, inadvertently, another.

With much flourish and flattery he presented me with a length of exquisite nainsook, fine combed cotton cloth which is excellent for the making of shirtwaists, undersleeves, and delicate chemises. I was well pleased. Then he handed me a large box wrapped round with rose colored ribbon. I guessed what might be inside. I untied the silken cords and drew out a bonnet of brushed felt, as gray and as soft as a dove's throat. The crown was shaped to sit back on the head with the brim tightly formed, with a length of shirred silk bordering it, to frame the wearer's face. Long crepe lisse streamers floated down either side. It was the kind of hat I could never afford for myself. I brushed tears aside, vexed at the unexpected rise of emotion.

"You'll wear it as prettily as any woman in Nauvoo," Julian said, to cover the awkward moment.

That same afternoon he came back from the bank muttering and sputtering. He threw down a copy of the *Nauvoo Neighbor.* "Just look at that."

One of his competitors had come up with some very fancy advertising: well-posed pictures with alluring descriptions beneath them, while his own plain, straightforward listing of goods was stuck somewhere at the back.

"I can't compete with this," he grumbled, striking his fist against the polished wood counter. "I'm creative with clothes,

Lottie, and I have the best value in town, but I'm a bumbler when it comes down to words."

"Let me try my hand at it."

"He raised his head and stared at me appraisingly. "You really want to?"

"I really want to."

"Think you could do a—" He interrupted himself, chuckling under his breath. "Well, I shan't lose a thing by letting you have a chance at it. Very well. Give it a try."

Thus innocently did I creep up to the edges of the dream I had entertained lightly this past year. By Christmas I had learned the hang of it. The descriptions of our goods read almost like a story:

Your husband has invited you to an evening at the theatre. Take off your stiff, pinching work shoes and slide your foot into one of our satin slippers. Buttercup yellow, Cinderella gold, Arabian turquoise, peacock and fuschia—every hue of the rainbow—petal soft . . .

At first Julian laughed at me and bellowed that no one would print such rubbish. But once they did our sales soared and he had to send to New Orleans for shipments to replenish his stock. It was harmless enough, though a bit overdone. But as Christmas approached I sent in a piece about loving one's neighbor being an essential part of loving the Savior, succoring his children, as he would if he were here. To my delight, they printed it. A little thing, really, but it infused me with a wonderful sense of satisfaction.

Perhaps Emma knew how difficult the holidays would be for us, for she surely went overboard, sending bright be-ribboned packages, bonbons and pralines in greater abundance than last year, and lengths of lace for Merin, who had admired her work. Late in the afternoon, two days before Christmas, when the air was crackling cold and smelling of snow, a wagon drew up to the house. Something very large was wrapped up in a crate in the back. I stood at the window, wiping flour from my hands, watching the men heave it out. It took several of them to carry it up to the house. It struck me suddenly, as they grew nearer, what it was they carried and where it must have come from. I put my hand to my mouth, overcome at the mere idea.

Sure enough, it had my name on it, with a note in Emma's own hand. "For you and your songbird," she had written, "and for quiet little Grace, who I believe has some music within her soul."

The piano was cherry wood. I ran my hand lightly along the rich grain. I could not take my eyes from it. When Merin came over that night we blindfolded her and led her to it. I think she smelled it before she had crossed the room. What joy and squealing and delighted laughter followed! She pulled out the polished bench carefully and sat down to the keys. We sang Christmas carols until we were hoarse. Then while I nursed Emma Roselyn and the four little girls sat down to cookies and milk and Winston to his studies, Merin played from the classics for us, ending with "Glory to God" from Handel's *Messiah*. The notes, when she was finished, still sent a thrill of pleasure through the house.

How hallowed is this season, as Shakespeare said. We made it through Christmas, but the worst, the real hurdle was yet to come.

We did not even attempt to pretend it away, Winston and I. But for some reason neither of us could face the outer world. I told Julian I would not be coming in. We baked Seth's favorite cake in the morning, read passages from books that we liked, plunked out a few tunes on the shiny piano, played simple games with the girls. In the evening, just as the pale sun was slanting across the low tree branches, we walked out to the grave. I recited Wordsworth's "Sonnet" and Scott's "Love of Country," two of Seth's favorites, and Winston, his voice thin and solemn against the cold air, read from the Book of Mormon scriptures that Seth had loved. Then we sang, the little girls with us, some of his favorite hymns: "A Mighty Fortress Is Our God," Parley Pratt's "The Morning Breaks," and "The Spirit of God Like a Fire Is Burning," hallowed by its use at the dedication of the temple in Kirtland when angels joined in the singing and heavenly messengers appeared.

When the icy air began to burn in our throats we knelt on the hard, swept floor of the earth and offered up a prayer, for his soul and for ours, and for the peace which we craved.

My fingers were frozen stiff by the time we got back to the house. I stirred up the fire, fed the baby, and put the children to bed. When I returned, Winston was sitting in the shadows; he had not lit a lamp. I sat beside him and realized he was crying. I drew him into my arms and the anguish I had held back all evening mingled with his—tears for the dead, and tears for the living, and that is how it should be. We grieve in our need and our weakness, because heaven is hidden from us, and the narrow view of today is sometimes too dreary, too dismal for our eternal spirits to bear—spirits that long for the shining realms which call to us in our dreams.

I held Winston fiercely against me and wept the blind, bitter tears of a mortal, feeling nothing beyond that misery, nothing at all.

CHAPTER SEVENTEEN

THE MAN WAS A STRANGER TO ME; I saw nothing in him that looked familiar at all.

"I supposed you might have known by now who I was." He spoke with a certain arrogance which I found offensive.

"Pray enlighten me, sir," I said, glancing purposefully behind me to where customers wandered the aisles.

"This is not the time or place," he replied, as though remembering himself. "I will come in search of you later."

With that he turned on his heel and left. The irritation of the moment faded as I became immersed in the demands of the day.

I did not at first recognize him as he approached me on the street and tipped his hat respectfully. He was not really a bad-looking man, light of hair, with good brown eyes, but his face was too narrow for me, with a prominent nose, high cheekbones, and a chin that was weak.

"We are well met," he beamed. "Now I can introduce myself. I am Seth's cousin, Aaron Taylor. I hail from Bainbridge, Massachusetts. He must have told you of me."

"He told me he had an uncle in Massachusetts. I had the impression he both respected and admired him."

"That is us!" The arrogance was back again, chilling the effect of his enthusiasm, at least for me.

"That is your father, you mean," I amended pointedly. "How long have you been in Nauvoo?"

"These six months and more, but I thought it not seemly that I call upon you before."

"Not seemly?" I could not help repeating him, though I did not quite mean to mock him. It was now May, so he must have been here for Christmas, for the anniversary date of Seth's death.

"Seth's death was a grievous loss to all of us," he intoned. "He was held in the highest esteem among his own people."

"Did you, yourself, know Seth?" I asked.

He winced a little, which gave me a perverse pleasure.

"No, no, I cannot say that I did."

"Then do not quote to me the opinions of others; they are of no interest to me."

He seemed duly subdued. I should have felt ashamed of my rudeness, but for some reason I did not. He walked with me all the way to my house. When we reached my front pathway he paused.

"I hope you prosper well here in the city," I said politely, by way of dismissal.

"It has been a pleasure conversing with you, Cousin Charlotte," he responded, as though I had not spoken at all. "Please, when would it be convenient for me to call upon you again?"

"Convenient?" I echoed.

He appeared a bit discomfited and drew his breath into his narrow chest.

"I should like to come as a suitor. . . . I should like your permission to . . . that is . . ."

My chilling gaze was at last getting through to him. "For what possible reason?" I asked.

He squirmed a little, and I saw that if I offended his pride too much further, he would become little and mean.

"It is not right for a woman as young and attractive as yourself to be left a widow. I am moved with compassion for you. I felt, being part of the family . . . I felt it right and appropriate . . ."

I could not help myself. "How can you possibly know what is appropriate, sir, where I am concerned?"

"I only thought, I only hoped—"

I bit my lip. "I am touched by your thoughtful and honorable attentions, Aaron Taylor. But you do not even know me, and is too early . . . too soon for me to even think of another husband . . ."

He groped for my hand. "Say no more. I am sorry to have grieved you by even mentioning the matter. But I may call upon you again?"

"In time . . ." I was amazed that my voice could sound so gentle when I was seething inside.

"That is sufficient!" He kissed the gloved hand he held, then let it drop. After a little more obsequiousness he turned and left me. I was nearly weak with relief.

So much for Seth's family, I thought as I turned in my door. *So much for the lot of the strange, narrow creatures. How did such a fine spirit as his come to settle among them at all?*

We had made it through the dark winter to spring and its renewal of the back-breaking cycle of planting and harvesting, garnering the earth's fruits against yet another winter when no such work can be done. But, oh, the earth was sweet and tender with life that year, and the renewal of the spirit accompanied the renewal of labor.

I had received replies back from my English friends, and they had been very much what I had expected. May could not help saying "I told you so." Her words were cruel, but behind them stood a sincere concern for my sanity and well-being, so I could not entirely fault her. Marion, though less cautious in expressing it, felt much the same way. "You have wasted this precious time," she wrote. "Do you intend to come home now and begin where you should have two years ago?"

It broke my heart, and in truth, it tried me sorely. I went out to Seth's grave and sat alone beneath the swaying green branches and poured my soul out to him. *Baddenwell mine!* A life of ease and comfort, a secure, respected station, the fruition of the daydreams I had cherished since I was a child.

Seth would have understood; he understood while he was living, and he possessed the power to gently nudge me aright, or to somehow shame me into judging issues honestly without hurting my feelings—he was a master at that. It was not that the deep, committed part of myself was wavering, only that the human portion longed for the lighter, easier way. I stayed there for a long time, but I did not come back really comforted, rather resigned, perhaps even determined to do what was wise and honorable, though not thoroughly reconciled to the decision and its demands.

With the letter from Marion came a note from Ernest to Winston. When I wrote back Winston handed me his own carefully penned response. "Don't read it," he cautioned, so I resisted the temptation and slipped it in with my own. At Christmas Marion had sent some handkerchiefs of my grandmother's to Sita. Sarah was six now, and Winston had taught her her letters, but I was surprised at the skill and care reflected in the note she wrote back in thanks. As I sealed the packet and gave it to Winston to take to the post office I wondered if this would be the last of it, if they would wean themselves away from their frail hopes regarding us and steel their hearts against us. I wondered; but I prayed it would not be so.

I did not receive an answer from my brothers until April, and then it was penned by Hugh to inform me of the inevitable: Arthur had been sent to India at last, based in Calcutta for the present, and adjusting well—which meant the reality had blasted his boyish expectations, and he did not find it either magical or easy, but rather another rough step toward manhood. I prayed for him even harder than I had been given to doing before.

Another hot summer in Nauvoo. How could any of us guess it would be Joseph Smith's last? He was *the Prophet*, he was as mighty as the heavens, as good and gentle as I pictured the Savior to be. He was the heartbeat of the restored gospel, and he would go on and on, despite the combined powers of earth and hell that had always raged over his head.

The experience of many of the Saints in the city went back to Kirtland, or at least to Missouri. When the rumblings of persecution grew loud enough, like thunder over the still cornfields at evening, they began to take notice; they began to show fear. Polygamy was a natural target. All women and men of honor shrank from the prospect; and mispracticed, misrepresented, it could be used to ignite dozens of fires of righteous indignation and wrath. Joseph's political aspirations were another irritant, though men of integrity and sound judgment easily recognized the superiority of his nature. The *Iowa Democrat* wrote: "If superior talent, genius, and intelligence, combined with virtue, integrity and enlarged views, are any guarantee to General Smith's being elected, we think that he will be 'a full team of himself.'"

Most of us were only vaguely aware of the gathering forces and the heavy shadow they would soon cast over Nauvoo. Such is the nature of people who choose to see only that which they want to, disregarding all else.

When the *Nauvoo Expositor* was printed every heart in the city was sickened with disgust at its lurid evils and lies. But when the city council declared it a public nuisance and ordered it to be removed, Julian prophesied dire consequences.

"They had every right to do that, legally and morally," I argued.

"Of course they had," Julian agreed. "And if this had happened in any other American city the action would have been supported, even lauded. But not in the city of the Mormons— not the city of Joseph Smith."

I felt a cold shudder run all the way through me. "They can do nothing against him. He hasn't broken the law."

"Lottie, my dear"—Julian's countenance was so dark with misery and concern that it frightened me—"do you not know that the Whig party has formed an alliance with men who call themselves 'the anti-Mormon party'? Their major resolve is to crush Joseph's power any way that they can. This incident will flame into nightmare, for all of us."

I had been there the day last summer when the Prophet returned from Dixon with his enemies, Reynolds and Wilson, in his custody—treating them humanely, even graciously, in contrast to the crudeness and cruelty with which they had used him. I had been there in the afternoon when thousands of his people gathered to hear him speak. With great feeling he declared that he would suffer unhallowed persecution no more. "To bear it any longer would be a crime!" Those were the very words he had cried. Now they echoed in my memory with ominous tones.

I remember walking home on the night of June 11 following my discussion with Julian. The *Expositor* press had been dismantled the evening before. We were hovering as in the eye of a tornado where all appears calm and the raging winds, so powerful and destructive, had not touched us yet. I felt it. I remember looking out to the river where the first pale sunset colors were beginning to spread. The still, suspended peace of twilight had just begun to descend. I felt suddenly frightened as I used to in Dacca, for no apparent reason at all. My skin prickled with the sensation. Once I was safely inside my own home I bolted the door, got down on my knees and prayed. But the sense of foreboding stayed with me, until I at last lost it in sleep.

Each separate, individual history became for a time one history, one story: the story of Joseph Smith.

Joseph was accused of riot, and when he was acquitted on a writ of habeas corpus by a non-Mormon judge, his enemies were incensed with rage. Alarmed, Joseph placed the city under martial law—and the season of twilight began.

Governor Ford would not admit our delegates, insisting blindly, ludicrously, that the Prophet submit himself to arrest. Late on Saturday, June 22, Joseph left the city he loved, under cover of night, under a great weight of sorrow. But the following day many of those nearest to him sent word begging him to return, disturbed by the threats of the state militia to surround the city until Joseph and Hyrum were found.

This pattern was not a particularly new one—Joseph had survived such scenes before. Many of the Saints yet went about their business with little concern. Many, like myself, could simply not conceive of horrors such as some others described.

Julian Winters did not fit into either category. Julian prepared for the worst, the muscles of his face tightened into grim lines, his eyes dull with foreboding.

Of course I partook of his mood. I had endured enough concerns of my own over the past years to not worry myself much about others. But Seth's death had altered me somewhat, as had Merin's coming. To me Joseph the Prophet had been the one steady light upon my horizon. I could not imagine—I dared not imagine—

Then Joseph returned and was ordered to Carthage, though he accompanied Captain Dunn back and himself executed the governor's orders to disarm the Legion. Those men who stood in line and handed over their weapons, those men who for the last time looked into Joseph's calm and beautiful eyes—those men knew, those men sensed the danger that now stood bold and upright, in broad daylight.

The nights in Nauvoo, along the stretch of river, are humid and close. The night of June 27 it was too hot to sleep. Or perhaps it was not only the heat that disturbed men and women that night. An eerie spirit, black and disturbing, spread through the air. Dogs barked and howled through the silence to one another, and would not be still. Even the cattle were restless and bawling. And many a Saint, awakened for no apparent reason, stood at the window and watched, and wondered at the melancholy that gripped their souls. I was one. I checked on each of my children to see how they slept. I stared at the yard, patterned by moonlight, yet seeming dark as the tomb. I stood long, and wondered and trembled, before I went back to bed.

Of course—it was true. Joseph *was* dead, and the gentle Hyrum with him. Their bodies were brought back to Nauvoo the next day. We were stunned, stunned with grief like children, and just as concerned for ourselves. *What will become of us now? What will become of the Church without Joseph?* Men and women gathered in homes and on street corners to talk of it, every one with his own opinion, his own fears and complaints.

It was a dark time. Many people wavered, many revolted outright, many slipped away like so many shadows and were heard of no more. Perversely, my thoughts turned to Seth. How staunch he would have been, how busy in shoring up others' unsteady faith. I thought of it much during the weeks that followed as I worked in garden or kitchen, as I lay alone in my bed. I realized that times such as these not only tried men, but made each soul dig deep and discover what he was truly made of. Joseph's martyrdom had made me turn inward; for days I lived in the realm of spirit, performing my tasks mechanically while my inner self struggled, searched, and at times even soared.

Some, like Abigail Haven, had already been through their baptism of fire, and though they were devastated by the loss of the Prophet, their hearts and souls—the very fibers of their beings—had already been trained to stand firm. Merin was much like myself; she had suffered, and she had borne suffering nobly, and she desired to be strong, but we were both yet learning how to put desire into action, whatever the cost.

With purposeful intent I baked some fresh apricot pies and took one over to Seth's parents' house, and found things very much as I had expected: Victoria raving at everything and everyone, from the mobbers who shot the bullets, to Governor Ford, who was responsible for the treachery; to the Legion officers who stupidly allowed themselves to be disarmed; to Brother Markham and Dan Jones for leaving Joseph in the jail without further protection; to Willard Richards who had entreated the Saints to not strike back but submit meekly to the hand of the Lord. The girls dissolved into weak tears because they believed it would please their mother and because they were dismayed and confused. Under pretense of examining a rip in my horse's saddle I drew Kenneth out into the yard with me and tried to coax his views from him, but he had little to say. He would not stray far from his wife's strong opinions and obvious lead.

I left feeling sad all over, and a little bit sorry for myself. How good it would be if his had been a strong shoulder to lean on, and Victoria's a wise, understanding heart. At times the sense of my aloneness, my personal, inner isolation, would surface unbidden and threaten to drive me to feelings of madness or depression. I hated it when such times would come. There was little I could do but grit my teeth and ride through them. But I felt weak and exhausted afterward, with a weary sense of having to start from the beginning, all over again.

When I heard that Sidney Rigdon was back in town making himself sound important I began to really wonder how the Church would be organized now that we were forced into making a change. *Guardian for the Church,* Brother Rigdon's term, did not sound quite right. I was in the grove on August 8, myself and Merin and Winston. We could have left Winston home to watch the children, but I wanted him there. Indeed, I'd have stayed myself before I'd have denied him the experience, as spiritual a boy as he was. They say there were six thousand Saints gathered that day, and I believe it. One could not move enough to even get breathing space. I saw Mary Fielding Smith, an English convert like many of us and widow of the Patriarch, Hyrum, leaning on the arm of her young son, Joseph. Her face looked serene and calm. And light—there was no light about Sidney Rigdon when he stood in the wagon and held forth for an hour and a half.

When Brother Brigham stood to speak he was blunt and to the point, as always, but the Spirit was there. He reminded us that we have a head, that the Twelve had been appointed by Joseph, by the hand of God, to bear off the kingdom, holding the necessary keys of the priesthood. His mind seemed clear and sure, but you could feel the tenderness in his heart. Everyone knew the love he felt for the Prophet, everyone knew, when he said, "Here is Brigham—have his knees ever faltered? Have his lips ever quivered?" that his devotion to principle, to service, was as perfect as any man's devotion could be.

When he called for a vote of how many desired to sustain the Twelve as the First Presidency of this people I felt a thrill travel through my whole system as I raised my own hand. I remember—I remember glancing from side to side, all about me, coming to realize that every arm in that vast throng was raised. The spirit was sweet; one could feel Joseph's presence, as though he stood beside his disciple with his hand on his shoulder . . . as though he walked among us, cheering and blessing his people as he always had done. It was then that I came to realize that the Prophet Joseph's ultimate sacrifice sanc-

tified the principles of truth he had revealed to the people—
sanctified his testimony, and even ours, with his blood.

It was not until later that evening when Merin and her
daughters had left and the girls were settled into bed that Winston approached me. He seemed nervous, even ill at ease.

"What is it, dear?" I asked. "Is something bothering you?"

He gave me a long look of consideration and appraisal.
"Did you see . . . did you think anything strange happened
there in the meeting this afternoon?"

I thought for a moment, knowing he was getting at something. "Not really. I felt many strong impressions of the Spirit,
I felt the presence of Joseph—"

"Felt it?"

I knew my son well by this time. "Did you more?"

He could hold it no longer. "I *saw him*, Mother! Saw the
Prophet Joseph—well, not really. I was looking at President
Young as he spoke and suddenly *it was Joseph*—Joseph's voice,
Joseph's face—"

"Even his voice?" I was beginning to feel a tingling sensation along my skin.

"Yes, everything all together. It was wonderful! But as soon
as I recognized it was happening, it was gone."

I drew him to me, just for a moment, feeling the solid puls-
ing warmth of his youth and vitality. Then I held him at arms'
length with my hands on his shoulders. "It was a testimony, a
sacred testimony given to you straight from God."

"I know, Mother."

"Cherish it—I know you will cherish it."

"But why, Mother?"

"Because he loves you and is pleased with you, Winston.
Because sometime, later on in your life, he will need you to be
strong—he will need your testimony to be sure."

He understood. He went up to his room. I sat alone in the
dim room pondering the events of the day, going over them in
my mind for Seth, as though he sat here, too. As I sat, a gentle
warmth seeped into me, pleasant and comforting, as invigo-
rating as energy—or light. "I know, Seth," I whispered. "I
know this means you are near."

CHAPTER EIGHTEEN

𝔍

THE CITY OF JOSEPH—SO NAUVOO WOULD be designated from this time forth; so it would remain when we turned it over to the lusting hands of our enemies and walked into the unknown, with naught but our faith in God leading the way.

In October Brigham called a conference, the last to be held in Nauvoo. Here he announced his bold decision to take the Saints west. That alone would have been overwhelming, but there was the temple to finish, thousands of us longing to receive our endowments in this holy place. Brother Brigham, with his mind for detail and organization, laid out very specific requirements that must be met before anyone could consider himself prepared to begin this journey into the unknown: an outfit for a family of five should contain one good wagon, three yoke of oxen, two cows, two beef cattle, three sheep, one thousand pounds of sugar, one rifle, ammunition, a tent, and tent poles. The requirements staggered me. Yet Brother Pratt assured us all could be procured for the sum of $250. I still had some little money put aside, but Merin had none. Nevertheless, we two decided to pool our families and travel as one—two adults, five children, one of them a baby. We would require a few more supplies, but would have to fit somehow into one wagon. President Young had admonished the priesthood brethren appointed leaders of companies to each take an equal portion of the poor, the widows, and the fatherless. I prayed they would heed his counsel and be merciful unto us.

The entire city was turned into a hive of activity—one large machine shop, as someone put it. 'Tis almost impossible to describe it if one had not been there to see. Wheelwrights, blacksmiths, carpenters-turned-wagon-builders finding or making room anywhere, even in their own front parlors. Women sewing, reaping, preserving, drying, and performing many of the chores their husbands usually saw to in order to ease the demands upon their suddenly over-burdened time. Children often ran dirty-faced and ill-kempt because their mothers only had two hands instead of the ten required. Everyone was strained near to the breaking point, and sometimes tempers ran short, especially since we did all with a sense of fear upon us, under the eyes, under foot of those who despised us and wished us harm.

Those were not pretty months to look back upon. We could not even gather together in numbers over ten without exciting the attention and anger of our enemies. The government of Illinois, which had once shown a humane compassion toward us, repealed the charter of our city in January of the new year, 1845, leaving us entirely at the mercy of low and unprincipled men. The organization of the Church and priesthood took over, to the astonishment of onlookers, and the City of Joseph continued to stand. But we were hard-pressed; day and night we were hard-pressed.

Seth's family, by and large, continued to ignore me, and I had neither the time nor the heart to force them into anything more. I had nearly forgotten about Cousin Aaron and his magnanimous proposal, when he showed up one day at my door.

"I thought you had forgotten where I lived," I chided him, deciding to take the lead.

He was well dressed in a light summer suit, with vest and top hat and immaculate kidskin gloves. He preened himself for a moment before replying.

"I have been occupied, cousin dear, courting—nay, being courted by a widow who did not seem distressed by my attentions."

"How lovely for you!" I cried, genuinely relieved. "Is this person someone I might know?"

"She is a person of great influence and no little means. You may have heard of her—" He spoke the name with deliberate emphasis, "Suzanna Beck, widow of the late—"

"Of course I know Susie Beck!" I cried, both amazed and delighted. "She truly has settled on you?"

"To my good fortune and gratitude."

"To her credit," I smiled, trying not to laugh at him. I invited him into the parlor and let him dandle Emma on his knee a bit while I prepared him a glass of cold ginger beer which Janet Dibble had contrived to make, imagining to myself all the while how he and "little Susie," as we affectionately called her, would appear together, she being at least three times his size. We had a delightful visit of fifteen minutes; then he stood, smoothing the creased line of his pants, and gracefully took his leave. Susie was a dear sort, and she would make him happy, even if her money did not, for she possessed a tidy sum left by her husband when he died five years before—that and much property throughout the city, which sadly would be of no value now.

How strange life is. I wished them both well of one another, I truly did.

I would never have dreamed what Abigail Haven had in her mind when she appeared unexpectedly at my door. But as soon as she suggested it, 'twas as if she had offered me a port in a storm, a prize I had not even been seeking.

"You wonder if we'll have you?" I nearly laughed out loud at the prospect.

"Well, I thought, seeing there are only two of us—Abbey and myself—we would not take up a whole wagon together. So if you and Merin would not mind having us travel along with you—"

"Mind? Mind the incredible luxury of space in another wagon? Mind your kindness and competence, mind the joy of your company?"

She waved her hand for me to stop, thoroughly red-faced and embarrassed, but I had meant deeply every word that I said. I had not wanted to admit to Merin, even to myself, how frightened I was. I had hungered for someone to lean upon, someone even a little bit older and wiser than myself. It is so lonely to have the entire burden of your own life and the lives and well-being of other little human beings on your shoulders. "I am honored and grateful," I told Abigail, shaking my head against the tears in my eyes.

I owned my home and property outright—an enviable position, except where tyranny reigns. We were beginning to discover that none would give fair value for our lands and possessions, reasoning that they would bide their time and simply take possession after they had forced us to leave. Only some who were a little wise and more circumvent than others were willing to pay a portion of the value that they might hold title freely, and sleep securely in their—or our—beds.

I was not alone. It was a problem we all faced. In the end many of the leaders merely gave their farms and homes to Church agents to dispose of for as much as possible, with instructions to distribute the amount gained to the poor. *The poor.* I truly was not among them, so I strove to count my blessings as I labored to prepare.

One of the requirements for the journey was to possess a firearm. Seth had a gun of some sort, stored in the blanket chest. In the back of my mind I thought I would draw it out when the time came and find ammunition for it, if I must. I knew there was danger, but I did not think a weapon in my hands would serve much good. I was not afraid of firearms—I had lived among military men too long for that. Perhaps I simply possessed a healthy respect, and at the same time no interest in such matters at all.

I could not believe the amount of stir made about us. Sisters with non-Mormon families still living back East received tearful letters, moved to distraction by varied reports that flooded the newspapers. We were an oddity; people were interested, even fascinated, but nobody cared that homes and farms were being attacked, even destroyed on a regular basis and terrified families forced to move into the city, which was already bursting at the seams. We did our part by forming our new family organization early. Abigail and her Abbey came in early November. By two weeks before Christmas, Merin and her daughters, Rachel and Drusilla, had also moved in. This freed up precious living quarters for those who were homeless and destitute and, perhaps selfishly, I had friends with me, rather than strangers as the Christmas season approached.

We surely did not celebrate the holiday in any grand manner. Every cent people could get their hands upon went into supplies for the impending journey. The brethren printed a checklist in the *Times and Seasons* which included flour and breadstuffs to be packed in good sacks, sugar, rice, cayenne pepper, black pepper, beans, beef, bacon, peaches, pumpkin, seeds of all kinds, and an ample supply of candles and soap. If I thought of it in a broad sense, I panicked. I had to force myself to take everything one day at a time.

But for Christmas we did have music! Merin never refused a request if one of us had need of a song. Abigail could work nearly as many wonders in the kitchen as she could in the sickroom, so we were well blessed that season, our last in Nauvoo.

I looked back, remembering how aware I had been of *the last* about everything as we prepared to leave London. That had been as nothing, child's play, compared to what we were undertaking now. My heart was sore. I longed for Seth as I never had. The year 1845 came in cold and punishing. When I tried to write letters to May and Marion I discovered that my ink had frozen and could not be used. I wore fingerless mitts Emma had crocheted for me years ago on my hands day and night, for they were always aching with cold. On the anniversary of Seth's death I did not even go out to the tree and the grave beneath it. The day was bitter, and I was ill with a cold— but that was not the real reason. I could not face the idea of leaving him here. I was afraid of going so far away without him as though, by so doing, I would shut him out of my life, close in some irreparable way the chapters that had him in them, and go on forever alone.

It was singular that Winston was the only male member of our rather eclectic household. Sometimes we teased him about it, but he took it, as he did all things, most seriously. Yet I had no idea, no clue of what he was doing until one Saturday late in March.

The weather had cleared, a warm sun breaking briefly through the layer of clouds which seemed as thick and dense as the black river they shrouded. Winston announced that he had some chores to do and went off about three o'clock. I let him go without thinking; I seldom questioned his movements: he was very nearly thirteen now and entirely trustworthy. I did feel some concern when the clouds closed in again about five o'clock, more dense and dark than before, and a thin, freezing drizzle wet the city. *This will drive him home,* I remember thinking, then bent again to my work.

I lost track of time for awhile, until Merin came in, tense and white-faced, to tell me that five strange men were riding into the yard.

"Five?"

"I counted them."

"You are sure?"

"I recognize none, Lottie, and at least two of them are cradling rifles in their arms."

I remember feeling fear then, such as I had never experienced in the early days of London, or even in Dacca. I felt as if all the forces of evil had concentrated themselves upon me. As I followed Merin to the front of the house I hissed, in sudden panic, "Where is Winston, Merin? Dear heaven, where is he?"

Something within me knew. I drew a shawl around my head and shoulders and walked out to meet the men. I did not see him at once, for he was flung across one of the rider's saddles, both head and feet dangling down.

"Does this here worthless piece of—" the man used a terrible obscenity, "belong to you, missus?"

He pulled Winston up by the hair and literally threw him onto the ground at my feet. I bent down quickly, fear nearly strangling me. He had landed on his back and his eyes were open. "Winston!" I whispered. "Can you hear me? Can you answer me?" He nodded his head and moaned. I rose to my feet unsteadily.

"This is my son," I said. "What have you done to him?"

"Taught him a lesson or two." The man laughed low under his breath and the sound shuddered through me, making my stomach feel sick. Then I realized, dimly, that one of the others had dismounted and was pushing his way through the door. I shivered. The rain was coming down heavier than before. A nasty wind came in gusts to drive it against my bare arms and my cheeks.

I bent over Winston again and began to lift him. "Leave him where he is, miss," spoke another. "He'll fare just fine where he is until we're through here."

The man at the door must have entered the house, for I looked up to see him returning. "Nothing much inside. No man around—just took care of a few things these ladies won't be needing."

"Must be something for us in the barn," answered one of the others, spurring his horse in that direction. I wrapped my arms around my body and stood watching them dully. Abigail's tap on my shoulder seemed like a bolt of lightning. I cried out involuntarily and put my hand to my mouth.

"You take his feet, I'll take his head and shoulders. Be quick about it!" she ordered. In less than a minute we had shifted him and carried him safely inside the house. She took him all the way into my bedroom, laid him down carefully, then turned to me. "Cover him, but do not touch him, Lottie, do you understand me? And you stay here."

She walked out of the room in purposeful strides, shutting the door behind her. I stood stunned and frozen. When I turned my face to my son I saw that his eyes were watching me, and the relief made me weak.

I snatched up a blanket from the bed and laid it gingerly over him. Then I touched his forehead briefly with the tips of my fingers. "Are you badly hurt, Winston? Can you tell me anything?"

"My arm's on fire," he rasped. "I think it may be broken. Otherwise, I'm all right."

It was a statement bravely made, for my sake. I reached for matches to light the bedside lamp—but Abigail had not given permission—perhaps it would be wiser to wait.

That became one of the longest half hours of my life. When I heard rifle shots from the direction of the barn a sick panic rose up in me and Winston's whole body twitched, so that my heart ached at the thought of what they had done to him! At last things grew quiet, deathly quiet. I turned a mute face to Winston and waited a few more minutes. Just when I thought I could bear it no longer the door squeaked and swung inward. For a moment my breath stopped, until I saw Merin's white face. She held a lamp high above her, its golden light shaky but welcome.

"Everything's all right now, my dears," she said. "It's all right, it's over."

She came and sat on the edge of the bed beside me. Tears streaked her cheeks, and there were tears in her voice.

"Is . . . are . . ." I choked on my words and my throat was too dry to swallow.

"We're all fine, no one is hurt, Lottie." She reached for my hand across the coverlet, grasping it with a grip that hurt.

How grateful I was to see Abigail's solid, competent shape appear in the doorway. She shut the door tight and leaned against it.

"The girls are safe in the loft. The men have been gone these ten minutes; I do not think they'll come back. As soon as I see to Winston I'll run over to Brother Matthews."

Brother Matthews lived two doors down. He was an officer in the Legion, a capable, yet compassionate man.

"What happened? Please tell me."

I did not miss the quick glance Merin and Abigail exchanged. But Abigail was already bent over Winston, an excuse, I knew, for ignoring my request.

"What were the shots?" I pressed. That would be a good starting point.

Again the quick glance and hesitation.

"Merin!" I turned on her, both pleading and imperious. "Please."

She sighed. "You must know. Of course. We lost two sheep, three hogs, and . . . Seth's horse was shot."

I drew in my breath softly and clenched my fists beneath my gown. "What else?"

"They tore open a few sacks of grain, tipped over the milk bucket, not much damage, really . . . not after Abigail put a gun to the head of one and threatened to pull the trigger."

I turned to her, aghast and amazed. "You did that?" I blurted.

She continued serenely with her work. "I've done much worse before."

Missouri—I had not even thought of Missouri and what black memories this nightmare must have stirred.

She kept us busy for the next few minutes boiling water and tearing clean bandages, giving terse, detailed instructions. "I'm going for a doctor; his arm will have to be set," she announced. "I'll stop and alert Brother Matthews at the same time. Do not move him. You can give him sips of sorrel tea with a spoon, Lottie." She smiled wanly. "I'll be back in a jiffy."

It was not until later, much later, that we heard Winston's story and pieced together what had happened. The boy had set a grim errand for himself that afternoon, though he looked upon it as fun. He took the country road way out beyond Brother Wilson's fields, which Seth used to rent, to a long open space down by the river which he and some of the other young boys used for target practice. He had gone intently about his business, not hearing the men approach down the lane that ran behind the cornfields. But they had seen him from their positions on top of their mounts. As soon as they cleared the fields they galloped toward him full tilt. One swooped past and kicked him down with the pointed toe of his shoe. As he was staggering to his feet another lifted him up by his shirt collar, pulled his horse up short by the river, and threatened to throw Winston in.

Here he stopped. I knew there was more, but it pained him to tell it and to see the distress it caused me. "They threw the gun into the river. I am sorry I lost it, Mother. I will work extra hours to pay for the purchase of another."

Winston did odd jobs about the city for half a dozen different people. I accepted his offer with a nod and a smile twisted with the threat of tears. Would he take this incident in the same light in which he had taken Seth's death? I wondered.

He answered the question himself. As I rose to leave him to the rest Abigail had ordered, and bent over his bed to kiss him, he said solemnly, "I was all right, Mother, really. The pain was not too much to bear."

"Were you frightened awfully?"

"I thought of Joseph and Hyrum and prayed," he replied.

"Prayer has always worked with you." I kissed him on the forehead. An ugly bruise, green and purple, had nearly shut his left eye.

"Christ forgave his enemies, and so did Joseph," he said, unexpectedly. "Remember Dixon and the Missouri marshals?"

I nodded.

"I am sorry for the evil they brought upon you and Merin and Abigail," he said. "Do you think I can ever come to forgive them as Joseph Smith did?"

"Your heart is gentle enough and your faith strong enough for it," I answered. "Now, get some rest."

Good, I thought. *He is beyond blaming himself; he has grown up these past years.*

But my sense of reassurance, almost contentment, delicate though it was, became instantly shattered the moment I walked into the parlor and took one look around me. Merin sat on the floor, her face in her hands, sobbing uncontrollably. The beautiful cherry wood piano had been hacked and smashed by the heavy strokes of an axe blade. I heard the mobber's voice echo: "Just took care of some things these women won't be wanting." I sank down onto the floor beside Merin and gathered her into my arms, weeping as I did so, feeling as if my own heart would break.

I truly believe that every man, woman, and child had not only contributed but sacrificed to build the temple. Most of us gave contributions in kind, men donating one workday in ten, women sewing, washing clothes, cooking, contributing prized possessions brought from England or handed down from generations: jewelry, linen, fine china, even pieces of furniture which could be translated into cash.

In May of 1845 the final stone was laid and President Young prayed that the Almighty might protect and defend us until we had all got our endowments. Of course, the interior now had to be finished and furnished, which included the making of rugs and curtains and fine cotton veils, as well as fine embroidery and upholstery work. I wished often for Emma's skills; I wished often for Emma herself. She had written two or three scathing epistles over the past several months, begging, then bullying, but never wanting to be reconciled to my going away. She did not make it easier, but well she knew that, and would have laughed boldly in my face if she had been here on the spot to accuse.

The temple became more and more the focal point of all our activities: marriages were held there, even our innocent parties and socials took place within the safety of its walls. There, as Saints, we danced and sang unto the Lord, and felt his yearning over us, and were renewed.

As we headed into the new year, with only weeks left until the exodus would begin, the pace of the sealings picked up. Brigham began staying in the temple day and night, and then for several days on end before returning to his family. Because of his devotion I was one who became privileged to enter those holy rooms and be sealed to the man who had made me a Latter-day Saint. I did not think that this was happening only days before that dismal January afternoon when I had lost him; I did not think that, in less than four weeks, I would walk away from Nauvoo. For those brief hours Nauvoo no longer existed, the world outside held no meaning, no substance at all. What I felt and experienced was the most real thing that had ever happened to me. And it remained, for many days, like a shield around me, like a strength bearing me up. When reality tugged at me, demanding its just dues—even then that power did not desert me nor leave me entirely to the fluctuations and wiles of the world. Thus I was able, with the help of heaven, to make it through to the end.

I was able to sell my home and property for a yoke of oxen, two sheep, two pigs and a hundred pounds of flour thrown into the bargain; I was much more lucky than some. This came about through Julian Winters's good offices, looking out for my welfare even after his goods had been spoiled and his lovely store burned to the ground.

"I still had some favors I could cash in on." That was all he could tell me, and I had not the heart to ask more. I did not really wish to see the faces of those people who, like thieves in the night, would come and inherit my house, who would reap where they had not sown, who would walk hallowed ground without knowing at all.

Emma did not make it, and perhaps that was all for the better. Could either of us have borne such a parting as that would have been? She sent, in her stead, the magnificent sum of a hundred dollars. "You shall not go a beggar!" she said. Even on paper her words snarled with that mixture of love and defiance which characterized her.

There were bright spots; there are always bright spots, be they ever so small. When Abigail, who had been supervising the building of our wagons, took us to see the finished product we laughed out loud with delight. She had instructed that the wooden boxes be painted a bright apple red. "We will not lose each other this way," she said with a slow little smile.

I do not like to tell this; I do not know how to tell this, how we turned our backs on Nauvoo, walking down Parley Street to the river that February morning when the thermometer read seven degrees below zero. Those who had gone for the last few weeks before us had been ferried across on flat boats. But the river had frozen again, solid enough for us to drive our wagons over the ice.

I was cold. Merin's girls were sniffling a little and Grace was whimpering and the wind blew tiny ice particles into our faces. I noticed everything: the glint of cold sun on the rooftops; a pale, scruffy black bird pecking at a puddle of mud that had turned quite solid; the face of a child at a window as we passed by; Seth's tree standing against the brown fields, its stripped branches tracing a pattern as delicate as a painting—I noticed everything, and nothing. There was not one particle within me that wanted to go; yet I did not, for one day more, for one hour more, wish to remain in Nauvoo.

Winston held my hand and steered me carefully, all the way over the river, and I thought that was symbolic of how his life and mine had been: hand in hand, no matter what else was destroyed or lost to us. Hand in hand, with all our yesterdays tucked safely where they belonged: in our hearts.

CHAPTER NINETEEN

𝔍

WE SPENT OUR FIRST NIGHT ON THE IOWA side of the river. The following morning it snowed. It was still snowing two days later when we reached Sugar Creek. The ground was messy with snow and standing water. The children's clothing was damp. I noticed Drusilla was shaking, so I put my shawl over her shoulders and sent her back to the wagon, away from the winds. I tried to help Merin and Abigail set up camp, but I was clumsy and unaccustomed to most of the tasks they had both learned to perform before. My heart felt heavy and despondent until Abigail jumped down from the wagon, a large bundle in her arms, and sat herself down by the fire, propped a huge black umbrella over her head, and began to stir up a pan of her light biscuits right there in her lap. Then I could laugh with Merin, then I could keep on going, at least for a little while longer, walk back to the wagon and locate the plates and utensils we would need in order to eat our supper that cold, windy night.

I cannot tell of those early travels, of our first days in Winter Quarters, without an almost dreamlike quality, for that is how they appear in my mind.

We were lucky—we were among the first. The land Brigham found for us belonged to the Potawatomi Indians, but we were allowed to camp there, hundreds and hundreds of us, and more arriving each day. The worst of winter was over now, though all was still dreariness and mud. We had traveled and traveled—I hated to think that what we had been through was only a beginning! And who could have dreamed that Council Bluffs and Winter Quarters, on either bank of the Missouri, would house our people for years to come, as more and more Saints prepared for the journey to the land of promise, which only the hand of the Almighty could have prepared.

We built a community—what other choice had we? It was a far stretch from Nauvoo: log cabins, tents, and huts that were not even tents yet; poverty and bickering, death and sickness, stranger and friend jostling together for survival. At times the spark seemed to go entirely out, and we forgot what we were there for, feeling only the cold and the suffering, and the putting of loved ones under the ground. I did not like it, but people do what they have to and, as in Dacca, we all learned to get by. Winston thrived; this experience was tailored for youth, if for anyone. He was needed; day after day he had work of a vital nature at hand. He was our salvation, in his way, and so was Abigail, in hers. Merin and I gave wherever we could, but at times I felt so inadequate, even empty-handed compared to this woman who knew healing and patience, and many of the arts of the spirit which were little more than sweet words to me.

That first summer is not one I wish to remember. Somehow we lived through it until the cooling vapors of autumn came to restore our sanity and paint with the blazing colors of its glory those scenes which had been gray with dust and blisters and fatigue. On the tenth day of October Seth's clan, noisy and quarrelsome as ever, pulled into the camp.

Victoria had refused to leave, shouting defiance to those mobsters who dared to stray too close to her house, clinging on till nearly the point of madness before she was forced to let go. I tried to deal gently with her; I had learned some things from Abigail. Victoria would have no part of me, but the girls were grateful, and I think truly glad for the sight of me, fussing over the children, exclaiming at how much little Emma had grown. Kenneth, without seeming to have shrunk in size or girth, yet appeared gaunt and spent, his big suits hanging loose on his frame. *Victoria is too full of spit and vinegar to get ill,* I thought, *or to even slow down.* But I worried a little about her pale, quiet husband.

Aaron and Susie, I learned the day following the Taylors' arrival, had come with their company, too. I was eager to visit with her, and curious to see Aaron and discover how marriage agreed with him. I asked Kenneth to point out their wagon, and he did as I bid him, without a word. Perhaps he was too tired, too stunned by what he found here to give one thought to the matter, perhaps he had grown accustomed, inured to whatever might happen. Nevertheless, I wished later that he had been kind enough to warn me, at least.

I walked up merrily and cried, "Hello the house!" an old British form of greeting, all "hail thee fellow well met" and high spirits. But there came no reply from within. I tried again, and Susie's head popped out between the back flaps. "Hush, you'll wake him," she half whispered then, seeing me, she threw her head back and lumbered down to greet me properly. I do not know how long we chatted before I asked, "And Aaron—has he taken to sleeping in the middle of the day now he has you to care for him? Is he ill?"

Susie's face contorted; I watched her expression alter. "He *is* touchy, he is not himself since that day—he cannot really help it," she ended in robust defense.

"Since that day?" I had no idea what she was talking about, but suddenly there came a great rattling from within the wagon, as though someone were banging two pans together, and I heard a voice cry out in high irritation.

Suzanna Beck was ever a quick one. She saw my confusion and guesses, and guessed accurately. "No one has told you?"

"No one has told me. I have no idea what you are talking about."

She knit her brow, trying to decide how to handle this, but Aaron took it out of her hands. He threw the flaps open, cursing like the worst of the sailors I remembered, demanding that she see to him right now. I did not think what I might be risking, but strode close to the wagon and stood indignant, hands on my hips.

"Who taught you such rudeness?" I glared up at him. "Whatever your need may be, Aaron Taylor, you shame your parents, you shame your good name, you shame yourself with language such as I just heard come out of your mouth."

He stood agape. Without knowing any differently, he believed I had heard all about him. His countenance was a perfect struggle between anger and self-pity; I could see that the pity had won when his lower lip began to tremble and he put out a hand to steady himself.

"Well! Are you not going to apologize to Susie—and to me, for that matter?"

He looked at me darkly and pulled his crumbling face together. "Go to the devil!" he said, and turned back to the tent.

I looked at Susie, my eyes asking the questions I was fearful to voice. She waved me to follow her and walked off a short distance. "'Tisn't a pleasant story," she warned me as we settled, with little comfort, on a rough fallen log.

"In his own way Aaron became as crazed as Victoria those last days in Nauvoo. I have some little money Samuel left me, as half the city knows, and we fit ourselves up a splendid outfit, but that wasn't enough. He couldn't bear to see all my properties just melt away from us, falling into the greedy waiting hands of the—well, you can imagine what he called them."

We smiled, and I wondered at her wisdom that could lighten a mood so heavy.

"He became obsessed, going out before daybreak and again after dark to protect 'his Susie's property,' his Browning loaded and in hand. Three houses, Charlotte! He prowled like a ghost back and forth between them, just asking for trouble."

I nodded.

"Well, of course, it finally came."

"Oh, Susie."

"Yes, I told you 'twas not pretty. A group of five or six of them came upon him, drunk as lords. Baited him a little—you know how easy Aaron would be to bait. Finally took to shooting up the dust at his feet, making him dance for their pleasure—" I shuddered. "At last one of them aimed a bit higher, his foot at first, then his knee, then his thigh. He went down pretty fast, I suppose, and it was the darkness that saved him— that and the men's stupor."

She put her hand on my arm, the way a child would to punctuate his feeling. "He crawled all the way home, Charlotte. Can you believe it? I heard him out there, moaning, and I thought it was one of our dogs that had been caught in a trap."

"Stop, Susie!" I covered her cold hand with mine.

"Yes, well, you see how it's been with him then ever since."

I covered my face with my hands; I was sick with pity for both of them. "'Tis a shame, that's certain," I said, "yet no cause to abuse you who has—"

"No, he must abuse someone at the times he can't stand it," she defended him. *Which is always,* I thought bitterly. *Which is how he has been all his life.*

"Nevertheless, whenever it gets to you, Suzanna, you know where you can come. We have a small cabin full to the gills with sympathetic women."

She smiled, but she had taken my meaning. "God bless you, my girl," she said as I rose to leave.

God bless you, I thought, *for showing mercy to one of his creatures such as only he, himself, would show.*

I walked home quickly, but the shadows of misery trailed after me, unwilling to loosen their hold.

The winter was not as bad as I had expected it to be. The society of the Saints is rich and warms the cockles of the heart, no matter how cold the weather, no matter how cold the world outside. Yes, there were problems still; the pettiness of human nature reared its head, even there. But given the circumstances, I believe many among us were Saints in every true sense of the word. Eliza Snow, Emmeline Wells, and some of the other leading sisters of the Nauvoo Relief Society went about the encampment tirelessly, administering comfort, uplifting spirits, sewing, mending, sitting with children and sick mothers— angels of mercy they were, they and the midwives, like Patty Sessions and our own Abigail. She would go weeks on end sometimes without sleeping an uninterrupted night. She went out in all kinds of weather, never thinking of any sort of comfort or gain for herself. Come mid-January when all the babies of the spring decided to present themselves I became worried about her, and begged her to awaken me when she received a call in the night.

"No need," she would reply succinctly. "I've learned how to handle it, but you would suffer, Lottie, and for no reason at all."

I thought back to the days when she had nursed me, a stranger, and I had returned only unkindness. I wrapped my arms around her. "It is a proof of God's love for me," I murmured, "that he brought you into my life."

She pushed me gently away. Both praise and affection openly shown embarrassed her. But the shine of pleasure was there, sitting behind her soft eyes.

One night I did awaken, by happenstance, and stumble upon a small secret that was meant to be kept from my eyes.

Emma had been restive with a cold and fever, and I was up with her for the second time, walking the floor and crooning Merin's old lullabies. When I heard the doorknob rattle and turn I knew it must be Abigail coming back from a call. When I saw Winston stumble through the door, bleary-eyed and a bit disheveled, I stepped back into the shadows.

"Shall I put the kettle on?" he called behind him. "I'm fair chilled to the bone."

He lit the fire even as he spoke and quietly set out two cups and saucers, pulled off his mittens, and chaffed his cold hands. By the time Abigail followed him the sweet lemon balm tea was already brewing in the cup.

She sat down wearily and wrapped her fingers around the china to warm them. "I do not know what I should do without you, dear boy," she sighed. "But you have worn yourself out these past nights. Drink quickly, Winston, and hurry back to your bed. I'll do my best to contrive a way for you to sleep in a bit tomorrow."

He threw her a grateful smile, downed the drink in two or three gulps, and was on his way to the lean-to in the back where he slept, without noticing me. I would have pulled it off altogether if Emma had not chosen that moment to cry out in her half-sleep. Abigail's head went up and she looked around her with a dazed expression, so that I knew she had been dozing and mistaken the cry for that of a newborn she had just helped bring into the world. I stepped forward.

"There is no work for you here, my dear." I put my hand out. "Let me help you to your bed. That's right, hold onto me."

She roused a little as we walked through the still house. "You saw?"

"I saw."

"Do you mind awfully?"

"Why should I mind? I have offered such assistance myself, you remember."

She sat down on the bed and sighed as I placed Emma beside her and knelt to untie her long laces.

"He came to me, Lottie. I did not ask him."

I smiled into the darkness. "I did not think that you had."

"He's a lad in a million," she said as she undid her bodice and sash.

"He is that." I gave her a quick hug, then lifted the limp Emma into my arms. "We are lucky to have him, you and I—each of us sonless right now, in her own way."

I slipped out quickly, as grateful this time for the darkness to cover my weak tears and tremblings as Abigail was.

We meant to leave the following summer for Zion, but our plans are not God's plans. Victoria, in her perverseness, held the trump card for the last time, and kept us in Winter Quarters another year.

I was wrong; my gifts are not prophetic, nor even my hunches right. She took ill right after Easter but ignored it and went about her business, securing the best plot for a garden, bullying miller and butcher and blacksmith into prices that set them grumbling at their own ignorance after she had wheeled out of their shops. Mary Jane told me that she woke them in the night with her coughing, but still she ignored it until she began coughing up blood. Then she conceded so far as to allow Kenneth to consult a doctor on her behalf. He ordered her straight to bed, and, in justice to her, she might have meant to comply. But a shipment of shoes had been brought from New Orleans by an English convert who had just arrived from St. Louis, and she must be the first to examine them and wheedle from him her choice.

She went alone, telling no one where she was going or when to expect her back. But she never made it to her destination. After the spring rains the mud was like glue down by the river. It was clear to see where she had slipped and lost her footing and gone down in the bushes, where the evening shadows hid her. She struck her head hard when she fell, but not hard enough to kill her. She had lain on the wet ground half the night before anyone discovered her whereabouts and carried her home to her distraught family.

She was burning with fever, but she regained consciousness the next day. "It is only a matter of time," the doctor said, shaking his head.

Time indeed. The fever racked her for three weeks, and she racked the rest of us, raving against earth and heaven, against the God in that heaven himself. The wagon company we had been assigned to pulled out and headed west. I do not mean to appear unmerciful, but it was hard to stand by and see my hopes ruined, to face living in this place that was neither a real city nor a real home for another long year.

She died in early August, her face forever frozen in its austere, acrimonious lines. Her daughters at first reacted as they had been taught to, but after a time that died down. Mary Jane began to pull out of her shell a little. I made it a point to visit them daily, and I saw Phyllis soften, now there was no one to bite and snap at her when she ventured out of the mold.

Kenneth was beside himself. Who would have expected it? He had the look of a lost soul with no direction, no sense of purpose, no soul of his own.

"We'll change that!" I told Merin and Abigail. "If we must stay here to properly mourn and bury her, if we must drag her poor family with us, at least we shall do it our way!"

They laughed at my vehemence. Perhaps they knew, as I

did, that I was only covering the frustration and disappointment I could do nothing about.

Time passed. We went through the process again of accumulating supplies for the trek. Kenneth and the girls would be traveling in our company, as would Aaron and Susie; but they had accommodations that far outshone most. I had spent much of the little hoard of money I had brought with me, but Emma's hundred-dollar bill was sewed into the lining of my best dress and tucked safely away. Spring came again, muddy, but warm, with the insects stirring in the wetlands by the river and the soft prairie grasses beginning to wave in the breeze. I liked to awaken to the voices of the meadow larks singing in the new day. The fruit trees blossomed and the trees leafed out and the scent of lilacs, for a few brief weeks, perfumed the air. I felt hope, and a terrible itch to be moving. We were doing little more than treading water here, betwixt and between a world that was ruined and a world that was unknown.

We made it somehow. Wheat and potatoes, rice and raisins, salt and sugar, soap and candles—all the necessities all over again. Abigail contrived to have the red wagons given a fresh coat of paint and that touch of gaiety lifted our spirits and made the difference. I made sure Phyllis and Mary Jane were organized; Kenneth did best, I fear, when he was told what to do. I felt few regrets in leaving Winter Quarters behind. What lay ahead was all that mattered now, and I was eager to go.

CHAPTER TWENTY

I DO NOT WISH TO CHRONICLE OUR JOURNEY across the plains—
that is a volume in itself. Organization was very strict, and the
same for all. Each company was divided into groups of hundreds, fifties, and tens, with a captain over each. John Mason,
our company leader, appointed Winston captain over our nine,
and I knew he did not do so merely to humor the boy or to get
us off of his hands. Winston's qualities were there to notice for
anyone who possessed eyes to see. Besides, he placed us under
Elder Myron Mecham as our Captain of Fifty, and none of
Seth's people were in our lot.

The bugles awoke us at five o'clock every morning. Winston arose first and joined the other men for prayers. He was
sixteen and held the Aaronic Priesthood. "The power is there,"
he told me, "enough to help us through any need." By seven
o'clock the cooking and eating and cleaning up was accom-
plished, the teams fed and hitched, and all things ready to heed
the call to move out. If one had small children who had been
sick in the night, or a cow who was balky and would not milk,
slight adjustments were made, but only slight ones. For all
dreaded the prospect of being left behind, and none desired to
travel as the last in a wagon train that churned up rivers of
dust, dust that never lifted for those near the back. We traveled
from eight to twenty miles a day, and if we found a suitable
camping spot in good order, the bugle for prayer time would

be sounded at half past eight, and we were expected to be retired by nine o'clock.

There were good days and there were bad days. Living quarters in wagons as crowded as ours were very cramped. But the large wooden chest holding tools, dishes and the like was packed in one wagon with the pots and pans and cooking utensils. Most of the larger chests rode there as well. So we were able to make one wagon into comfortable sleeping quarters for women and children. Winston slept in a corner of the supply wagon, or outdoors underneath the wagon bed if the weather was nice.

Cooking was terrible, what with the dust and the red ants which, bad as they could be, were preferable to rain and high winds. I never did become accustomed to the use of buffalo chips for fuel. Whenever Winston had time, he would gather them for us. But neither Merin nor the little girls minded as much as I.

Evenings around the wagon circle could be nice, with the fires softly sighing and etching patterns against the immensity of sky that seemed to reach down and meet the horizon with nothing between. I liked the rise and fall of men's and women's voices on the gentle air of evening, like the faint echoes of a lullaby carried on a sweet wind. We were a group blessed with an abundance of musicians and, more evenings than not, the men would build a big bonfire, then clear off as level a piece of ground as they could find, dampen it a little to keep the dust down, and the dance would begin.

Abigail's Abbey was a girl of thirteen now and looked very much the young lady. Her hair, falling in thick, natural waves, was of a rich auburn hue, her brown eyes burnished to a warm shine, as though both hair and eyes had been cut from the very same cloth. She had tiny wrists and hands, and a petite little waist. Besides that, she was light on her feet and, therefore, never wanting for partners. Winston was well aware of this, and it amused me to see how ill it pleased him, how keen an eye he kept out for her. Was it the protection of a brother, or of one who would come courting, I wondered, or perhaps a mixture of both.

Susie, despite her respectable size, loved dancing; it was one of the few pleasures she would not allow Aaron to cheat her of. Night after night you could find her down in the thick of things, twirling and stomping with the best of them, until the musicians gave out and went reluctantly to their beds. Aaron, left to himself, hobbled off into the shadows to nurse his grievances, often as not with a bottle of liquor. I suspect he had brought a goodly supply with him, nor was he too discreet about it. I was relieved that Brother Brigham, or Brother Kimball, which would be worse yet, were not here to see.

Two things only about that journey are worth mentioning here. The first incident took place about twenty miles out from Fort John or Laramie ford—a fort where there were to be found other civilized white men, where those in desperate need had a chance to replenish supplies. We had just crossed over the halfway mark between Winter Quarters and the Salt Lake Valley and we felt to rejoice at this milestone we had finally made. But the forts, far-flung as they were, drew Indians as well as settlers. I remember seeing a goodly number lounging about the buildings, racing their ponies and playing some game of their own making, driving a rawhide ball with sticks between them, accompanied by much shouting and excitement. I noted all this: the colorful attire of many, the doe-hued skin and sleek black hair that were similar, and yet different, from my own people in India. I remember there were several who, upon catching sight of me, would stop dead in their tracks and stare. Their manners were very different from ours—they meant no offense by it. Once or twice I got the impression that they took me for one of their own, sensing both confusion and indignation as I stepped on by. I was neither drawn to them nor repulsed by them, but I did feel a wariness.

"That is your nature, not theirs," Merin teased me when I confided my reservations to her. "They stick rather close to the fort, I think. They should not bother us much."

She was not right in her assessment. The native people, harassed and, in many cases dispossessed, found it easy to justify demands, even depredations upon the innocent white people passing over their lands. Often they begged food, clothing, even animals and rifles—at times they demanded rather than begged. By and large, since the Mormon companies dealt justly with them, they returned the favor. But there was a trade, a very lucrative trade they practiced between themselves, and at times individuals among them were tempted, and acted upon that temptation.

About fourteen miles out from Laramie ford, just past the warm springs, we came to a pass through a narrow ravine over half a mile up. It was a steep ascent over cobblestones and between ragged bluffs. Those who had gone before provided maps and instructions, and on the strength of their knowledge our company camped for the night just past the spring at a green, pleasant site.

There occurred nothing unusual to alert attention; we went about making our routine preparations for the night, save that the hour was a bit later than usual and the sun was already slanting athwart the low land. Abbey had gone with Sita and Drusilla to gather buffalo chips, but Drusilla stepped on a sharp stone that cut her skin, so Abbey sent the two younger girls back. I do not know how Winston saw what happened so quickly, save that he was tethering horses for some of the brethren and was wont to keep his eye on Abbey at any and all times.

A single Pawnee brave swooped down noiselessly upon the lone girl and swept her up to his horse without breaking his stride. In the blink of an eye she was gone, as if she had never been there—but in that blink, Winston saw, and moved. If he had not seen, if he had not had his hand on the pommel of a saddled horse—there were many ifs that would have assured tragedy that night if things had arranged themselves differently. But within seconds he was after the rider, pressing close but not overtaking him, the skill of the Indian and his pony, as well as his knowledge of the terrain, giving him an advantage that maddened his frantic pursuer. That might have assured him the victory if Winston had not felt for the gun that rode at the side of the saddle and drawn the long weapon out.

The captor saw and bent low over the body of the girl he carried, but Winston aimed well. His first shot grazed the bronze arm; the Indian turned in the saddle and fired his gun in return. At that same moment the pony swerved, the long arm jerked, and the girl jumped free.

All in an instant. The slender rider pressed forward without his prize and Winston slipped from under the horse who had received the shot intended for him. When he reached Abbey and found her to have suffered only bruises and scratches he was overcome with relief and gathered her for a moment tenderly into his arms. She explained what had happened—how when the brave raised his weapon to fire she had sunk her teeth as deep as she could into his other arm.

"You have some of your mother in you!" he had teased, both pleased and amazed. But the troubles they believed had ended were only begun.

The night shadows were deep now, especially in this narrow mountain passage, and they had no way back save the tedious and painful one of using their own legs. The trail was narrow, the surface dangerous with obstructions and loose stones, and to slip, to veer too far would mean a fall from the bluff to certain destruction below.

They offered a prayer before they began their precarious journey, but still the going was slow, and soon night's cloak inked out the pale evening light they had used to guide them.

"Perhaps I was not the only one who saw what happened," Winston suggested, hoping to comfort her. "Perhaps even now they are riding in search of us."

But that was not so. After leaving Abbey, the girls, feeling their freedom, wandered in search of flowers to bring back to the wagon as unexpected treats. By the time they arrived, Merin had already started a fire with what fuel we had.

The first matter of business was to hear of the injury and have it lovingly cared for by Abigail. Then with sudden awareness we wondered where Abbey had gone.

"In that direction," Sarah offered, indicating a grassy knoll where a few shady trees huddled.

"Do you suppose she has met up with some of her friends," I asked, "and forgotten the time?"

We delayed a bit longer, then served the now-scorched

food to the little ones and went off, in separate directions, toward the wagons of those girls Abbey was closest to. When she did not turn up at any of them, we felt the first pricklings of real concern. It was then we began scouring the fields and stands of trees that eventually led to the river we had followed until the road turned less than a mile from the stream. When we did not find Abbey we still did not think to connect her absence with Winston's; Winston went about his affairs nearly as freely as the grown men shouldering, as he did, the same responsibilities. It was dark—it had been dark for some time— when we realized that Winston was missing, too.

Meanwhile the two were struggling slowly through the thick darkness, only inching their way, it seemed, fear weakening them more than their weary feet.

Winston told it well, how they came to an apparent turn in the path and took it, but the path ran straight, after all. The bend, as they saw it, was only a curve of rock jutting toward a tall point of bluff lined with juniper hedges and therefore bearing the appearance of a legitimate path. They traveled only a few steps when Winston saw a light in front and just above him to the right. "I think they are coming for us. Look, Abbey!" he cried.

She looked and saw nothing. They moved a few cautious steps further, then the light appeared, brighter this time, and closer. A figure stood in the midst of it, the figure of a woman. "Go no further," she told Winston. "A few steps more and you will go over the cliff."

He stopped, pulling Abbey close to him. The woman had spoken to him without moving her lips. He had heard her clearly, yet when he questioned Abbey she had heard or seen nothing at all.

"Wait," the woman said. "Wait here until help comes to you." Then she had smiled upon him with such love in her eyes, such love radiating from her whole being, that he felt it enter him like a warmth, like a light.

He obeyed her instructions. An hour later some of the brethren found them. They were carrying torches and had brought extra horses. Abbey, badly shaken and weary, was returned to us unharmed. Once her mother had assured herself of that, we fed the girl hot tea and biscuits, cleaned her up a bit, and sent her to bed.

Winston had moved off a bit from us women and our proceedings. The menfolk shook his hand heartily and made much of him in the way and manner men do. I wished to assure myself of his well-being before I could, too, seek my bed. I found him with his blankets rolled out under the wagon.

"Do you not think you should sleep within tonight?" I asked him; then I noticed the long narrow shadow that lay stretched at his side. "Do you really think you will need that?" I asked, indicating the rifle.

"No. But it will not hurt to make certain." His voice was calm, his voice held some quality. . . . He had told us, when he first placed his precious parcel back into the arms of her mother, of the strange visitor who had warned him and saved both their lives. I bent down close to him and kissed his forehead. "I am glad that your mother came to you," I said. "It seems only right that she should."

He closed one hand around my wrist. "It was not my mother," he said. "I remember my mother. It was *her.*"

I knew at once. He had seen the portraits hanging on the walls at Baddenwell: curly hair, a strong forehead, dancing eyes that masked only lightly the tenacity within. We simply looked at one another for a long time. "She did it for love of you, Mother," he said. "I felt it at the time."

I did not even try to stop the tears. "In some very real way you were meant to be mine, Winston—meant to be ours."

"I know. I know that."

We sat there, his hand slipping from my wrist to my fingers, his eyes, clear and beautiful, boring into my soul until a dog barked somewhere in the camp and I sighed, and rose on my stiffened legs and walked to the wagon and my soft bed, and sleep.

Winston was a hero in the camp for a while, especially in Abbey's eyes, which was the only thing that mattered, as far as he was concerned—though it strengthened yet further the bond existing between her mother and Winston; how could it not? So we lived, in harmony and gratitude, as we walked our way west.

We reached the north fork of the Platte River, then the Upper Platte ferry, less than four hundred miles from the Great Salt Lake. At places the buffalo passed us in great herds, and though their meat was desirable, we had to use caution around them, for the sound of guns firing seemed to infuriate them into stampede. They run in a strange, loping way—a black shaggy wall, breathing and snorting, crushing everything in its path. I liked to watch them from safely off in the distance, swaying and shimmering like great black rock formations under the sun.

The Sweetwater River and Devil's Gate—the Sweetwater, which we were to ford time after time. I cannot hear the name without a shudder of despair passing through me.

We had endured days of heat; breathless, beating down upon us, with no way of relief. Several in the camp had come down with cholera, and by nightfall we realized that Merin's Rachel was one.

To add to our misery a thunderstorm broke upon us with terrible winds that drove the loose clay into thick, choking swirls. When the rain came it was a downpour. The fires sizzled briefly, but were soused within seconds. We were forced to take shelter in our wagons which creaked and swayed under the sheets of water that struck their sides. Several tents which had been set up were blown over, their contents ruined with water and mud. All were miserable, but those with sickness upon them faced a special fear.

As the storm darkened into night Rachel was seized with violent spasms. As the battle of the elements raged outside, the battle of spirit against flesh raged within. Two of our number died that night, but Rachel was not one of them. Although weakened and still feverish, she was with us as we wound our way through the slippery gullies, choked now with mud, as we reached the broad, gentle upland valley of South Pass and the Continental Divide.

We passed Green River, less than two hundred miles from

the Valley, less than forty miles from Fort Bridger, and our spirits quickened at how close we were! We sang "Oh, Susannah," and "Whoa, Haw, Buck and Jerry Boy," and "Shoot the Buffalo," a lively square dancing tune. On the red fork of the Weber River mountain fever invaded our camp—a scant forty-five miles from the Valley! Those weakened from the cholera were the hardest struck.

We could do nothing to abate Rachel's fever. It grew higher and higher until delirium set in. The skills of hand and heart were not sufficient, nor did our prayers avail.

"We are in God's hands," Abigail said, her eyes sick with the failure of her own.

We buried the girl in a beautiful spot where a small spring echoed against green banks and the air was filled with the music of the mountain warblers amid the solemn stillness which God alone can create. Merin said nothing, gave no show of emotion. It was my arms that comforted Drusilla, it was Winston who walked alone with Merin, and listened when the anguish at last poured itself out in a tumble of words and hot tears.

We crossed Last Creek nineteen times before reaching the mouth of the canyon where the road was at first rough with ruts and stumps. But it opened up and descended in gradual good order to the valley floor, broad and wide and nearly empty. But the life that was there—a smattering of homes, a log fort, neat squares of farmland laid out—spoke of familiar, well-loved things. I walked with an eagerness that had not been in my step these many days. For the first time since leaving India—for some deep, inexplicable reason—I felt as if I were coming home!

CHAPTER TWENTY-ONE

🌿

THE WHOLE WORLD STRETCHED BEFORE US, untrammeled, untaken, unspoiled. Each Saint was given his or her own inheritance in the Valley where none could molest them, where they could build and plant to reap with their own hands and raise their children in peace.

That was reality, but it was the ideal side of it. On the practical hand we had a shelter to build, a need of food for our bellies, clothes worn and faded by traveling to be washed or replaced.

For all intents and purposes we had one man among us, who could do the heaviest tasks; we three women could handle all else. But where to build, and should it be one house, at least in the beginning, for all of us, as it had been? Then there were Kenneth and the girls to think of as well. Would he wish to dwell near us, or separate and apart?

At last we selected a site for our lot of an acre and a quarter, which size Brigham had set. But outside the city limits we were to have a five-acre plat where we might grow what we needed to sustain ourselves. Kenneth chose a spot in the same block, and that was agreeable—the same block, several acres away from us. Nothing but space here, with tiny made-man cabins which were dwarfed by the stands of sagebrush, wide and bushy, that could grow from eight to ten feet tall.

Merin and I would share a cabin for the time being, it was

decided. But Abigail hedged, for reasons of her own, which she would not yet state to us.

At first we camped in tents on our own land, using our wagons for storage. The summer was hot and dry, with no shade anywhere to protect us from the driving rays of the sun. Up this high, in this thin atmosphere, they could burn the skin within minutes. I had more experience with this kind of heat than most of the Saints had known. Nevertheless, those first few weeks were miserable—and would have been despite the unexpected tragedy that struck.

We were cooking out of doors; it was an accident, really. Grace, nearly seven, had a penchant for animals of all sizes and types. She was chasing a black-spotted baby rabbit around the camp, convinced she could catch and tame the small beast. I had ordered her to stop and so had Merin, but she paid us no heed. Suddenly the thing darted right for the stove with its little pile of burning coals, scattering the embers and hot, burning pieces every which way. In a breath fingers of flame trailed paths through the dry brush, like veins in a hand. I snatched Emma first and ordered Drusilla, the oldest, to take the children to the bank of the stream near where the wagons were parked and wait for us there.

Abigail was off delivering a child for a sister several miles from us, and both Winston and Abbey had gone to the mill. There were only Merin and myself to fight the bright, flaring blazes, and we were almost helpless against them and the dry tinder of weed and bush they consumed. I gave out a shriek as I saw one side of my tent go up in a sheet of orange flame. I bolted for it, and would have crawled within the cauldron if Merin had not held me back. In a matter of minutes we retreated to the river and let the flames burn themselves out.

As we stood watching I heard the sound of horses approaching, a man and two boys who dismounted quickly, drawing their saddle blankets with them and calling out as they came. Under their instructions we beat at the worst of the flames while they cleared a wider and ever wider swath of land, trapping the fire, as it were, on an island, attacking any stray sparks that jumped the ring and threatened new damage, until there was nothing but acrid smoke left.

"You are fortunate, ladies," the older one said as he dropped to his knees by the stream and gulped the cool water with his blackened hands.

Merin began to thank him with great feeling, but I turned my back on the lot of them, tears stinging my eyes worse than the smoke. I heard him introduce himself and his two sons to her, but I caught nothing more than his first name, Maurice, and the fact that he spoke with an accent which was not British. Perhaps German, I guessed.

"It is lucky we had most of our supplies in the wagon," Merin chatted, "and have lost very little." I ordered Sita to watch her sisters and started walking, arms folded, down the line of the thin stream and away from the rest.

By the time he approached I was crying too hard to hear anything. He came up suddenly and placed his hand on my shoulder, and I did not even jump. It seemed the most natural thing in the world to say, between gulps, "Our laundry was in that tent, all our clothes went up in flames."

"Clothing can be replaced, and sooner than most things."

"A hundred-dollar bill cannot."

He drew his breath in sharply; even in my misery I took note of that. "This is much money, one hundred dollars."

"I sewed it into the hem of my best dress and have carried it all across mountain and plain that way, only to lose it senselessly here."

"Such a large sum?" He was obviously curious.

"A gift from my best friend who came over from London with me. But she stopped off in New Orleans and made a fortune there. I have guarded it so carefully—it meant a home to us, a bit of security!"

"You are English?"

"I am British," I replied without thinking. Then, feeling his gaze still searching me, I met his brown eyes and remembered. "My father was English, my mother Indian. I was born in Calcutta."

"Ah-h-h." It was a long-drawn-out sound, with much of pleasure in it. "You are a long way from home."

I did not answer, but he appeared not to notice.

"I come myself from the Rhineland, where they know how to make rivers." He kicked a clod of dirt into the slow, shallow water that stretched at our feet. "Where they know how to grow trees, for that matter."

His words were drawn from deep feeling, I could tell that, but he clothed them in a hopeful, almost playful tone, perhaps to make them palatable.

"Did you join the Church in your homeland?" I took the clean handkerchief he had dug out of a back pocket for me and dipped it into the cooling water, then rubbed it across my hot face.

"I did. I came first to Liverpool, then to New Orleans, as you must have done."

I nodded, confirming his surmisal.

"My wife died aboard ship," he said, "giving birth to our third child."

"And the baby?"

He shook his head. "These fine boys who are with me are Emma's from a previous marriage. My two remaining daughters died of cholera the first spring we were in Nauvoo."

I felt my shoulders sag at his words, as if he had sent poisonous darts through me. I found a low log to sink down upon and sat with my face in my hands.

"I am sorry if I distress you!" he cried, crouching and resting on his heels close beside me. "You must have suffered similar losses yourself—how unthoughtful of me."

"Who of us has not?" I asked. I knew my voice sounded both tired and discouraged, but I did not care. "As Saints we live only for the next world. There is nothing but misery in this life for any of us!"

I do not remember that he gathered me into his arms, that I wept against his strong shoulder. I was not aware of the way in which he looked upon me as he led me back to the others— the look that would haunt and torment Merin for long years to come.

Maurice Keller, with his Teutonic energy and genius for

organization, became our savior, the blessing that blossomed out of adversity. When he happened upon us that day, he and his boys had just completed their own house. "Our tools are still warm and honed," he joked. They started right in on ours. In exchange we did laundry for them and cooked their meals. They showed Winston how to plow and sow the arid land and helped him to plant the first acres; in exchange we cleaned windows, made curtains, mended bedding, even painted walls. It was a system that seemed to work flawlessly. Hans and Eric were good boys, stolidly built and quiet, but with a gentle light in their eyes. I found myself wondering often what their mother had been like. Her name had been Emma, and when I told Maurice that this was the name of my friend as well as the name I had given my youngest, he looked upon it as another link between us.

I saw in time the expression that lit his eyes when he looked upon me. He called me his lotus flower, because in his mind, as he explained it, this stood for something both delicate and exotic, something both gentle and proud.

That first winter was difficult as we pulled together our scanty means and fought rats and hunger and the cold that came in through the chinked log walls. By the spring Julian Winters had set up a modest dry goods store and offered me work. By the spring Abigail had accepted her dead husband's brother in marriage and gone off to the northern settlements above the Valley with him.

Winston was devastated. "You will see Abbey," I assured him. "It is not as if she has dropped off the edge of the earth."

He began to talk restively of the acreage available for young homesteaders, of the various kinds of work he could turn his hand to, and I realized with a pang of real pain that he would not be with me for long.

Abigail was the first; it seemed she started the whole string of changes that fell into place after her like a gambler's deck of shuffled cards.

That autumn, when the mountain trees were in glory, and even the valley floor both mellowed and sharpened, as autumn has the power to do, Mary Jane became wed to Maurice's Eric.

It was a love match, and I was glad of it. The three Keller men built an adobe for the couple not far from the fields where the boys enjoyed working, on the southerly stretch of the valley. Maurice, gifted as a carpenter, finished a mantelpiece and a headboard for their marriage bed. "I could do the same for you," he said bluntly. "This city is growing too crowded. Come out to the country with us."

I demurred; I pretended I did not understand him when he made such comments as these. He was patient, but I knew by his nature he would not always be so.

As cold snapped through the dry air and the narrow creek beds swelled with moisture from the rains and first wet snows, life, always two-sided, showed the other side of her face to us: first joy and the promise of new lives, now bitterness, sorrow, and the enigma of death.

Susie, still managing affluence somehow, half-filled her city lot with a house that dwarfed all others, bringing in glass windows, lace curtains and fine oak furniture from the East. No one minded, not as they might have with some. Susie was too effulgent of spirit, too easy to love. She hosted parties and dances and Pioneer Day celebrations, and reminded her friends of the pleasant effects a good time can have. But there was no place in such a life for Aaron; or at least, in his eyes there was not.

He took to spending the bulk of his time with low, benighted creatures who viewed life much as he did. He could not walk, he could not work, he could not dance; therefore, he *would not* enjoy. Drink was his consolation, anger and cruelty his recompense. He was disgusting but, despite that, I felt sorry for him.

One thing Aaron could do, with minimal assistance, was ride. With Susie's money he purchased a costly, high-spirited stallion, whom he drove with bit and spur relentlessly. Once when a groom tried to stop him he got a slash with the whip across his cheek for his troubles. Susie refused to see, refused to check his cruelty. Perhaps it was, after all, only a matter of time.

He was bold with drink when he tried to force his animal

over one of those swollen creek beds. When the horse shied and attempted to turn he lashed out at him, but the pace had been checked, just enough—the hind legs did not quite clear, but scrambled for purchase along the slick bank as the horse went down on his knees. Aaron was thrown forward; they say he broke his neck instantly with the force of the fall.

It was merely one death among many—not a woman in childbirth, or an innocent babe scarce born, or a promising child, not a golden young man risking his life for others. But it was the loss of a life, the final stroke of darkness to one who had turned his face away from the light. With what we knew and understood as Latter-day Saints there was more tragedy here, more cause to mourn than in the death of the faithful. I felt it. I felt a sad, lonely pity as they laid him into the grave, and I felt the shadows of all my own dead crowd round me: the loved and the hated, the cherished, the feared, each with his own claim upon me, his own place in my days. I moved away, wishing the sensation of death would not follow me, like a cold hand on my heart.

The fallow winter set in. We enjoyed pulling taffy and roasting apples over the fire, singing and sewing and reading poetry by candlelight. But Winston was making his plans. Soon after the new year he came to me, suffering so visibly that I took pity upon him and did what I had vowed I would not: made it easy for him.

"You love Abbey and I am glad of it," I assured him. "She is a girl worthy of your love and esteem."

That pleased him and he waxed a bit bolder. "I have all things in order, Mother. Brother Perkins has offered me a position in his mill up in Weber County. He needs an assistant, Mother. His only son was killed in a rock slide last spring. He has high hopes of me—"

"As we all do."

"We have a piece of land—"

"Yes, and Maurice has promised to start your house just as soon as the ground thaws. All things are in readiness, I know that. . . ." *All things*, I thought achingly, *except my heart.*

"I have waited this winter for your sake, Mother, and for your sake only." The words were softly spoken, but they sent a stab of guilt through me.

"Forgive me for holding you back," I cried.

His smile came slowly. "Can't you see yet, Mother, that I am nearly as loathe to leave you as you are to let me go?"

My heart pounded painfully. I searched the clear depths of his wonderful blue eyes with my gaze.

"You and you alone have been life to me these long years," he said, "starting far away, back in India. You are more than friend, more even than mother."

I shook my head, afraid of what tears would do if they started.

"I suppose it does not have to be said that I will carry you with me wherever I go. But I do want to tell you that I will love this woman as you have taught me to love. I will reverence and protect her as I watched Seth do those few years with you."

"You will take the best of both of us and make something marvelous of it," I added, trying to lighten the mood a little. My heart was aching with a joy more painful, more consuming than anything I had felt in my life. I knew when the spring came I would be able to let go of him, as God intended me to. I had remembered how much I trusted Winston, and how much I trusted my Father in heaven where he was concerned.

The same summer that Winston and Abbey married, Sita met a young man. She was only a child of twelve, but as if to mock me, to shake the fragile fabric of my mother's security, she fell head over heels in love. His name was Parley Haslam; his father was a blacksmith who was beginning to build up a rather substantial ranch on the side. They were good people, kindly in their ways, and Parley was their oldest, fifteen or sixteen, so it was conceivable—Sarah was not really too young for him, given a few more years.

In her frustration she turned to an unexpected source: the solace and encouragement of her correspondence with Marion, the great aunt on the other side of the world who had been taken with her as a child. I thought it singular that the two could fulfill some need in the other in this way. The pull of my father's family, which had always been strong in me, was somewhat sanctified by that which Winston had experienced in the mountain pass. Then, too, I was grateful the girl had something so harmless to occupy her thoughts and her time.

Merin's Drusilla was two years older than Sita; soon she, too, would be marrying age. I was unable to reconcile myself to the subtle changing of roles. *Is this all for me, then?* My mind asked over and over. *Have I had my day? Must I move aside for those who are yet children, at least in my eyes?* 'Twas not that I begrudged them their own opportunities as they came to them. But I was still young. Perversely I felt more alive and aware at thirty-one than I had at nineteen. I would like to have discussed my feelings on the matter with Merin, yet I dared not. Chances were she would snap at me as she had of late, "There are those who think you just right for marriage, Lottie. You play the fool to be blind."

Did I? Maurice was a good-looking man. I liked the way his dark hair curled around his temples, I liked the strong line of his jaw. When he turned his eyes upon me, liquid and burning, I cannot say they did not stir things within me that had lain dormant these past years. And yet . . . and yet there was something missing. He was not enough like me, though that might sound strange. He enjoyed making decisions and controlling those around him, and that might have been easier for me if his ways were more like my ways. Whatever the causes, I continued to hold him at arms' length, he continued to allow it, and Merin continued to yearn and struggle with her desire and resentment; thus poorly are mortal affairs often arranged.

CHAPTER TWENTY-TWO

🎵

THE LURE OF GOLD REPRESENTS MORE than mere wealth; it is the splendor of dreams, the gleaming, indestructible substance that crowns mortal man when he makes himself a god upon earth. I had seen much of gold and fine, glittering gems in India, but I had never seen men go mad for it until now.

Those hundreds and thousands bound for the gold fields of California streamed through Salt Lake. Most of them were near to destitution when they reached us, and bedraggled in spirits; yet still they pressed on. I felt sorry for most I saw, gamblers in spirit, who would end up with nothing but sand running through their fingers, and the farm back home forever lost to them.

I was at Julian's store one afternoon, working—I will say those few who made money with gold dust or nuggets knew how to spend their wealth well—and I did not recognize the well-dressed woman who walked toward me. Indeed, I thought her clothes gaudy and in rather poor taste.

"Don't stick yer nose up at me, you snotty little Mormonite!" she bellowed. "I've seen you when your feathers were dragging, dearie, I have."

I stared. Not until she threw her head back and laughed did I know. "Emma? . . . Emma!"

I ran to her. She hugged me, then held me at arms' length to take a good look. "You age well, Lottie. You may even be prettier than the last time I saw you."

I could not help but color at her praise, flushed as I was with the pleasure of seeing her.

"Husband number three," she whispered, drawing me aside a bit. "And he's got more money than the other two put together."

"Then what in the world are you doing here?"

She laughed at my directness.

"Chasing the rainbow; what else, lovie? Life gets stale if you sit still for too long."

I thought of the room Maurice had helped us add to our adobe cabin, of the rug Merin and I had labored over, of the garden coaxed out of the hard desert clay, of the many small improvements that had come only with labor and years. I could be content to catch my breath in this one spot for a long time without moving on.

I took her home to inspect her precious Sita, and Grace, and her own little namesake. She made a great to-do over everything and everyone, even Winston's new wife, teasing her over what a scrawny girl Emma remembered her as. Winston now ran Brother Perkins's mill for him, since he was in the process of opening two others at different sites. Abbey had a child due in early spring. "That makes you and me on the way out, Lottie!" Emma moaned, winking at me. "Make way for another generation!" But she possessed more energy than Merin and myself put together, an energy that glowed with some vibrancy of her own.

I could see as soon as she entered that she noticed the absence of the piano. In fact, I watched her open her mouth to say something, then shut it again. Sure enough, as soon as we were alone together, which was not until late, she demanded an explanation.

"Did you have to sell it for wheat," she asked, "or that faded red monstrosity parked outside?"

"I would not have sold it for wheat, or for anything else; not if we all half starved to death."

She leaned forward in her chair as I explained what had happened, her robust face reddening in righteous indignation. "It's a bloomin' shame, Lottie! If I'd have only been there to put the fear of God into 'em."

We could almost laugh about it, but not quite. And unspoken, too, was her continuing incredulity that I would choose and prefer such a life.

We showed Emma and her Daniel the salt lake and took them to bathe in the hot sulphur springs. She handed out lengths of her exquisite lace effusively, as though it were no more than coarse burlap, but we were all overcome with her generosity. And during the two weeks she stayed with us, she was instrumental in saving me from one of the strangest experiences of my life.

Walkara and his Indians were by and large friendly with the Mormons. They liked Brigham Young and trusted his dealings with them. They took more advantage of the Mormon people than the other way round, trading on their tender, long-suffering nature and pushing it at times to the limit.

The worst thing they indulged in, the most difficult for our people to understand, was their dealing in human beings—the slave trade that existed from tribe to tribe. Many a small family struggling for survival in a frontier cabin would be induced to give nearly all in their possession to save the life of a captive child, whom they would then raise up as one of their own, after the manner of the whites. As it happened this time, an Indian got the whole process reversed.

As it fell out, Emma and I were alone at the little orchard Maurice had helped me to plant, gathering the first ripe peaches and, in her way, she was scolding me roundly.

"Spoiled you, he has! Jumps at your slightest wish, love, waits on a word from you—"

"Emma, really!" I protested. "You do not know what you say."

"I know full well. He is a good man, and well favored. Marry him, Lottie. Or are you just too afraid?"

I whirled at her when she said this, upsetting my basket of fruit at my feet. The Indian who had been watching us saw me put my hand to my mouth, but he did not hear me laugh. He did see Emma shake her finger and bellow at me and, not comprehending English, believed she was scolding me still.

"Don't you know a good thing when you see it? Take what

you can get, silly, awkward woman, while there is still someone asking."

We would have dissolved into laughter if a strong arm had
not encircled my waist tight enough to startle me and put a
catch in my breath. He held a long rifle in his other arm, which
he waved wildly at Emma.

"Squaw come with me . . . no more slave to white woman
. . . I take her back to her people."

He walked backwards, keeping his eye on Emma, dragging
me with him, though I screamed in protest, "I don't want to go
with you! Put me down, put me down!"

Seeing me frantic only made him believe all the more that
this large, red-faced woman had abused me. He shook his
weapon menacingly. "Stay away . . . Indian woman go back to
her people . . . you no stop her . . . hear?"

We were approaching the pony he had left standing and
ready. A real panic rose within me and I glanced pleadingly at
Emma, whose face was as stunned as my own. Then all at once
she began moaning, holding her hands to her head as if in misery. The Indian slowed his steps, hesitated.

She began talking a mile a minute and held her hand out to
say, "Stop! Wait!" All Indians understood that language. But I
was too distraught to realize what she was saying.

"Do not take her," she pled. "I love her . . . as a daughter."
She hugged her own arms to her and began to wail. "If you
take squaw my man . . . my husband . . . will beat me . . ." She
picked up a stout stick from the ground and made as if to hit
herself. I thought she had gone a bit mad. Then she dug into
the large carpetbag she carried and pulled out a lace scarf, long
and intricately worked. She approached the hesitant warrior
and draped it across his extended arm, gun and all. "For you
. . . leave squaw with me . . . I will be kind to her . . . my husband will not beat me . . ." She picked up the stick again, then
dropped it. "Take presents instead."

She drew out another fine shawl and placed it over the
other. The brave's face was still passive, his hold round his
prize still secure. Swearing like a Louisiana planter, Emma
pulled out an exquisite gold necklace from which swung the

largest pearl I had ever seen. It quivered and gleamed in the glow of the sunlight. The Indian reached for it, but she drew it back. "I give you necklace, you give me squaw," she said, with a beckoning motion of her hand. She held it forth again; he stood poised between duty and desire. At last, with a grunt of resignation, he gave me a firm shove forward. I ran like a frightened girl and hid behind Emma's skirts. He grabbed for the chain and she loosed her hold on it; then we both scuttered to the furthest end of the small orchard, not even waiting to watch him mount his pony and ride away.

Emma got as much mileage out of the adventure as she could, telling and retelling it for everyone's pleasure.

"So I gave up my prize pearl," she would boast, "which is worth more money than any of you would want to know." Then she would snort and point a finger at me. "Do you believe that little slip of a girl there is worth it?"

Of course, when Maurice heard the tale he stated the obvious—"Charlotte is worth it many times over"—his moist eyes beseechingly seeking mine.

"I do not know about that," Emma countered, her eyes all a-dance, "but I do know she needs somebody who can take care of her." I could have given her a good shaking for that!

It was not until after she had left that it really struck me. Without her quick thinking, her ingenuity, her sheer brass, who knows what might have happened? In retrospect, I shuddered at my possible fate.

I missed Emma the minute she was gone; it was as if she took all life from the house. Despite my efforts, I was restless and moody for the rest of the day, feeling generally unsettled and uncertain in a very discomfiting way.

That night I dreamed, and in my dream I walked through India with Emma at my side. In my dream there were tigers and runaway elephants, angry rajahs, poisonous snakes that curled round our feet—we walked through all of them, unafraid and unscathed. As we proceeded, the narrow path along which we were walking broadened into a meadow lush with grasses and springs of water, and the flowers that only my native country can grow. Sitting in the meadow, surrounded by these flowers, were my mother and my grandmother, as I imagined them, and Karan, as I remembered him.

The dream awoke me with its vividness and power. I lay in bed my whole soul aching, wondering why this dream of Karan had come. Perhaps it was merely brought on by memories which Emma's presence had stirred; perhaps my submerged fear of abduction such as my mother had suffered roused hidden desires and fears. I knew not, but my spirit was in turmoil and for days knew no rest.

When poor Maurice attempted to improve upon the opportunities Emma had opened for him, my heart went out to him, for perhaps the first time. He had never attempted to touch me, but this time he put his hands on my shoulders. "I am not necessarily a patient man, Charlotte, yet I have been patient with you. I have waited, when my own desires—" At that point he drew me to him and, before I realized what was happening, pressed his lips over mine. The anguish of that kiss would have stirred a soul less passionate than mine.

"Maurice," I breathed, pushing him gently away from me, "I have not meant to torment you. I have tried, above all, to be honest."

"That is the torment!" he cried. "There is something you will not let go of. I know if you did—"

I put my fingers to his lips. "You do not know." When he began again to protest, I added, "I know if you would cast your eyes elsewhere there is one who would love you as you wish that I could."

He knew my meaning precisely, but he chose to ignore it. "It is not devotion I want," he said between clenched teeth, "it is you."

"That right now, especially on the terms you desire, cannot take place."

I thought his anger and passion would consume him, and I felt wretched inside, wretched and somehow guilty. As he left me, stiff and bitter, I wondered how many more times he would ask.

❦

Abbey was safely delivered of a child on the last day of March, 1852. Her mother attended her; Winston and I stood waiting a room away. The child had curls on her head, and the curls had a red tinge to them.

"We are calling her Charlotte Elizabeth," Abbey said after she had sent for me, and I cradled the soft new life that had been drawn from her within my own arms. "It is only fitting," she smiled, "considering the great influence of those two women in Winston's life."

I could not trust myself to speak, but I thought of what a good wife she was to think foremost of her husband's desires in naming her first child.

"And it is not Winston who has asked this of me," the girl said. "It is what I want, Charlotte, as much as he."

When I bent to kiss her she whispered, "Would you mind if we called her Lottie sometimes?"

So spring this year for us was truly a celebration of rebirth and renewal. And to round off the season, Merin's Drusilla was wed, and that left only the two of us, the little girls, and my Sita, more restless now than ever before.

The cycles came and went, in an ever continuing circular pattern, and I began to perceive that the pattern was good. Winter came and passed, and before spring had really announced itself, Maurice stood at my door. He looked tall and imposing, and I knew by his manner that this moment had a solemn stamp to it which had not been there before.

"I have been called by Brother Morley to settle Sanpete County, perhaps two hundred miles south of here. I am to leave in a month's time. I mean to establish a fine home there. Will you marry me, Charlotte, and come with me as my wife?"

He had not expected the response he desired, and certainly not from the start. "I must know. It has come to that moment."

I hesitated, searching for a way to express what I felt. But he gathered me to him, as tenderly as I might gather one of my children. "Do not kiss me and confuse things," I entreated.

With a smile he ignored me, and was a long time in releasing me, breathless and trembling. "My desire for you clarifies things, Charlotte," he said with his lips against my hair. "It is what God intended." He kissed my cheeks, then found my mouth again. "I will make you happy," he said. "Please trust me, Charlotte, please give me that chance."

I was in agony. I paced the floor for hours, unable to settle to any task. Merin knew as soon as she entered the room and looked at me. "Why have you refused him?" she asked bluntly. "What madness is in your head?"

Then she walked through to her own room and shut the door behind her, and we were like two moths shut in our own cocoons of darkness and misery, with no passage out.

I have never spent more time on my knees, more energy petitioning heaven than I did those few days following. Emma's words kept echoing and re-echoing. "You say you don't love him, dearie, but he loves you. That's enough at this point. Many a decent marriage has been built upon less." I reasoned with myself, knowing I hesitated in part because of a reluctance to leave friends, to leave Winston and my new grandchild behind. But that, in the long run, was not a deciding factor. I pleaded, I agonized, I attempted, all to no avail. I could not do what it was not in me to do.

I went to Maurice myself; the sooner the better, for his sake. He knew as soon as he saw me, before he had even looked into my face.

"Would to heaven I could give you the answer you deserve," I said.

He shook his head, and it was a gesture of understanding. But he could not speak. I left him standing there, watching after me, his eyes as sad and empty as if something within him had died.

That winter not a week passed without Sarah and Parley contriving some way to meet. There was a natural sympathy that existed between them which was touching to see.

"Other girls have been married at fourteen," Sita pressed.

"Yes, and they were as much children as you are. I will not do that to you."

"There is nothing in life for me until I am with him. Why do you hold me back?"

"You will be fifteen before the summer. Let us see what happens then."

Perhaps I was wrong, perhaps I should have remembered how I felt at eighteen, but four years' difference at that stage of life is a huge gap. And I was not saying *no*, I was just saying, *wait*.

What happened is that Parley was sent on a mission to the Lamanites, down in the far southern counties. He was happy to go, reconciled. "My first duty is to God," he told Sita, "and then to myself. I will make you a better husband when I come home."

Yes, I thought, *and my child will be grown then, and able to make you a wife.*

But he did not come back. The Walker War started that summer, and Parley was one of the casualties to the ignorance and anger of others—he simply got in the way. He did not come back, and Sita turned the whole force of her anguish on me.

I did not mind the fierce anger that felt like hatred. It was the suffering in her eyes that distracted me. I have never been able to see those I love in pain without feeling it, too. That first week I did not know if we would hold on to her. She would not eat, would not sleep; she tried to do all in her power to force her life to end, too. But hunger for life is inherent in youth, whether they like it or not. One day she simply rose from the chair by the window which she had nearly become a part of, and walked into her room. A moment later she reappeared with gloves and bonnet and walked out the front door. She was gone for the better part of two hours, most of which I spent praying, and watching out that same window where her torment had been spent.

When she returned her face was composed, and somehow different. She appeared as though she had matured two years in the space of two hours.

"I have been to the missionary office, Mother," she said. "I meant only to make inquiries, but a group of missionaries, as it happens, leaves for England next week. Two wives, older women, will be accompanying their husbands. I have secured permission to travel with them."

As it happens! "To England?" How small my voice sounded in my ears. "To do what?"

"Aunt Marion has invited me—pled with me to come. She is older and cannot get around so well. I could be a companion to her; I know it would please her immensely."

"Even if you come unannounced?"

"That would be of no matter to her. She would understand."

I nodded. I realized that I was digging my nails into the palm of my hand, lest I cry out, lest I speak out and harm my own cause more. I knew nothing of this intimacy between them. It stung deeply to think that Sarah would not have confided at least part of these feelings to me.

"How shall money for your fare be provided?" I was choosing my words carefully, keeping them neutral, impersonal.

Here she hesitated, but only slightly. *You did what you thought you must do,* her eyes told me. *I only do the same in return.* "Emma sent money last Christmas, remember?"

"No, I do not remember, and you know that I don't."

"It was meant for my wedding—a gift of encouragement. You know Emma." She shrugged her thin shoulders, and the gesture sent tears to my eyes. "I may as well use it for this. It is . . . a generous sum."

Of course. If it came from Emma, it would be so. Yet I could not help but feel the smart of betrayal. Why would Emma do such a thing as this behind my back? She knew my feelings concerning the matter. She ought at least to have told me, in that blustering, overriding way of hers. Deception and intrigue were not like her. . . .

"If you are sure."

"I'm sure, Mother."

I felt my lips begin to tremble. *Heaven, help me,* I prayed. *I must not cry now.*

"I must do this. I must get away from this place, Mother, before I go mad."

She spoke the words simply, with no show of emotion, no feeling. And somehow they seemed more terrible that way.

Somehow I went to her. Somehow I placed my arms very gingerly around her and whispered, "I love you." Then somehow, somehow—I let her go.

CHAPTER TWENTY-THREE

𝓕

WORK. THERE IS ALWAYS WORK FOR THE HANDS to do when all else fails. I begged Julian for more hours at the store, which request he was happy to accommodate. Then I canned the fruit of my own orchards, made pies and preserves, put up beans and tomatoes, pickles and beets. I made more hated candles and more soap than we could hope to consume in a year. Merin saw, but it was her way to say little and let me work things out. From time to time I wondered if, indeed, I had played the fool in letting Maurice go off without me. What life was this? Each child who left would take a part of me with her, and when it was over, what would I have? A soul in tatters and a half-life, with no one to make me whole.

I did not always think thus. But in the dark times, the lonely and sad times, such thoughts would come.

After three months I received a letter from Sarah Elizabeth. I could tell, reading between the lines, that the healing had started, and I had to be content with that. For on the surface all was a gay round of teas and parties, dances and introductions. A note from Marion was tucked in with Sita's letter, like a knife in my ribs.

Sarah Elizabeth is lovely, Charlotte. Now that she is a young woman and no longer a child, her resemblance to my mother is quite arresting. Whatever in the world the dear thing has suffered, we mean to make it up to her. She is already becoming a favorite, looked upon as a beauty. . . .

What in the world had I done, letting her go like an innocent into the jaws of mammon? Merin, watching my face as I read, said, "You did not let her go. Nor could you have stopped her, if you'd had a mind to." She came over to where I was sitting and placed her hand on my arm. "She must find her own way, Lottie. A painful process—more even for you than for her."

Christmas came. I had never spent the holidays with one of my children missing. I tried to push my sense of emptiness, the nagging worry out of my mind and approach this blessed season with the faith I had learned back in London, that first dismal, haunted year. Emma's greeting did not help, effusive in praise, as it was, for Sita's beauty and cleverness, pleased at the prospects her aunt was opening up for her. Panic, like a dark weight, closed around my heart whenever my daughter came to my mind.

Merin was gentle. "Emma's life has taken new, more worldly directions time after time, Lottie. They are bound to affect her. She is a rare and delightful person. But because of what she meant to you in London, you hold her almost sacred. No human being can help but disappoint expectations like that."

"You have grown wise while I have grown foolish," I answered her, and though my tone was light, I meant it. Her words snapped me back. What abundance I possessed in comparison to Merin, who had only one child left to her and no more prospects than I, as well as the horrifying awareness that her sons existed somewhere, living some kind of life, unknown, and lost to her. Yet she never complained. She never demanded of others—of life, of God himself—pity and justice, the way I did.

That made a difference. I sensed a growing equanimity I was grateful for. Then Winston made an announcement when we were all gathered together Christmas morning—Abigail, even Kenneth and Phyllis, whom I had invited, and Mary Jane, with her husband and new baby son.

"I have been called on a mission to Italy," he said.

I glanced at Abbey. There were tears in her eyes, but her smile seemed real, deepened as it was with pride in him.

The young people gathered round, congratulating him, asking questions, but I sought Abigail and a quiet corner. "There is something else," I said, for I had seen a certain look in her eyes.

"She is with child again."

"Does Winston know?"

"No. She'll not tell him. She says he will not leave if he knows, and she is probably right." She smiled. "We were right about Winston, dear Lottie. He has made her so happy. There is not one fault I can find in him, not one weakness to mar his kindness and integrity."

I smiled in return. "Hasn't he a right to know?"

"Surely he has. But Abbey fears that he will refuse the mission to remain here with her, and then regret it forever after. 'He is without guile, Mother,' she told me. 'He has so much faith, so much to give. If I held him back from serving God, how could I live with myself—or, for that matter, with him?'"

I nodded. "We must leave it in their hands, then, and in God's."

"I will be here when her time comes," Abigail said, as if assuring both of us. "Will you come and be with us as well?"

I clasped her hands and smiled mistily. "With all my heart, Abigail! You know that."

It was nearly a year to the day since I last had seen him that Maurice showed up at my door. I let him in willingly, eager to hear of his adventures.

"You look well," I said. And he did, his skin tanned and seasoned, his thick hair worn a bit longer, so the curls were even more prominent. I watched his mouth as he spoke, thinking of the times his lips, sweet and demanding, had covered mine.

"The land is kindly," he told me. "The crops I have planted are growing well."

"And your house is the largest and finest."

"To date," he laughed.

"I am pleased to hear that you like it there, Maurice, that you do not regret the move."

He told me details, as men will, of things I cared little about, and I told him of Winston's call, and we spoke of Mary Jane's baby, who was his grandson, though that thought seemed strange to me. I did not tell him of Sita, and if he knew what had happened, he did not broach the subject with me.

It was not until he rose to take his leave and we were standing together that he tilted my chin to meet his eyes, his warm brown fingers on my cheek and throat.

"I must marry, for many reasons. There are those who would have me . . ." His touch made me ache, and I knew he was struggling with deeper emotions than mine. "But I could not make that decision without asking one last time—here, where my heart lies . . . I have to make sure."

I sighed, and the little sound trembled between us. He nodded his head slowly and, with the tips of his fingers, caressed my face. "I will not ask again, Charlotte."

"I know."

His kiss was nearly enough to undo me. "With all my heart I wish you the very best," I whispered against his cheek.

"I am leaving the very best behind," he said, his voice gruff with emotion.

I let him go because I had to—because, for some reason I could not fathom, I was unable to do otherwise.

It is an old statement taken from the Bible—I have sung the words often in hymn form: *God moves in a mysterious way His wonders to perform. . . .* Heaven knows I had seen it in my own life, time after time. But never like this—never before touching this.

He had my address from the letters I had sent, though very few had reached him, and when he knocked on my door and learned from Grace that I would be at Julian's for the next two hours he intended to come at once and surprise me there.

It did not work out that way. Merin came in from the garden where she had been working, her red hair falling in loose curls about her shoulders and down her back. Her hair was still long and thick and she liked to wear it thus, free and unrestrained, in the privacy of the house. She offered him some mint lemonade, our own concoction, and scones freshly baked.

"I did not expect scones," he exclaimed, piling on our homemade peach jam.

"Lottie's influence," she smiled. "Tell me of yourself. We get little news of the outside world here, and I know how dear you are to Charlotte."

"And that piques your interest?" He had smiled amicably, settled back in his chair, and begun.

When I arrived home to see him ensconced in my parlor, looking comfortable and at ease there, I could not believe my eyes. He gathered me into his arms.

"Oh Lottie, the sight of you, after all these years—after all I have been through!"

"Arthur!" I clasped him to me, smoothing his hair back as I had when he was young. I could feel pain and relief mingling in him, and remembered those times we were together after his father's death, and again after Constance, and thought, unaccountably, *He has come home.*

Things came about bit by bit, as they do in the living, though I must tell them all at once, as it were, attempting to capture feeling and expression, and what my face must have looked like when Arthur said, "I have not traveled all this way, through the wastes of the American desert, just to see you, sister, though that would have been nice. I have come to Zion—I am an immigrant, a convert, much like yourself."

I did not believe him; I truly did not, until all of his story came out. "India was not what I remembered—" The lines of his face twitched. "Not what I expected."

"That is because you were not what you expected," I told him, and he knew what I meant. "You had less of the soldier in you than you had imagined." Though he was, in many ways, like his father: serious about life, slow-thinking, one to consider much before action yet, once decided, to give all he had.

"I was two years in India when I became ill and was sent home on leave. As it happened, Aunt Alice conveniently died while I was about to take care of things and settle her estate. I would have gone back. . . . I intended to go back. . . ."

"Why?"

He shrugged his shoulders, and I knew there was something to the matter he was not yet ready to tell.

"Then I ran into two missionaries tracting on the streets of London, where I had gone for business, and I was reminded at once of you and Seth, and our brief visit with you, and the thought came into my head: *Lottie is one of the few truly good people I have ever known. Perhaps I will stop and listen a minute.* I have lived in India, you remember, both as a child and a man. I possessed a mind more open to new and different ideologies than most Englishmen."

"And those few innocent moments were your undoing." Merin spoke so softly that we both turned our heads toward her.

"Yes," he replied, with a curious expression on his features. "You have the right of it."

"It was much that same way with me," she continued speaking half to herself. "I did not wish it, especially after my husband's cruelty. I wished I could walk away. . . ."

She shuddered a little, and to my astonishment Arthur was on his feet and beside her. Acting on the vaguest of hunches I said, "Merin, some of those tomatoes at the end of the garden are getting ripe, I noticed. Wouldn't they be nice for supper?" I took one of our baskets from its hook. "Why don't you go out and pick some, and take Arthur along to show him the garden."

She did not need further urging, and, for that matter, neither did he. When a quarter of an hour passed and they did not return, I was not unduly surprised. When the time stretched into an hour I hesitated, but at length, though reluctant, was forced to call them to a scorched and overcooked dinner, missing the tomatoes that never found their way into the basket.

Thus it went with the two of them for several days, until I could bear it no more. Finally one evening I determined to talk to Merin myself, once we got Arthur safely in bed. But she came to me, slipping silently into my bedroom, and I thought with some surprise, *She looks as young and blooming and vulnerable as a girl.*

She settled herself on the foot of my bed, drawing her knees up to her chin, her blue eyes as soft and dreamy as the ocean on a mild summer's day.

"What is happening here?" I asked, and the warmth I felt for both of them was plain in my voice.

"More than I dare hope!" she sighed. "From the moment I came through the door and looked up and saw him there. . . . from the moment his eyes found mine, Lottie, and held . . . do you think it strange?"

"I think it wonderful!" I said, reaching out for her hand.

"He was in love before, did you know?"

"I know nothing of it—much less, I am sure, than you do."

"A girl in England who was supposed to be waiting for him. When he came back unexpectedly, because of his illness, he discovered that she had married another, and not even cared enough to inform him."

"Poor, gentle Arthur," I murmured.

"That is why he intended to go back—drown his sorrows in misery and self-punishment." We both smiled wanly. "The gospel rescued him, Lottie."

"Yes, I know. It does that, in one way or another, for all of us."

"So he resigned his commission and joined the Church." Her voice was full of wonder."

"And came here and found you."

She blushed like a maiden, and I realized that the wonder in her voice was the wonder of love.

And I remember feeling as happy for her as I would have been for myself. She was only three years older than he, and they were well suited for one another, of that I felt sure. Her travail had been long; her blessings would be well merited, well deserved.

The letter came like a blow, entirely unexpected. *Going to travel to India with Aunt Marion!* "The deuce you are!" I said under my breath.

At first I was consumed with her selfishness and betrayal, and then with worry concerning the dangers in which she may be placing herself. I could think of nothing, torn every which way, as I was, by the emotions that played through my soul.

At length I let Arthur read the letter. He did so, then returned it to me thoughtfully. "Well, what do you think?" I demanded.

He leaned forward in his chair while addressing me, as though he were yearning toward me. "She is traveling with a colonel, his wife, and servants, Lottie. Did you not read that? If it were 'Aunt Marion' alone, I, too, would be concerned. But this is a different story."

"She is going," I retorted, "to the other end of creation, without so much as a by your leave."

"Yes. You are a mother; I cannot imagine how much that would hurt you."

His sympathy, natural and undemonstrative, began to calm me. "I must wait," I cried, "wondering what is happening to her, what effect all these influences are having upon her life, upon her spirit."

His face reflected my misery, but he had little for me by way of comfort, by way of answers.

When night fell I found myself walking, past the lots where people and animals sheltered, to the bare moonlit plane beneath Ensign Peak. I sat in silence, feeling dead inside, empty. Then I became dimly aware of a sensation, a growing assurance that I was not alone. I glanced around me: nothing but occasional clumps of sagebrush with the evening shadows playing over them, and the dim glow of the houses below. "Seth!" I cried, expecting to hear his bright whistle at my elbow, missing him with a hunger suddenly as new and acute as it had been when he died.

I closed my eyes. Behind my dark lids I saw clearly an image which I knew was my mother—I saw my father's red hair and his laughing green eyes, and emerging, as if from around and within him, a woman with dark curls and a small mouth, both strong and tender at the same time. . . .

I blinked my eyes open and stood, and paced back and

forth in agitation, because the images would not go away. Then, from amongst them, filmy and insubstantial, rose a bronzed face whose brown eyes filled with tenderness and compassion—eyes my own had not gazed upon since I was a girl. Suddenly, unaccountably, Karan's words came back to me, as from a great distance.

"I saw you in a dream," he had said. "I saw you in a place other than India, but strangely like her. A land of deserts, barren and treeless. . . ."

Why had I never once thought of his words before? They came to me now, perfect and effortless, as though he were speaking them to me in the even, musical cadence of his voice.

"A great empty basin, bounded on the east by high, snow-crowned mountains, and set off in the west by a lower range and a sprawling blue lake. . . ."

The Great Salt Lake City. How had Karan seen it, when it came from a future that existed only in the knowledge of God?

"You were where you belonged," he had said. "That was the one thought that stayed with me, even when I awoke. . . ."

"Then I will keep it with me!" I whispered, "even if it is all I have to hold onto right now."

I belong here. Even as I thought the words, the truth and power of them poured through me, as if my whole being and the dark, silent hillside were enveloped in light.

I belong here—and God will ordain my life, as he always has, to my good.

I walked back toward the house where my children— where Merin and Arthur—where happiness waited for me.